Praise

"A sprawling, sparkl... ...Robbins's literary legacy ...y much alive, and fans should experienc.. a pleasant sense of déjà vu as they race through this latest installment."
——*Publishers Weekly* on *Heat of Passion*

"Splendid pulp . . . Stunningly well written."
——*Kirkus Reviews* on *Heat of Passion*

"An intriguing story . . . fascinating."
——*RT Book Reviews* on *Heat of Passion*

"Tight-packed plot and inside detail on gambling cheats in Las Vegas gives off blue rocket fire . . . Seminal Robbins. The pages go *whoosh*."
——*Kirkus Reviews* on *Sin City*

"Robbins's faithful fans will be lining up for this one. . . . The plot is spiced with loads of fantastical sex and nymphomaniacal women."
——*Booklist* on *Sin City*

"*Sin City* moves quickly and is great fun. . . . Packed with vintage Robbins boudoir scenes, it follows a street-smart youth clawing his way to wealth and power. Robbins fans . . . will be rewarded for their devotion with this unexpectedly lively offering."
——*Publishers Weekly*

"Harold Robbins is a master!"
——*Playboy*

"Harold Robbins is one of the world's bestselling authors. . . . Each week, an estimated 280,000 people purchase a Harold Robbins novel."

—*Saturday Review*

"Robbins grabs the reader and doesn't let go."

—*Publishers Weekly*

"His characters are compelling, his dialogue is dramatic, and his style is simple and straightforward."

—*Los Angeles Times*

HAROLD ROBBINS

❖

The Piranhas

A TOM DOHERTY ASSOCIATES BOOK
NEW YORK

This is a work of fiction. All of the characters, organizations, and events portrayed in this novel are either products of the author's imagination or are used fictitiously.

THE PIRANHAS

Copyright © 1991 by Harold Robbins

Originally published in 1991 by Pocket Books, a division of Simon & Schuster Inc.

A Forge Book
Published by Tom Doherty Associates, LLC
175 Fifth Avenue
New York, NY 10010

www.tor-forge.com

Forge® is a registered trademark of Tom Doherty Associates, LLC.

ISBN 978-0-8125-7788-4

First Forge Edition: June 2010

Printed in the United States of America

0 9 8 7 6 5 4 3 2 1

For Jann,
with all my love and gratitude

The Funeral

IT WAS PISSING rain at eleven o'clock in the morning in front of St. Patrick's Cathedral. The police had blocked all traffic down Fifth Avenue from Fifty-fourth Street to Forty-ninth Street except buses, and they were only in a single line close to the sidewalk near Rockefeller Center across from the Cathedral. The street itself was crowded with blackened-window stretch limousines. The sidewalk and the steps leading up to the entrance of the Cathedral were jammed with television cameras, reporters, and the morbidly curious crowd that always managed to show up for death and destruction.

Inside the Cathedral all the pews were filled with black-dressed mourners, some very expensively dressed and others in threadbare black—but each looked down toward the altar to the front of the ornate gold coffin with a simple wreath of flowers at the foot. There was an expectant air as they waited to hear the mass that would be given by Cardinal Fitzsimmons. They wanted to hear what he had to say, because he had always hated the dead man.

I was seated in the first seat off the aisle reserved only for relatives of the deceased. I glanced over at the open coffin. My uncle looked fit and relaxed. Better, actually, than he usually had in life. Even as a child I realized that he was taut and always thinking. But most of all, I could always see, peering over his left shoulder, the Angel of Death, who would disappear the moment my uncle would talk to me. There were five other members of the family in the pew with me. Among them were my Aunt Rosa, the sister of my uncle and my father, who had been his brother. Then there were Rosa's married daughters and their husbands. I had trouble remembering their names because over the many years we had rarely seen each other. I think their names were Cristina and Pietro, and Luciana and Thomas; the latter couple had two young children of their own.

Across the aisle, also in the front pew, were the important people and close friends of my uncle. My uncle had many friends. He had to have many friends because he died in bed of a massive cardiac seizure and not by a bullet as was the usual form of death for his compatriots. I looked across the aisle. I recognized some of the men, somber in black suits, white shirts, and black ties. Next to the aisles, Danny and Samuel were seated. They were young, maybe about my age, fortyish. They were my uncle's bodyguards. The man sitting next to them

I recognized from his photographs in newspapers and magazines. He was very handsome, with silver-gray hair, and wearing a carefully tailored suit, a black handkerchief in his breast pocket matching his tie falling neatly across the front of his white silk shirt. The CEO. The Chairman of the Board. Fifteen, twenty years ago they would have called him the Godfather. The Capo di Tutti Capi. That was what they used to call my uncle. That was forty years ago. They used to kiss his hand. But not today. The CEO was fourth-generation American. And it was not the Mafia. The Mafia, maybe still, in Sicily. Here in America it was a conglomerate comprised of Sicilians, blacks, Latin Americans, South Americans, and Asians. But the CEO held the reins tightly in hand with the board consisting of the five original families. The head of each of the families sat in the same pew as the CEO. In the few pews behind them were the others. The Latins, the blacks, the Asians. The pecking order never changed. Not in all the years.

The Cardinal rushed the mass. The whole thing was over in less than ten minutes. He made the sign of the cross over the coffin, then turned his back and started to walk away from the altar. At the same time, a thin, small, black-suited man seated toward the center of the church began running down the aisle toward the coffin waving a gun wildly over his head.

I heard my Aunt Rosa scream and saw the Cardinal dive quickly down behind the altar, his robes flapping. I left the pew and went after the man, and I saw others running after him. But none of us caught him before he emptied his gun into the coffin; then he stood there and cried loudly: "One death is not enough for traitors!"

My uncle's bodyguards wrestled the man to the ground. I was just in time to see them begin to break his neck, but the CEO was already there. He gestured with his hand and shook his head. "No," he said.

The bodyguards rose to their feet, and by that time the coffin was surrounded with uniformed police. Two plainclothes detectives were in charge of the officers. One pointed to the small man still on the floor. "Get him out of here." The other detective picked up the gun lying on the floor and dropped it in his pocket. He turned to me because I was closest to the coffin. "Who's in charge here?"

I glanced around. The CEO and my uncle's body-guards were back in their front-line pew. My aunt was crying loudly. She broke away from her two sons-in-law, ran to the coffin, and screamed again as she saw the mess inside the coffin. My uncle's head had been almost obliterated; what remained was more a gargoyle than a man's face. The silk sheet in the coffin was stained and spattered with brains, pieces of torn skin, and a pale pink fluid that the embalmer had used to replace the blood in my uncle's body.

I pulled her back and pushed her into the sons-in-laws' arms. "Get her away from here," I said.

Aunt Rosa did the right thing. She fainted, and the two men dragged her back to the pew as her daughters rushed to her aid. At least now she was quiet. I turned to one of the undertakers. "Close the coffin."

"Don't you want us to take him back and clean him up?" one of them asked.

"No," I said. "We go right to the cemetery."

"But he looks terrible," the man protested.

"It doesn't matter now," I said. "I'm sure that God will recognize his face."

The detective looked at me. "Who are you?" he asked.

"I'm his nephew. My father was his brother."

"I don't know you," the detective said curiously. "I thought I knew all of his family."

"I live in California and just came in for the funeral." I took out a business card and handed it to him. "Now, let me get the funeral on the road. I'll be at the Waldorf Towers if you want to get in touch with me this evening."

"Just one question. Do you know anything about the nut who pulled this stunt?"

"Nothing," I said.

The Cardinal came toward us. His face was pale and drawn. "Sacrilegious," he said huskily.

"Yes, Your Eminence," I agreed.

"I'm very upset," the Cardinal said. "Nothing like this has ever happened in here."

"I'm sorry, Your Eminence," I said. "But if damages have occurred, please give me the bill and it will be taken care of."

"Thank you, son." The Cardinal looked at me. "I've never met you?" he asked.

"No, Your Eminence," I answered. "I'm the prodigal. I'm from California."

"But you are his nephew, I understand," he said.

"True," I replied. "But I never have been baptized. My mother was Jewish."

"But your father was Catholic," the Cardinal said. "It is not too late for you to come back to the faith."

"Thank you, Your Eminence," I said. "But there is nothing to come back to because I have never been a Catholic."

The Cardinal looked at me curiously. "Are you of the Hebrew faith?"

"No, sir," I answered.

"What faith do you profess to?" he asked.

I smiled. "I'm an atheist."

He shook his head sadly. "I am sorry for you." He paused a moment, then gestured to a young priest to join us. "This is Father Brannigan, who will accompany you to the cemetery."

THERE WERE TWO flower cars and five limousines following the hearse down Second Avenue, under the Midtown Tunnel to Long Island, through the gates of First Calvary. The family mausoleum shone brightly in the noonday sunlight, the white marble columns in front of the iron grillworks in the doors set with stained-glass windows. Over the door the family name was chiseled in white Italian marble. DI STEFANO. The doors were wide open as the cortege came to a stop in the narrow roadway.

We stepped out of the cars and waited for the men to roll the coffin onto a four-wheeled trolley and push it up the pathway toward the mausoleum. The flower cars were immediately unloaded and followed the coffin up the pathway. Aunt Rosa and her family, who had been in the first car of the procession, were led by Father Brannigan to the coffin. I had been in the second car with my uncle's bodyguards, and we followed Aunt Rosa and her family. From the three cars behind emerged the Chairman, his bodyguards, then my uncle's attorneys and accountants. Following them were six men, all older Italian men, probably friends of my uncle.

The flowers were piled high at the side of the open mausoleum doors as we entered the cool of the mausoleum. The coffin was still on the trolley in the middle of the room. In the far corner was a small altar over which the Christ looked sadly down at the coffin as it sat at the foot of the cross upon which He agonized.

Quickly the priest, his voice echoing hollowly in the room, gave the Blessed Sacrament and the last rites over the coffin, then made the gesture of the cross and stepped back. One of the undertakers handed each of us a rose, and after Aunt Rosa placed her rose on the coffin we followed with our own.

Quietly, four men raised the coffin and slid it into its place in the wall. A moment later, two men fastened the bronze plaque over the opening. In the light streaming in from the stained-glass windows, I could see the etched lettering. ROCCO DI STEFANO. Born 1908. Died ———. R.I.P.

Aunt Rosa began crying again and her sons-in-law escorted her out. I glanced around at the walls of the mausoleum. I saw names of other relatives I had never known. But my father and mother were not there. They were buried in an interdenominational cemetery north of New York City on the banks of the Hudson River.

I was the last man to leave the mausoleum. I watched for a moment while one of the cemetery workmen turned the big brass key to lock the door. He looked at me. I caught the message. I took out a hundred-dollar bill and pressed it into his hand. He touched his cap as acknowledgment. Then I followed down the path to the roadway.

The hearse and the flower cars were already gone. I went to Aunt Rosa and kissed her cheek. "I'll call you tomorrow."

She nodded, her eyes still filled with tears. I shook hands with her sons-in-law, kissed the cheeks of my cousins, and waited until their limousine took off.

I turned to my car, where the two bodyguards were still waiting. One of them opened the car door for me deferentially. The Chairman's quiet voice came from behind me. "I'll take you into the city."

I looked at him.

"We have many things to discuss," he said.

I nodded and gestured to the bodyguards to go on. I followed the Chairman to his stretch limo. This was his own car, black all over and blackened windows in the passenger compartment. I followed him into the car. A dark-suited man closed the door behind me and got into the front seat next to the chauffeur. Slowly the automobile began to move.

The Chairman pressed a button and the blackened window between the passenger compartment and the front seat closed. "Now we can speak," the Chairman said. "We are soundproofed. They cannot hear anything we say."

I looked at him without speaking.

He smiled, his blue eyes crinkling. "If I may call you Jed, you may call me John." He held out his hand.

I took his hand. It was firm and strong. "Fine, John. Now what do we have to talk about?"

"First, I want to tell you that I had much respect for

your uncle. He was an honorable man and never went back on his word."

"Thank you," I said.

"I'm also sorry about that stupid incident in the church. Salvatore Anselmo is an old man and hasn't all his marbles. For thirty years he has been saying he would kill your uncle but never had the balls to try. Now it was too late. He couldn't kill a dead man."

"What was the vendetta about?" I asked.

"It happened so long ago I don't think anyone remembers or knows."

"What happens to him now?" I asked.

"Nothing," he said casually. "They'll probably put him in the Bellevue psycho ward at first. Disturbing the peace or something. But no one will bother to press charges. They'll send him home to his family."

"Poor bastard," I said.

John leaned forward and opened the bar behind the front seat. "I have a good scotch. Would you join me in a drink?"

I nodded. "With ice and water."

Quickly he picked up a bottle of Glenlivet and poured it into two glasses. He added ice cubes and water from the small bottles of Evian lined up at the back of the small bar. We held up our glasses. "Cheers," he said.

I nodded and sipped the drink. It was good. I hadn't known how much I needed it. "Thank you," I said.

He smiled. "Now down to business. Tomorrow the lawyers will inform you that you're the executor of your uncle's estate. That estate, except for several personal bequests to your aunt and her family, is placed into a foundation that will distribute to various charities. A grave responsibility. About two hundred million dollars."

I was silent. I knew Uncle Rocco had a great deal of money but I didn't realize it was that much.

"Your uncle didn't think that he had to leave you any money because for one, you are rich in your own right, and two, as executor of the estate you will earn between five and ten percent of the distribution of the funds from the foundation as ordered by the probate court."

"I don't want any of the money," I said.

"Your uncle said you would say that, but it is simply a matter of law," John said.

I thought for a moment. "Okay," I said. "Now how do you fit into this?"

"In his estate—nothing," he said. "But there are other considerations. Fifteen years ago, when your uncle retired and moved to Atlantic City, he made an agreement with the De Longo family and the Anastasia family that they would give him Atlantic City as his territory. That was long before gambling had ever been thought of there. Since then, all the unions and various other businesses have been under your uncle's control. Now they would like to take over that part of his business."

I looked at him. "It's a lot of money?"

He nodded.

"How much?" I asked.

"Fifteen, twenty million a year," he said.

I sat silent.

John stared at me. "You're not interested in taking it over?"

"No," I said. "That's not my game. But I feel they ought to contribute something to Uncle Rocco's foundation—if for nothing other than respect for his memory. After all, as I understand it, Uncle Rocco took over those businesses when Atlantic City was nothing but a broken-down town, and helped it grow to its present importance."

John smiled. "You're not stupid. If you wanted to keep his organization you would be dead in a year."

"Probably," I answered. "But I have my own business to attend to and am not interested in Uncle Rocco's affairs. But I do think that they should donate something to his foundation."

"How much?" John asked.

"Twenty million dollars would be about fair," I said.

"Ten million," John bargained.

"Fifteen and you have an agreement," I said.

"Done." He held out his hand. I shook it.

"The money has to be placed in the foundation before we go into probate," I said.

"I understand," he said. "The money will be transferred tomorrow."

He refilled our glasses. "You are very much like your uncle," he said. "How come you never did go into the family business?"

"My father didn't like it," I said. "And I had a touch of it when I was young and I realized it was not my game as well."

"You might have been in my place," he said.

I shook my head. "In that case, one of us would be dead." I was silent for a moment and then nodded my head. "I was very young then," I said, remembering going up the Amazon with my cousin Angelo, many years ago.

Book One

❖

ANGELO AND ME

1

❖

I WAS SWEATING from every pore, even though it was supposed to be cooler in the late afternoon. I wiped myself with the soaking towel dipped in warm Amazon river water. It didn't help. Nothing helped. It wasn't the heat, it was the humidity. But this wasn't humidity, this was wet. And hot. I stretched out on the shelf of the stern.

I had fucked myself. I never should have listened to my cousin Angelo. It was two months ago, June to be exact. We sat in the Pool Room of The Four Seasons in New York, at a poolside table. Just Angelo and me. I had just graduated from the Wharton School. "You don't have to go to work right now," Angelo said. "What you need is a vacation, an adventure."

"You're full of shit," I said. "I have offers from two

of the best stockbrokers on Wall Street. They want me right away."

"What are they offering you?" he asked, finishing his vodka rocks and ordering another.

"Forty grand a year for starters."

"Chicken shit," Angelo said. "You can get that anytime." He looked at me. "You hurtin' for money?"

"No," I said. He knew as well as I that my father had left me more than a million dollars.

"Then what's the rush?" Angelo looked across the pool at a girl on the other side. "That's class," he said appreciatively.

I looked at her. I didn't know what he was talking about. She was ordinary Radcliffe. Long brown hair, large eyeglasses making her eyes seem enormous, no brassiere, soft titties. I didn't say anything.

He turned back to me. "I'm going to South America next month," he said. "I would like you to come with me."

"What the hell for?" I asked.

"Emeralds," he said. "Worth more than diamonds in today's market. And I have a line on a suitcaseful of them for pennies."

"Illegal?" I asked.

"Shit, of course," he said. "But I have arranged everything. Transportation. Customs. We walk through."

"That's not my game," I said.

"We could split two million," he said. "No hassle. The family's covering me. Blanket all the way."

"My father walked away from that many years ago. I don't think I should go into it."

"You're not going into anything," he said. "You're

just being company for me. You're family. Anybody else I might take along might get some big ideas." He looked across at the girl again. "You think it's okay if I send a bottle of Dom Perignon to her?"

"Forget it," I said. "I know that type. Cold ass."

"That's what I like. Warm them up and turn them on." He laughed. He turned back to me. Serious. "Coming with me?"

I hesitated. "Let me think about it." But even while I said that, I knew I would go with him. Burying my nose in books for the last few years wasn't my idea of great living. It was fucking dull. Wharton was not excitement, no action. Not like it was in Vietnam.

My father was pissed off when I enlisted. I was nineteen and had just finished two years in college. I told him that the draft would get me even if I didn't beat them to it. At least this way I had the choice of services. That's what I thought, but that was not the army's idea. They didn't need PR men. There were enough people shoving bullshit to the media. What they wanted was grunts, and that was I. Grunt number 1. Asshole.

I took all four months of basic training. I jumped out of planes and helicopters, dug foxholes until I was sure that South Carolina was slipping into the ocean. Then to Saigon. Three whores and five million units of penicillin. Seventy pounds of armament: an automatic rifle, a Colt automatic .45-caliber pistol, a disassembled bazooka and six hand grenades.

I jumped into the middle of the night, four hours away from Saigon. The night was quiet. Silent. Not a sound except for us assholes groaning as we hit the ground. I got up and looked for the lieutenant. He was nowhere to be found. The grunt in front of me turned around. "This is a cinch," he said. "Ain't nobody here." Then he stepped into a field mine and pieces of him and shrapnel blew back in my face.

That was the end of my career in the army. Four months later, after I got out of the hospital where they fixed up my face, leaving only two small scars on either side of my chin, I walked into my father's office.

He sat behind his big desk. He was a small man and he loved his big desk. He looked up at me. "You're a hero," he said without expression.

"I wasn't a hero," I said. "I was an asshole."

"At least you're admitting it. That's a step in the right direction." He rose from his desk. "Now what are you going to do?"

"I haven't thought about it,' I said.

"You had your turn, you went into the army." He looked up at me. "Now it's my turn."

I didn't answer.

"When I go, you'll be rich," he said. "Maybe a million or more. I want you to go to the Wharton School."

"I haven't the credits to get into it," I said.

"I've already got you in," he said. "You start in September. I figure that's the place to learn how to handle your money."

"There's no rush, Dad," I said. "You're going to live a long time."

"Nobody knows," he said. "I thought your mother would live forever."

It was six years since my mother had gone, but my father still hurt for her. "Mother's cancer is not your fault," I said. "Don't be so Italian."

"I'm not Italian, I'm Sicilian," he said.

"They're the same thing to me."

"Don't tell that to my brother," he said.

I looked at him. "What's happening to the Godfather?"

"He's okay," my father answered. "The Feds couldn't lay a hand on him."

"He's something else," I said.

"Yes," my father said disapprovingly. When my father was young he split with the family. It was not his way of life. He went into the car-rental business and in a short while had thirty locations in airports around the country. It wasn't Hertz or Avis, but it wasn't bad. Twenty million gross a year. He hadn't heard from his brother for years, and didn't hear from him until my mother died. Then my uncle sent a roomful of flowers. My father threw them all out. My mother was Jewish and the Jews don't have flowers at their funerals.

"Do you know what Angelo is doing?" I asked. Angelo was my first cousin, just a few years older than I.

"I hear he's working for his father."

"That figures," I said. "Good Italian boys go into their father's business." I looked at him. "Do you expect me to go into your business?"

My father shook his head. "No, I'm selling out."

"Why?" I was surprised.

"Too many years," he said. "I thought I would travel around a little bit. I never saw anything of the world and I plan to start from where I was born. Sicily."

"You got a girl to go with you?" I asked.

My father flushed. "I don't need anyone to travel with me."

"It would be good company," I said.

"I'm too old," he said. "I wouldn't know what to do with a girl."

"Find the right one and she will show you," I said.

"Is that any way to talk to your father?" he asked indignantly.

IT HAPPENED. I went off to Wharton and my father sold his business and went off to Sicily. But something went wrong. His car went off the curving, winding road coming down from Mount Trapani to Marsala.

My uncle called me before I left for Sicily to bring my father's body home. "I'm going to send two body-guards with you."

"What for?" I asked. "Nobody's going to bother me."

"You don't know," he said heavily. "I loved your father. Maybe we didn't agree but that doesn't matter. Blood is blood. Besides, I heard that somebody has tampered with the brakes on your father's car."

I was silent for a moment. "Why? Everyone knows that he was straight."

"That doesn't mean anything in Sicily. They don't know about those things, all they know is that he was family: my family. I don't want them to get to you. You're goin' to have two bodyguards."

"No way," I said. "I can take care of myself. At least I learned that in the army."

"You learned how to get your ass blown off," he said.

"That was something else," I said.

"Okay," he said. "Then would you let Angelo go with you?"

"If I'm hot," I said, "then he'll be hotter. He's your son."

"But he knows the game, and besides that he speaks Sicilian. Anyway he wants to go with you. He loved your father too."

"Okay," I said. Then I had a question. "Angelo's not doing any business over there?"

My uncle was lying. "Of course not."

I thought for a moment. It really didn't make any difference. "Okay," I said. "We'll go together."

My uncle was smarter than I was. I didn't need any bodyguards. But Angelo always had four men with bulged armpits under their jackets, and since he was always with me, we had bodyguards. There was no trouble in Sicily. The small funeral service we had in the church in Marsala was quiet, with only a few people attending, none of whom I knew, even though we were supposed to be relatives. I received their condolences and embraces as the hearse carried the coffin to Palermo, where it was then transported by plane to New York. My father's wishes were to be buried beside my mother. It was done.

A WEEK LATER I stood in the cemetery as the coffin was placed in the ground. Silently I threw a handful of dirt on the coffin and turned away. My uncle and Angelo followed me.

"Your father was a good man," my uncle said heavily.

"Yes," I said.

"What will you do now?" he asked.

"Finish school. I'll get my degree in business administration in June."

"Then what will you do?" my uncle asked.

"Get a job," I answered.

My uncle was silent. Angelo looked at me. "You're an asshole," he said. "We have many businesses that you could fit into."

"Legitimate business," my uncle added.

"My father wanted me to go my own way," I said. "But I thank you for the offer."

"You're exactly like your father," my uncle growled.

I laughed. "Exactly. As Angelo is exactly like you. Like father, like son."

My uncle embraced me. "You are my family. I love you."

"And I love you," I said and watched him go to his car, then turned to Angelo. "What are your plans?"

"I have a date in town," he said. He gestured toward the limousine. "I'll go in with you if you don't mind."

"Okay." We sat silently as the limo drove back into Manhattan. Not until we had gone into the Midtown Tunnel did I speak. "I want to thank you for coming to Sicily with me. I didn't know it then, but I needed your support. Thank you."

"It's nothing," he said. "You're family."

I nodded without speaking.

"My father means it," he said. "He would like you to be with us."

"I appreciate that," I said. "And I'm grateful, but it's not the way I'm going."

"Okay." Angelo smiled. "I was always curious— why did your father change the name from Di Stefano to Stevens?"

"That was far enough from the family name," I answered.

"But Stevens, that's an Irish name. I don't get it."

"My father explained to me," I said. "All Italians change their names to Irish when they change them."

"And your name, that's not Irish."

"It was my father's idea. He wanted me to be as American as I could." I laughed.

The limo came out of the tunnel. He looked out the window. "Drop me off on Park and Fiftieth."

"Okay."

"Want to have dinner tonight? I have a couple of cute chicks."

"I'm packing tonight. I'm going up to school tomorrow. But thanks anyway."

"You'll graduate in June?" he questioned.

"Yes."

"I'll be in touch with you," he said. And he did so. Almost before I knew it, I was sweating on the back of a dilapidated old riverboat on the Amazon while he was down in the cabin screwing a crazy, beautiful Peruvian girl he had hired as a translator in Lima.

I stared up at the sunlight shining through the trees hanging over the riverbank. I was soaking wet with perspiration. I reached for a cigarette. Angelo had to be a better man than I if he could fuck in heat like this.

2

❖

FROM THE BENCH at the stern of the boat, I watched as the monkey moved expertly through the dense greenery on the shore. It swung gracefully from vine to vine. Suddenly it stopped and sat down on its haunches. It eyeballed me. It knew I was an amateur. Then it quickly disappeared when Angelo came up from the cabin. He was naked except for his designer bikini shorts, and the hair over his chest, shoulders, and back was matted with sweat. He took a bottle of beer and sucked on it. Disgustedly he threw it overboard. "Crap," he said.

"No ice," I said, looking up at him.

"Balls," he said, throwing himself down beside me on the bench. He stared at me. "The bitch fucked me out," he said with disbelief.

I smiled and reached for another beer.

"Why are you laughing?" he said angrily.

"I wasn't laughing," I said.

"I don't believe it," he said.

"She's used to the heat. You're not," I said.

"Got a cigarette?" he asked.

I gave him the pack and watched him light up. "When are we getting out of here?" I asked.

"In the morning," he said. "We should be loaded by ten o'clock, then we'll take off."

"I thought we were coming up for emeralds," I said. "Now we're sitting on two tons of coca leaves."

"The Colombians don't want our money, they want coca. We give them the leaves and they'll give us the emeralds."

I stared into his eyes. "You're full of shit," I said. "Now that I'm into it, why don't you give me the straight story?"

"You won't like it," he said, returning my stare.

"Try me," I answered.

"It's the difference between two million and twenty," he said.

"How do you figure that?" I asked.

He didn't answer.

"There were never any emeralds," I accused.

He shook his head. "You're family," he said. "The only one I could trust."

"Did your father know about it?"

"He didn't want you to go. But it was my idea." He shot his cigarette overboard. It hissed as it hit the water. "Besides you owed me one for Sicily."

"Nothing happened there," I said.

"Because I was there. I had four men to keep a blanket over us. Alone, you would have been wasted."

I was silent. I didn't know whether to believe him or not. Maybe I would never know. But it was over. "Now what do we do?"

"We go downriver to Iquitos. I have a DC 3 to take us to Panama. From there a Cessna Twin takes us to Miami, where we make the drop. We're booked on Eastern to New York."

I shook my head. "I was really an asshole."

"I'll never tell anybody." He grinned. "It's all in the family."

"Do you know the people we're meeting?" I asked.

"Not personally," he said.

"How will you find them?" I asked.

"They'll find us. It's all been arranged. Customs has been paid off through Miami."

"I want out," I said, shaking my head. "It's not my game."

"You can't quit now," he said. "All the charters are in your name. I had to do it. My name is on too many lists."

"I still don't like it. Too much could go wrong. We could be hijacked, we could be fingered by some snitch. It makes me nervous."

Angelo looked at me, then went back into the cabin. He came up a moment later and placed a Colt automatic in my hand. "That's insurance," he said. "Do you know how to handle it?"

"I had one of these in Vietnam."

"If anyone even looks suspicious, waste them."

I handed the gun back to him. "No," I said.

"Okay," he said. He put the gun on the bench beside

me. "I'm going in for a swim," he said and dived off the back of the boat.

Alma came up from the cabin as he dived into the water. Angelo's cotton shirt covered her down to her thighs. She looked at the gun, then at me. "Why did he bring a gun?" Her voice reflected only a faint Spanish accent.

"He wanted me to have it," I answered.

She was a pretty girl, but her face looked worried. "Does he expect any trouble?"

"No," I answered. I looked at him swimming in the water. "How is it?" I called.

"Great," he yelled back. "Come on in."

"No, thanks," I said.

He called to Alma. "Come on, baby. The water's fine."

She hesitated, looking at me, then dropped his shirt to the deck and posed for me. "You like?" she asked in a teasing voice.

I laughed. "You're a cunt."

"And I think you're a fag."

"You're not my girl," I said.

"But you never even look," she said.

"I have rules." I reached for another cigarette.

She dived into the water. She disappeared beneath the surface and came up in front of Angelo about twenty yards from the boat. She grabbed him and pulled him down under the water.

"Loco," the heavyset Peruvian captain of the boat spoke from behind me.

I looked at him.

"Tell your friends to get in the boat," he said in his halting English. "It is not safe." Something in the sound of his voice meant business.

"Angelo!" I yelled. "The *capitano* wants you to get back in the boat."

"What the hell for?"

"He says it's dangerous."

"Horseshit." He laughed. "The water is as calm—" He turned in the water, searching for the girl. "You bitch! Stop trying to grab my balls!"

"I'm not anywhere near you," she called back to him from five yards away.

"Christ!" Angelo yelled—then screamed in pain. "What the hell is going on?" He thrashed about in the water trying to swim back to the boat.

"Piranhas!" the boatman shouted, picking up a boat hook and holding it out into the water.

Alma began swimming back to us. "They're after me!" she screamed. She grabbed the end of the boat hook, and the sailor pulled her toward us, then drew her onto the boat. Her legs were punctured with tiny bites from which the blood was already oozing.

The sailor left her lying on the deck and tried to reach Angelo with the hook. I looked at him. Angelo was still thrashing and screaming but was moving more slowly toward us. I grabbed the boat hook from the sailor and took his arm so that I could lean farther toward Angelo. "Grab the hook, Angelo!" I yelled.

Still screaming in pain, he reached and grabbed the hook. The sailor and I pulled him heavily toward the boat; then the sailor grabbed him under the armpits and hauled him onto the boat.

I had seen terrible things in Nam but never anything like this. His right leg was eaten away almost to the naked bone, the flesh of his left leg hanging in tatters to the bones of his feet. Angelo was staring at me, his eyes clouded with pain and fear. He looked down at himself. He couldn't form any words, only a moaning, screaming sound. His groin was a puddle of torn flesh and blood, his penis and testicles gone. He turned his head back up toward me and tried again to speak, but no words came from his mouth.

"He will die," the captain said without emotion. "I have seen this before It will take one hour, maybe two, but he will die."

"Isn't there something we can do?"

The captain shook his head. "Kill him," he said impassively. "Or let him die by himself in agony."

I turned to Angelo. He spoke with his eyes. He knew what the captain had said. He managed a word. "Family."

I knew what he meant. I reached behind me to the bench and took the automatic in my hand. With the gun still behind me, I flipped the safety off with one hand. Then I kissed him on the forehead. "Family," I said and covered his eyes with my hand. Then I pulled the trigger.

Slowly I rose to my feet and looked down at him. Angelo was gone. And part of me was also gone. But another part of me was reborn. Family.

"What shall we do with him?" the captain asked.

For the first time I realized that the two other sailors were standing near us. "There is nothing we can do," I said, gesturing toward the side of the boat.

"The watch," the captain said, pointing to the Rolex on Angelo's hand.

"Give it to me," I said. I knew my uncle would want it. I turned to the girl lying on the deck, her eyes staring in fear. I heard the splash of Angelo's body as it hit the water. I paused a moment and then spoke to her. "How do you feel?"

She was frightened. "You're not going to kill me?"

Then I realized I was still holding the gun. I closed the safety and stuck it in my belt. "No," I said. I turned to the captain. "What can we do for her?"

The captain knelt beside her. "She has not too many bites. The piranhas were too busy with your cousin. We will wrap some wet coca leaves on her, it will stop the pain, and she will heal."

"Take her down to the cabin and take care of her. Then come back to me."

"*Sí, señor,*" the captain said.

I watched as he lifted her in his arms and took her down to the cabin, one of the sailors following with a sheaf of coca leaves. I sat down again on the bench at the stern.

A few moments later the captain came up. "My sailor is taking care of her. What can I do for you?"

I looked up at him. "Do you have a bottle of whiskey?"

"I have rum," he said.

"Bring it," I said. "I need a drink."

3

❖

THERE WAS ONLY one large cabin below deck. A curtain was strung across the middle to separate my bunk from the larger bunk that Angelo and Alma had shared. Despite the half-bottle of rum I had swallowed, I was sober, not even the slightest buzz. The curtain was now pulled back, and I looked over toward Alma lying on the bed. She appeared to be sleeping, her eyes closed. A faint whisper of breath passed her lips.

I crossed the cabin and stood next to her bed. I touched her forehead with my palm. She didn't have any fever. Then her eyes opened.

"How do you feel?" I asked.

"Numb," she said. "No feeling in my legs at all."

"It's the coca leaves," I said. "The captain told me. It's natural cocaine, a real painkiller. He said you only have small nicks, you'll be okay in a day or two."

"I feel heavy," she said.

"He gave you some coca-leaf tea," I said. "It will let you rest."

She nodded. Then tears came to her eyes. "I feel sorry about your cousin."

I was silent.

"I liked him," she said. "He was crazy, but nice."

"Yes," I said.

"What will you do now?" she asked.

"I'll go on, I guess," I answered. "There is nothing else I can do."

She looked into my eyes. "You don't cry."

"Crying won't help. He is gone. It's over." I turned and walked back to my bunk. "Why don't you try to sleep? You will feel better in the morning."

"I am afraid I will have bad dreams," she said.

"Don't be frightened," I said. "I will be right here."

She nodded faintly and closed her eyes. In a moment I again heard the faint whisper of her breath as she slept. I pulled out the attaché case Angelo had placed under my bunk. It was locked. I found the key in a pair of pants he had thrown over a chair.

The attaché case was filled with bank-sealed packages of one-hundred-dollar bills. Quickly I checked it. One hundred thousand dollars. On the open top cover was a typewritten note:

> Pucallpa to Iquitos—Boat 10m
> Iquitos to Medellín—DC 3 20m
> Medellín to Panama—DC 320m
> Panama to Miami—Cessna 35m

I stared at the money. Angelo had it all laid out. He was not as crazy as he pretended. I took out a package of ten thousand dollars and closed the attaché case. I put the case under my bunk and opened Angelo's valise leaning against the wall. Under his clothing was another automatic and ten clips of cartridges. I pushed the gun and clips under my bunk next to the attaché case, then closed the valise and placed it back against the wall.

I stretched out on my bunk and put my hands behind my head on the pillow. I stared up at the ceiling—then it hit me. Angelo was gone. And whether I liked it or not, I had to go through with his plan. And even worse than that, at the end of it all, I had to tell his father of his death. And all I could give him of his son was a gold Rolex watch. It would not be easy. Angelo was the apple of his father's eye. I dozed.

I opened my eyes when I heard soft steps running on the deck over my head, and the soft whispering voices of two men. Quietly I slipped out of my bunk and onto the deck, the gun in my hand. The captain and another man were talking quietly at the stern of the boat. I watched them silently. The stranger gestured with his hand, and two more men came aboard behind him and bent down to the hold, picking up two bales, and started to take them off the boat.

I turned off the safety of the automatic and stepped around the cabin entrance toward them. "What's happening?" I asked.

The strangers stopped talking and stared at me. I spoke to the captain. "What the hell's going on?"

"The *señor* says that the deal is off. He hasn't gotten the money to be paid by your cousin." The captain was very nervous.

"Tell him that I already know the money has been paid. If not, the coca would never have been placed aboard," I said.

The captain spoke quickly. The man replied in Spanish, then the captain turned back to me. "Only part of the money. There was still one thousand dollars to be paid when all the coca has been delivered."

"Tell him that he will get the money as promised when he has delivered the rest of the coca."

The stranger understood me. He spoke quickly to the captain and the captain translated. "He says that he is a simple farmer and he has worked hard for his crops, and he does not want his labor to be stolen from him."

I looked at the captain. "How much is he paying you for this bullshit?"

"*Nada, señor.* Nothing," the captain said nervously. "On my family's honor I tell you the truth."

I stared at him for a moment, then at the stranger. "Tell the son of a bitch to get off this boat or I will kill him. He can come back tomorrow with the rest of the coca, and we will pay whatever else he is due."

The captain spoke quickly. The stranger looked at me, then nodded. He spoke to the captain and nodded again. "He will be back in the morning," the captain said.

I gestured with the gun. "Off."

The stranger and his two men scrambled from the boat. I watched them disappear into the trees around the lagoon. I turned to the captain. "How did he learn that my cousin had died?"

"They are watching. They are always watching us," he said.

"Why did you allow him to come aboard to take back the coca?"

"He is Indian. Mestizo. Very dangerous. He would have killed me if I didn't let him on the boat," he said.

"I see," I said, thinking for a moment. "Then he will come back tomorrow and kill us."

The captain was silent.

"But not if we are not here tomorrow," I said.

The captain looked at me. "They are in the trees hiding and watching," he said. "They will hear the engines if we try to leave."

"Then we don't start the engines. We use boat hooks. Here the river is not deep, and we can push us far enough so that the river current can take us downstream until it is safe to start the engines."

The captain stared at me with new respect. "You know about such things?"

"In Vietnam. Many times." I lied; I had only heard about it. I had never really believed it until now.

"Sí, señor," he said. "When shall we start?"

"Give them about an hour to fall asleep," I said. "Then we go."

"And if they come after us?"

"You have guns?" I asked.

"Two pistols, two rifles," he answered.

"Then we kill them," I said. "Bring the guns up to the deck and have your men get ready to cast off."

He nodded and climbed into the hatchway that opened

to his quarters. I went back to the cabin, got the other gun, and stuck it into my belt beside the one I already had. Quickly I stuffed several cartridge clips into my pockets.

Alma's voice sounded across the cabin. "What is happening?"

"We're taking off," I said.

She sat up on the bunk. "But we were supposed to get ten more bales of coca leaves in the morning."

"We're not waiting for it," I said. "The farmer was already aboard and wanted to take the bales back. He said that Angelo hadn't paid him."

"It's not true," she said. "I saw him give him the money in front of the captain."

"The captain saw it?"

She nodded. "He arranged it. He spoke to the farmer in the native Indian tongue.

My hunch was right. The captain had already made his deal. "How long will it take us to get downriver to Iquitos?"

"Five, six days," she said. "It's down on the Uyacali river where it joins the Amazon."

"Okay," I said.

"Will there be trouble?" she asked.

"I don't know," I said.

She looked up at me. "Maybe I can help. I can use a gun." She got out of bed.

I gave her one of Angelo's guns. "You keep it," I said. "I don't expect any trouble tonight, but if there is any, I'll holler."

She kept looking at me. "But you are worried about something?"

"Not about the mestizos, it's the captain, I don't trust him. He was ready to let the others take off the bales without even letting me know." I suddenly remembered. "Didn't we meet the captain in the market in Tingo Maria?"

"That's right," she answered. "Tingo Maria is the main source of coca and marijuana. It was the captain who made the deal with the mestizo to bring the coca over the mountain road to Pucallpa. The same road we came down on."

"It was also the captain who had us move the boat downstream about ten kilometers from the Pucallpa docks." It began to fall into place. "It was safer, he had said, we would not be found by the police."

"Yes," she nodded. "I hadn't thought about it but the mestizo came right to us. The captain had it all arranged before we left Tingo Maria."

"Okay," I said. "You stay down here. I feel we'll have no trouble here. If he makes a move, it will be when we are further downstream when he thinks that I believe we are safe."

"You'll have to watch him," she said.

"I will." I reached across her bunk to the shelf where Angelo had left his small bag. I opened it and took out a vial of coke. Quickly I had a snort. I felt my head open and my eyes widen. "I'll be awake now."

"You'll be stoned," she said.

"I'll be careful," I said and went up on deck.

The captain and his two sailors were waiting for me. He gestured, and I saw the guns lying on the shelf in front of the wheelhouse. I nodded. "Now pick up the gangplank," I said. "But carefully. No sound."

The captain motioned to the sailors. Quickly and quietly they pulled the gangplank aboard. Then the sailors picked up the boat hooks and began to pole us out of the small lagoon into the main current of the river while the captain held the wheel. I could feel the boat move with the current. It seemed strong, and we moved quickly downstream.

The captain turned to me. "Start the engine now?" he asked.

"Not yet," I said. "Another fifteen minutes."

"The water is strong," he said. "I don't know if I can keep it straight."

"Have your men use the boat hooks on the stern. They'll hold us straight long enough." I looked back to the lagoon. There was no motion on the bank. "Keep going," I said.

The captain held up a hand, and one of the sailors took the wheel. The captain walked around and went down into the hatch to the engine room. Fifteen minutes later I heard the engine roar, and the boat began to move faster in the water. I looked at the sailor at the wheel. He turned to look back at me. Mistake. When you have a wheel in your hand, whether you're driving a car or a boat, you always keep your eyes on the road.

I spun sideways, turning back. The captain was out of the hatchway, a rifle pointed toward me in his hands. I could almost see the surprise on his face as the automatic spit angrily at him. Then slowly his arms stretched out and he tumbled from the stern of the boat into the water.

I pointed the gun at the sailors and gestured toward

the wheel. Alma had come from the cabin, the gun in her hands. "What happened?" she called.

"We lost the captain," I said.

She stared at me.

"Ask the sailor if he can get the boat down to Iquitos," I told her. "Tell him if he does, he gets a thousand dollars; if he doesn't he goes swimming with the captain."

Quickly she spoke to the sailor. The second sailor came to the wheelhouse and spoke to her. She turned to me. "They are captains in their own right, he says. And if they do what we say, the two should get money."

"They can divide the money," I said. "I will also give them the boat for themselves."

She spoke again. They looked at each other, then nodded. They spoke to her and she translated again.

"They want to know if you would give them the papers for the boat?"

"They will have them," I said.

She spoke to them again, then turned back to me after listening another moment for their answer. "They want you to know that they are not *bandidos* like the captain, they are honest men and all they want to do is their job."

"Fine," I said and shook their hands. "It's a deal."

They grinned at me. "Deal," they said.

4

❖

I STARED DOWN at my plate. Rice and beans covered with a sickly brown tomato sauce and lots of oil. I'd had it. Day and night. It had been four nights since we left Pucallpa. Rice and beans. Rice and greasy yellow fish. Rice and canned meat that produced maggots the moment the can was opened. My stomach was either exploding with gas or threatened with nausea that never quite came.

I looked at Alma. "How can you handle it?"

"Drink more beer," she said simply. "We have no choice."

I opened a bottle of beer and gulped half of it down. "Are there restaurants in Iquitos?"

"Iquitos is a big city," she said. "Relax, we'll be there tomorrow."

I pointed at my plate. "Throw this shit overboard."

"You'll eat it," she said firmly. "You're not eating enough as it is. You look like you've lost ten pounds."

"I'm okay," I said.

"You'll need your strength," she said. "Nobody knows what you'll have to face tomorrow. We've been lucky so far, but you're like a babe in the woods. You don't even know what we'll be facing up there. Angelo never told you anything."

I took a large spoonful of rice and swallowed it. I followed it with a mouthful of beer. Even though it was warm, it killed the taste of grease in my mouth. I looked over at her. "Did he ever tell you anything about Iquitos?"

"Only that he was meeting a red-bearded man who would be waiting on the docks when we came in."

"Did he say anything else?"

She shook her head. "Angelo didn't talk much about his business."

I nodded. Angelo didn't talk to anyone. Even me. "Has Iquitos an airport?"

"Yes," she said. "Iquitos is the second-biggest city in Peru, but the only way to get out is either by boat up the Amazon or by air over the mountains. They are too high to cross any other way."

"How did the city get so big?" I asked.

"Years ago it was the center of rubber plantations and was important until they brought the rubber trees into Malaysia. When that business had been lost, the city barely existed on produce until they discovered oil. Now tankers can go down to the ocean by way of the Amazon."

"Is it a big port?"

"I've never been there," she answered. "But I think it has to be pretty big because ocean-going ships go in there from Brazil."

I was just going for another spoonful of rice when I heard the small engine stop, and the boat began to wallow slowly in the water. I reached for the rifle and climbed out of the cabin with Alma right behind me. I saw the two sailors on the bow dropping the anchor, the long rope slipping into the water behind it. I moved up behind the sailors. "Ask them what they're doing," I told Alma.

She spoke rapidly in Spanish. The sailors looked up at us nervously, both of them speaking at the same time. She asked them another question. Then the older one answered her. He seemed to be explaining something to us.

She turned to me. "They thought it would be better for us to anchor in this cove until morning. It is only thirty kilometers to Iquitos, and it would be better if we went in early in the morning."

"Why not now?" I asked.

Pablo, the older sailor, answered her. She relayed his words to me. "The fishermen are all going out in the channel. Their nets will be everywhere and we could become snarled in them. Many of them are mestizos and thieves. Look over at the channel and you will already see them. They have bright searchlights aiming at the river to attract the fish, and if we have trouble with them, they would all gang up on us."

"What time can we get in?" I asked.

"The fishermen go in at four in the morning. By five o'clock we could begin. We should be in Belén by eleven o'clock and be tied up to the dock a half hour later."

"What's Belén?" I asked.

"It's where the Pucallpa boats dock—the smaller boats like ours. They also live on the houseboats there. The big ships are ten kilometers beyond at the other end of the city."

"Where did the captain tell them they would dock?" I asked.

They shook their heads. "He never told them," she said.

I looked out at the channel in the center of the river. The fishermen's searchlights were like lightning bugs bobbing up and down in the water about three-quarters of a mile outside of our cove. It seemed as if there were hundreds of them. I turned back to the sailors. "Okay," I said to Alma. "Tell them I want to get underway as soon as the fishermen are gone. And to stay out in the river as far away as possible from Belén, and we will go in where the big ships dock."

Alma translated. Pablo shook his head. He said something angrily. She turned to me. "He says it would be dangerous. That is where the customs and police are stationed."

"I'll worry about it when we get there," I said. I turned again and looked at the fishermen. "Keep your eyes out for them," I said, nodding in their direction. "If any of them come toward us, let me know."

She translated and then followed me to the stern, where we sat down on the small bench. "What are you thinking?"

"I don't trust any of them," I said. "But if we are to

meet someone, it makes more sense that he would meet us at one of the more important docks than at the docks for crappy riverboats and fishermen."

"I would think the smaller docks would be safer than the big ones," she said.

"I remember something that Angelo once told me. The best place to hide is out in the open. No one ever thinks you would be doing anything wrong."

"Angelo was crazy," she said.

"Not that crazy," I said. "He got me down here. What did he promise you to come with him?"

She looked down at me. "I liked him."

I smiled. "Nothing else?"

She laughed. "Money. A lot of it."

I nodded. "How much?"

"A thousand dollars U.S."

"You just got a raise," I said. "We get out of this, you get ten grand."

She was silent for a moment; then she laughed. "Now we have to fuck," she said.

"First, we get out of here," I said, looking out at the fishermen's boats, their lights bobbing up and down in the channel.

"What are you watching for?" she asked.

"I don't feel right," I said. I pointed around the cove. "We may be hidden from the fishermen but we're less than a hundred yards from the shore around us. And on top of it, the forest is right up to the water and there is no way we can see into it."

She stared at the shoreline. "Do you think the mestizos have followed us along the river?"

"I don't know," I said. "Do you think they could?"

"There are really no roads," she answered.

"But they have horses," I said. "They could have made it on footpaths."

She gestured forward to the sailors. "Do you think they might know anything about them?"

"I don't know." I shrugged. "They weren't very upset about the captain. I'm sure they knew what he was planning and were part of it."

She turned and stared at the shore. Night had fallen swiftly, and the only light we had was from the sparkling stars and the yellowish full moon. "I can't see a damn thing in there."

I nodded. "Bring the rifles and the gun I gave you and let's keep them up here with us."

"You're going to stay up all night?" she asked.

"I'll feel safer," I said.

"I'll stay up with you," she said. "I'll feel safer with you."

I looked at her. "Then put on a pair of jeans instead of your shorts and get a hat and a bug veil as well as the bottle of citronella. I don't want the bugs to get us if the mestizos don't."

She laughed. "I'll be back in a few minutes," she said going down into the cabin.

She wasn't stupid. She came up from the cabin with blankets and pillows. "If we wrap up in these blankets the damp will make us feel soaked as if we are in a bath. But if we spread them out on the deck, it will be dryer than sitting on the bench."

"Good idea," I said. "We'll also be less of a target." I watched her spread the blankets on the deck. The pillows almost made it look comfortable. Too comfortable.

I had an idea. "There's a round three-foot wicker basket next to my bunk. Bring it up with another blanket."

She didn't ask any questions. When she returned, I set the basket on the bench where I had been sitting, wrapped a blanket around it and stuck my old panama hat on top. I turned to her. "What do you think?"

She giggled. "He looks exactly like you."

"Thanks," I said and slipped down to the deck beside her. "Now you can get some sleep. I'll keep watch."

"You're not tired?" she asked.

"I'm okay."

"If you need a lift, I've got a vial in my pocket."

"I'll keep it in mind," I said. "I might need it."

I watched her wrap herself in the blanket, and I turned back up to look at the basket, smiling to myself. She was right. In the black of night it looked exactly like me.

5

❖

I FELT HER hand on my shoulder and came instantly
wide-awake. She pressed a finger against my lips and
pointed forward to the bow of the boat. Keeping my
head down I peered behind the overhang of the cabin.

A man was climbing aboard from a rowboat tied to
a stanchion near the bow. In the dark I could not see
his face but I saw our sailors gesturing to him. He nodded and began walking silently on bare feet across the
narrow deck to where we had been sleeping.

I pushed her into the cabin doorway behind me and
raised the rifle against my shoulder. The man moved
quickly now. I saw the gleam of the machete as he held
it over his head and brought it down viciously into the
basket I had placed on the bench. The machete was
tangled in the blanket as the wicker basket collapsed
around it. I didn't wait for the man to turn toward us. I

pumped two shots into his back between his shoulders. He bent forward and slumped over the stern. I kicked him in the ass and he fell awkwardly over the small railing and into the water.

Alma's automatic roared in a series of staccato explosions. I whirled toward her. She had the gun held stiff-armed in front of her, pointing at the sailor running toward us on the narrow deck. He was still moving toward us as I pushed her out of the way and he fell forward. I pushed him away. A revolver fell to the deck from his lifeless hands. I shoved him off the deck into the water.

"It was Pablo," she said in a trembling voice. "He was trying to kill us."

"That's right," I said.

"Is he dead?" she asked apprehensively.

"Yes," I said.

She crossed herself quickly. "I have sinned. I have never killed a man before."

"You would have sinned more if you let him kill you," I said. I took the gun from her hand and replaced the cartridge. "Keep this. You might need it again."

I motioned to her. "Follow me," I said and started along the narrow deck toward the bow.

Just as I came in front of the cabin, I heard the splash of oars and the rowboat moving away. In the prow of the boat was the younger sailor, still holding a six-pronged grappling hook with the rope trailing behind it. He stared, almost frozen with fear. Slowly I raised the muzzle of the rifle at him. He didn't hesitate. In one motion, he dived from the boat and thrashed through the water after the rowboat.

I watched him for a moment, then turned to Alma. "I guess we lost our crew."

Alma looked at me. "Now what do we do?"

"We'll figure out something," I answered, sounding more confident than I felt. I touched her hand. It was trembling. I pressed her palm into mine. "Take it easy," I said. "We'll manage. We survived this far."

Her eyes filled with tears. "I killed a man."

"He would have killed you," I said. "It's okay."

She began to cry, and I pulled her head to my chest. "Calm down," I said softly, stroking her head. "It couldn't be helped."

She clung to me. "When we get to Iquitos, I will go to confession."

I felt her body pressing warmly against me. "Whatever you say," I said.

A note of surprise came into her voice. She looked up at me. "You have a hard-on."

I tried to move away from her but she held tightly to me. "I'm normal," I said.

"I thought you didn't like me," she said.

"I told you. You were Angelo's girl." I moved away from her and she turned her face up to me. I kissed her quickly, then stepped back. "I like you. But we have other things to do before we begin to play."

She began to smile confidently. "Did you ever have any Peruvian pussy?" she asked teasingly.

"No," I answered, smiling back at her. "The only thing Peruvian I've ever had is Peruvian blue."

"You're in for a treat. Peruvian pussy is even better than Peruvian blue. You'll never have a better high than that."

I laughed. "Stop. You'll get me crazy." I walked down the deck to the stern of the boat. I opened the small hatch to the engine room. I looked up at her. "Keep your eyes open and call me if any of them try to come over here. I'm going to check out the engine."

"Okay," she said.

There were only three steps to the ladder into the engine room and the room was no more than three feet high. I hunched over and found a small electric bulb next to the wall. There was no switch to turn it on with, so I turned the bulb into the socket and it lit dimly. I turned to look at the engine. It was a simple old-fashioned two-cylinder Harvester motor that had probably once belonged to a small tractor. The motor could be started by a flywheel pulled by a cord much like an outboard. Next to the motor was a bank of six twelve-volt car batteries, and above them was a gas tank. I peered at the gauge of the tank. It showed almost half full. I then checked the gears. There were only two positions—forward and rear. Simple enough, I thought—I could handle it. I unscrewed the bulb slightly and climbed out of the engine room.

She was standing at the stern and watching the land around the cove. "I don't see anything moving."

"Good," I said. "I think we'll be okay. I can handle the engine, and piloting the boat should be easy."

"Fine," she replied. "But do you know where we're going?"

"Iquitos is downstream," I said.

"Great," she said sarcastically. "But do you know anything about the waterfront down there? Which docks would be safe, which would not?"

I looked at her. "Don't you know anything about Iquitos?"

"I've never been there," she answered. "Why should I? It's the fucking ass end of the world. No one in Lima would ever go there except for business. Like I told you, there are no roads out of there because of the mountains. You get in by plane or by riverboat from Brazil and Colombia, and I've never had a reason to be there."

"Angelo had arranged for us to get out by plane," I said. "He had a contact."

"Do you know the contact?" she asked.

"No," I said. "But once we're in town, I figure we'll be able to make him."

She was silent for a moment. "You don't know Peru," she said. "Iquitos is a rough town, and they'll make you long before you make them."

"We have to take our chances," I said. "There are no other places to go."

She pointed out toward the river. "The fishermen are going in."

I watched them moving downriver toward Iquitos. They were leaving in a group. Only a few seemed to be hanging back. Maybe they were trying to fill up their nets. "As soon as they're all on their way, we'll start," I said.

"We'll be traveling in daylight," she said.

"We have no choice," I said. "We can't stay here. The fucking Indians will be coming after us."

She shook her head. "I'm frightened," she said in a tight voice.

"We'll be all right," I said, wishing I could feel as sure as I sounded.

She seemed embarrassed. "I have to change. I peed in my pants."

I laughed. "Don't feel bad. It's normal. You go below and clean up. I'll stay up here."

I stepped into the small wheelhouse. It was only two steps higher than the deck but it gave me a good vantage point to see anything moving toward us. I found a pack of cigarettes I had left on the bench yesterday and took one out and dragged on it. The smoke helped, even though the cigarette was old and damp. I coughed and kept my eyes on the cove.

My eyes were burning by the time she came up. I kept thinking that I had seen lights flashing in the forest against the shore, but then there was nothing.

"I feel better," she said. "I washed up. And fresh clothes help."

"You look good," I said. I rubbed my eyes. "I must look like hell."

"Not too bad. You didn't have much sleep."

I nodded. I looked out toward the river. There were about three or four fishing boats still out there. "I wish they'd get the hell out," I said.

"It will be dawn soon," she said. "They'll be gone then."

I grunted and didn't answer.

She took a vial from the pocket of her jeans. "Peruvian blue," she said. "I need some help." Quickly she took two snorts, then handed the vial to me. "We both need the help," she said.

I took the vial from her. Quickly I took two hits in each nostril. I felt my head open up, and my eyes stopped burning. I was wide-awake. Who needs sleep? I gave the vial back to her and laughed. "Party time," I said.

She laughed. "You're feeling better."

"Check," I said.

"Look!" She pointed at the river.

One of the fishing boats was coming into the cove, its searchlight pointing at us. I picked up the automatic rifle. We watched the boat coming slowly toward us.

I pressed her shoulder. "Get down on the deck," I said. "I don't want anyone to see you."

She stretched out on the deck, her automatic held closely between her hands. I waited until the fishing boat was near, then blew out its searchlight with a rifle shot.

The voice was in English. "What the hell are you doing?" the man said angrily.

"Who the hell are you?" I shouted back.

"Angelo?"

"He's not here."

"Jed Stevens?" the man asked.

I waited for a moment. "Right," I said.

"Vince Campanella," the man replied. "I have the deal with Angelo to take him to Medellín."

"You have the plane?" I asked.

"That's my business," he said. "Where's Angelo? You were supposed to meet me in the next cove downriver toward Iquitos. What the hell are you doing here?"

"Nobody told me."

"Get Angelo," he said. "We have to get moving."

"Angelo is dead." I didn't want to tell him how Angelo had died. "Our crew tried to jump us."

"Where are they?" he asked.

"Dead and gone."

"Is the girl with you?" he asked.

"She's here."

"Can I come aboard?" he asked.

I kept the rifle pointed at his belly. "Only you."

He climbed over the small railing and stood up straight when he reached the deck. He was a tall man, six feet two, with blue eyes and red hair and beard. He wore a green khaki shirt and pants. "I spoke to your uncle yesterday. He wanted to know if I had heard from Angelo. You were supposed to be in yesterday, that's why I started out to look for you."

Alma got to her feet. She still held the gun in her hands. "Now, what do we do?" she asked.

"We get you out of here," he said. "We're going to give you a tow and move into the next cove. Then we unload the cargo and I take you into Iquitos and put you on a plane to Lima; from there you go to New York."

"Angelo had a plan," I said. "What happens with that?"

"I'll take care of it," he said. "Your uncle told me to handle it."

"When can I call him?" I asked.

"This evening when we get into the hotel," he said.

"What happens with me?" Alma said.

"You go to Lima with him," he said. "You can be his tour guide."

6

❖

IT WAS EARLY morning and the sun was rising over the trees as we entered the other cove. There was a rickety old dock that came out from the shore. The men jumped quickly over the side of the boat and tied up to the dock. Vince took out a walkie-talkie and spoke into it. Ten minutes later an open two-ton truck pulled up beside the dock. Right behind it came a Jeep with two men and parked next to it.

Vince called out to his men in Spanish. One of them climbed up on the cab of the truck and sat there, a light submachine gun cradled in his arm as he kept watch. Then the four men, two from the fishing boat and the other two from the Jeep, began to unload the bales of coca leaves from the boat and load it onto the truck.

He turned to me. "Get your bags together. We're moving out of here."

I looked at him. "But what about the boat?"

He shook his head. "Screw it. Two of my men will pull it out in the middle of the river and scuttle it. I'm not taking any chances on that boat being seen in Iquitos. I have a hunch that the captain had also tipped off customs. He would have gotten a reward if he had turned in the cargo."

"Wouldn't it be dangerous if we showed up there?" I asked.

"We are not going into the Iquitos airport. I have the plane on an airstrip not far from here. It's cut out from a former rubber plantation. We're organized. We've been working out of here a long time."

I turned to Alma. "How do you feel about it?"

"Okay," she said. "I'll be happy to get home."

"We won't be landing in Juan Chavez International. There is too much paperwork for police and customs. We'll put you down at an airstrip about sixty kilometers from Lima. I'll come in low behind the mountains so that radar doesn't pick us up."

"Then how do we get into town?" she asked.

"Don't worry. We'll have a car there to take you in on the Pan American Highway. You'll be okay." He smiled. "Now get yourself packed. We need to be moving fast."

He watched her disappear into the cabin, then turned to me. "Angelo told me I would collect the fare when we met."

"Yes," I said. "Forty grand for you to Medellín and then to Panama."

"Sixty now," he said.

"You're being greedy, Vince," I said.

"No," he said. "Forget that we had to find you, no charge for that. That's for the family. But to Lima from here adds another two thousand kilometers to our flight. That costs money."

"How much?" I asked.

"An extra twenty," he said.

"I don't know if Uncle Rocco would like that," I said.

"He told me if I get you out I would get a bonus," he said. "I'm just covering my extra expenses."

I laughed. "You're a hustler. You remind me of my cousin."

He laughed with me. "Do I get the money?"

"Do I have a choice?" I asked.

He laughed again. "Your uncle wants you home."

"Okay," I said. Then I looked at him. "Who pays for the plane from Panama to Miami?"

"If you have the cash I can handle it for you."

"After the extra twenty I haven't got enough," I said. "I'll tell my uncle and he'll work it out."

"Good enough for me," he said. "You can give me the money once we're airborne."

IT WAS A few minutes after six o'clock when we began our descent toward Lima. Five and a half hours in a hard plastic seat behind the pilot wasn't my idea of comfort. But the DC 3 wasn't made for passengers. It was a freight carrier.

Vince looked back at us from the pilot's seat. "We'll be on the ground in a half hour."

I groaned and stretched. "Thank God," I said. "I don't think I could take another hour in these seats."

Vince laughed. "This ain't no 707, that's for sure." He turned serious. "Do you have the fare?"

"I have it ready for you," I answered. During our flight, while he was busy taking care of business, I managed to open the attaché case and get the sixty thousand out for him. There had been several large manila envelopes in the case, and I had put the money in two of them. I reached over his shoulder and gave them to him.

He slipped them down into the map racks beside his seat. "Thanks," he said.

"Don't you want to check it?" I asked.

He smiled. "You're part of the family. I trust you."

"Thank you," I said. "I don't know what I would have done without you."

"We all have our jobs," he said. "You just tell your uncle what I've done."

"I will," I said. We seemed to be skimming down over the mountains. Below I could see what seemed like a small town. "Where are we?"

"We're passing Huancavelica and heading toward the coast," he said. "If you look forward you can begin to see the Pacific."

I stood behind him. I could see the blue waters of the ocean. I turned to Alma, who had stood up next to me. "The water is sparkling like blue diamonds," I said.

"Better get back into your seats and belt up. It usually gets turbulent coming down from the mountains to the ocean," Vince said. "You made it this far—I don't want you to break your skull in the plane."

He hadn't been joking. The little plane tossed

around like a leaf in the wind, and finally, when I was almost ready to throw up, it suddenly straightened out, and a few minutes later I felt the wheels touch the ground.

As soon as the plane stopped, he opened the door and Alma and I rushed out. The cool evening air was great. I breathed in deeply. "Jesus," I said.

He smiled at me. "You have to get used to it."

"Not me," I said. "I'll stick with the big jets."

He gestured to his copilot. "Get their bags out." Then he turned to one of the men standing near us. He spoke quickly in Spanish. The man nodded and ran off to the small building at the end of the runway.

He turned back to me. "He's getting a car and driver for you and they're bringing a fuel truck over to me."

In five minutes an old '65 Chevy four-door stopped in front of us. The men began to slam the luggage into the trunk.

I turned to Vince and held out my hand. "Thank you."

"It's okay," he said. "When you talk to your uncle, please give him my condolences."

"I will," I said.

He turned to Alma and held out his hand. "You're a good lady. Take care of him."

She nodded and kissed his cheek. "I will," she said. "Thank you."

We got into the car as the fuel truck began rolling up. He waved his hand and we waved back, and the driver kicked the car into gear and moved toward the highway.

It was dark and after eight o'clock when the driver placed our valises in front of the Hotel El Gran Bolívar. Alma whispered to me. "Give him a tip."

I gave the driver a hundred-dollar bill. He touched his hand in a half salute. *"Gracias, señor,"* he said, smiling.

"Okay," I said and turned to pick up our bags.

She placed a hand on my arm. I looked at her. "No." She turned back to me. "We won't stay here," she said. "There are always police hanging around in the lobby. And the way we are dressed they will be very curious."

She had to be right. We were still wearing the same dirty clothing we had been wearing on the boat. "Where do we go then?" I asked.

"My apartment," she answered. "It's not too far from here. I have a large apartment in a new building near the Parque de Universario." She waved to a taxi waiting at the head of the line parked near the hotel entrance.

Twenty minutes later we got out of the elevator and walked along the narrow marble corridor to her apartment. She rang the doorbell.

I looked at her. "You have someone living with you?"

She smiled, nodding. "My mother."

I was curious. "Won't she be upset that you are bringing a man with you?"

She laughed. "My mother is very liberal."

I was puzzled.

She laughed again. "She's really not my mother," she explained. "She's my maid, but she's been with me so long I call her Mother.

The door opened and a small dark Indian-looking

woman looked out at me. She smiled when she saw Alma. Alma hugged her and kissed her cheek. They spoke rapidly in Spanish, then the small woman held her hand out and smiled shyly. *"Encantada,"* she said.

"Thank you," I said, reaching for the valises.

She shook her head quickly. "No."

"You come in with me," Alma said. "She'll bring the bags. Let me show you the apartment."

It was a large apartment. The living-room wall was covered with photographs of Alma and framed magazine covers with pictures of Alma. I looked at her. "You're really photogenic."

She laughed. "That's how I make my living. I'm a model."

"I didn't know," I said.

"You thought I was a whore," she said wickedly.

"No," I answered. "I just thought you were a party girl."

"I'm that too." She laughed. "Peruvian pussy."

"Okay," I said. "Whatever you say."

The living room was furnished with modern Italian furniture, plastic chairs, long white fabric couches, milk white-shaded lamps. "Come here," she said, gesturing to the long window. She opened a door and led me out onto a balcony.

We were on the seventh floor of the apartment house looking over a park. "It's really beautiful, isn't it?" she asked.

"Very," I said.

"Are you surprised that I could have an expensive place like this?" she asked.

"That's none of my business," I answered.

"But I want you to know," she said. "I like you and I don't want you to have the wrong idea."

I was silent.

"When I was seventeen I fell in love with a wonderful man. He was much older than I and also married. I was his mistress for almost eight years. He sent me to school and gave me an education and helped me in my career. Last year he died. He left me this apartment and some money. I was not only grateful to him for what he did, I also loved him. It's only been in the last six months that I started going out again. But it wasn't much fun for me until your cousin asked me to go on this trip with him. I thought it would be a wonderful change." She looked up at me. "I really wanted to get away from here and forget my yesterdays."

I took her hand. "And did you?"

"After the last few days, I'm beginning to think I did," she said.

"Good," I said.

She led me back into the apartment. "Let me show you to your room." I followed her across the living room. "Besides," she said, "I think you want a bath and a chance to clean up as much as I do."

"I do," I answered. "But do you have a telephone? I have to call my uncle."

"The telephone's in my room," she said. "You give me the number and I'll get it for you."

I sat on the edge of her bed as she gave the operator the number. We waited a few minutes, then she turned to me. "The operator says the lines to the States are backed up. They'll call you back in a few hours."

"Damn," I said.

"That happens here all the time," she said. "You have to be patient. Take your bath and clean up, then we will have some dinner, and by that time the call will come through."

7

❖

I FOLLOWED HER from her room to the bathroom. She gestured to the door on the opposite wall. "That's your bedroom," she said. "The bathroom is between us." She opened a mirrored cabinet over the twin sinks set in a marble counter. "You have everything you need here. Razor, shaving cream, cologne. I'll fill the tub for you."

I opened the door into my bedroom. My valise was open on the bed but the clothing was gone. I turned back to her.

She anticipated my question. "Mamacita is cleaning your things. She'll have them pressed and ready for you by the time you get out of the tub."

"I can't believe it. This is better than any five-star hotel."

"It's only the beginning." She laughed. She turned

on the faucets in the large oval bathtub, then sprinkled a handful of multicolor bath salts over the water. A strange exotic perfume began to fill the air. She found a small white wooden paddle and mixed the salts into the water, then turned to me. "Get out of your clothes," she said, "and shave. It must be at least three days since you have shaved."

I stared at her. "What should I do with these clothes?"

"Throw them on the floor," she said. "Mamacita will throw them away. They're no good for anything."

I was still looking at her. "Then what are you going to do?"

She began to take off her clothes. "I need a bath too. It's a big tub, made especially for two. Are you shy?"

"No," I answered. "But I am surprised."

"I don't know why." She laughed. "You've seen me naked before, and I've seen you."

"How come you've seen me?" I asked.

"Don't be silly," she answered. "We were all in that tiny cabin. There was no place we could conceal ourselves. Now get going." She crossed to the side of the bathroom and straddled the bidet. "I'll have my pussy washed before you finish shaving."

She was already in the tub by the time I began to step into the water. The water was warm and soft. It felt good against my skin.

"Okay?" she asked.

"Perfect," I said.

She stood up and held out a large cream-colored plastic bottle with a plunger spout. "Stand up," she said. "It's a special bath soap. I'll spread it over you. It will make your skin soft."

Slowly she spread the soap over me with a light hand. "Now it's my turn," she said, handing me the bottle.

I felt clumsy. My touch was not as light as hers. She turned slowly and let me do her back, and then turned again to face me. I looked at her questioningly. She smiled. "Don't be silly. Finish." Quickly I spread the soap over her. Her breasts felt heavy in my hand and her belly strong and flat. Very lightly I spread the soap over her pubis.

"Harder," she said. "Get it into my hair."

I did as she asked and then brought the soap down between her legs. She was looking into my eyes as I gave her the bottle. She squirted more soap over my penis and testicles.

She was breathing heavily. "Did you feel my love button sticking out?"

I nodded.

She began massaging my genitals. "You're getting hard," she said.

"You keep on doing that and I'll come in your hands," I said.

"I've come twice already," she said. She put an arm over my shoulder and began to pull me down to her.

We made it to our knees; then I couldn't hold it any longer. The spasm tore through my body. It felt as if it would never stop. "Jesus!" I said. I looked down at her. "I've come all over you."

"That's beautiful. That's the best skin lotion ever made."

IN THE DISTANCE I could hear the telephone ringing. Then I felt her hand shaking my shoulder. Slowly I sat up. We were both naked in the bed. "Oh, boy," I said. "I really passed out."

"You were entitled to it." She smiled as she spoke in a soft voice. "I thought you would never stop coming."

I shook my head. "Did I hear the telephone?"

"It's your States call," she said. Quickly she held out a vial. "Take a snort," she said. "You're still half asleep."

I nodded. As I packed my nose, my head opened up. "Where's the phone?" I asked.

"Here," she said, picking it up from her bedside table.

I held the receiver to my ear. It was a female American voice I heard. "Mr. Stevens?" she asked.

"Yes."

"I have Mr. Di Stefano for you," she said.

There was a click; then I heard my uncle's voice. It sounded heavy and sad. *"Angelo è morto,"* he said. It wasn't a question; he already knew.

"Yes," I said. "I'm sorry."

"When did it happen?" he asked quietly.

"Almost a week ago," I said. "The captain tried to hijack us. He shot Angelo in the back. It was over in a minute."

"Where were you?" he asked.

"I was down below, in the cabin. When I heard the shots I grabbed the automatic just in time to put the captain away as he came down the cabin steps. I took out one of the other sailors. We made it downstream into a cove with the other two sailors until they got ambitious. I got rid of them before Vince found us. If it weren't for him we would never have made it."

"You said 'We.' Was there someone else with you?"

"Yes," I said. "Angelo brought a girl from Lima. He wanted an interpreter."

"Angelo wanted to get laid," my uncle said mirthlessly. "Can we get him back to the States?"

"No, Uncle," I answered. "He's five hundred kilometers up the Amazon in the jungle."

My uncle was silent for a moment. "I told him not to go," he said. "But he never listened to me. He always wanted to prove himself."

I had no answer.

"I didn't want you to go, either. I told Angelo that you had no part in this," he said.

"Angelo was my cousin and I loved him," I said. "Of course I would go with him. He came to Sicily with me."

"I want you home," he said. "When can you get a plane?"

"It's night now," I said. "I'll check the first thing in the morning."

"Get on Braniff," he said. "I don't trust any of the foreign airlines. You fly American."

"Yes, Uncle," I said.

"You call me the moment you book your flight."

"Yes, Uncle," I said.

"When you get home, we'll arrange for a mass for Angelo," he said.

"I'll be there," I said.

His voice was husky. "The girl? Is she all right?"

"Yes, Uncle."

"Was she a nice girl?"

"Yes, Uncle," I said. "Angelo had good taste. He didn't go with tramps."

"Take care of her," he said.

"Thank you, Uncle," I said.

"Take care of yourself, too," he said. "Don't forget that you're the only man in the family that I have left. And call me tomorrow."

"Yes, Uncle," I said.

"I love you," he said.

"I love you too," I said. The telephone clicked off in my hand. I gave Alma the receiver.

There were tears in her eyes. "How is he?" she asked.

"Heartbroken," I said. "Angelo was the light in his eyes."

8

❖

WE HAD BREAKFAST on the balcony. The sky was blue, the sun bright, and the air fresh. The old lady served us a large plate of fried eggs, onions, and tomatoes, and thin slices of grilled meat covered with a spicy salsa. The bread was hot and dark and the slices were covered with butter. The coffee was strong and hot. I was starved. I ate like there was no tomorrow.

Alma laughed. "Do you always eat like this?"

"Only when I'm hungry," I mumbled through a mouthful. "At least it's real food, not that shit we had on the river."

"Mamacita is a great cook," she said.

"I'll agree to that," I said. I looked at her. "You don't eat much."

"Girls have to watch their diet," she said. "Peruvian women tend to get fat."

"Like Peruvian pussy." I laughed.

"That's good fat." She laughed with me. "You didn't seem to complain."

"Beautiful," I said. "The best."

She leaned across the table and kissed my cheek. "You're sweet."

The old lady stood at the balcony railing. She turned to Alma and spoke.

Alma rose from her chair and looked over the railing. She gestured to me and I joined her. "Down there across the street. That car with two men standing next to it. They might be police."

"You don't know?" I asked.

"It looks like a police car but I don't see any insignia," she said. "Could be plainclothes men. Their cars are not marked."

"How do you know they're looking at us?" I asked.

"I don't know," she said. "But Vince said that the Iquitos police might have been tipped off about us. If they had, they would have notified Lima headquarters because it's the national headquarters."

"And if they are not police?"

"Then they are the *cocainas* still looking for the property." She raised her hand to mine and took my arm away from the railing. "Get dressed," she said. "I have some friends in headquarters. My *patrón* was a general in the army and was once the *jefe* of police. At one time we were all close. I'll make a few calls and see what I can find out."

I went to my room. The old lady was better than any valet. She had my clothes all laid out on the bed: a dark blue blazer with gold buttons, gray flannel slacks, a light blue shirt and a narrow black knit tie. My black oxfords were polished to a high shine and the silk socks carefully placed in each shoe. It took me less than five minutes to dress. There was only one thing I thought I might need. I opened the attaché case and took the automatic from it and slipped it into my jacket pocket. Then I took the ten thousand dollars I had promised Alma and put it into a manila envelope. I placed my passport and visa in my breast pocket and a few packages of bills in my pants pocket. I walked through the bathroom into her room.

She was still speaking on the telephone. The old lady was taking a dress from the closet and laying it out for her. I waited in the doorway until she put down the telephone.

"They are the police," she said. "But they are not looking for you."

"Then we have nothing to worry about," I said.

She shook her head. "They are looking for Angelo. And they think that you are him." She dropped her dressing gown to the floor and stepped into lace bikini panties, then quickly fastened a matching lace brassiere over her breasts. She looked up at me as she sat on the edge of the bed and pulled up her nylons. "You're staring," she said.

"You're a tease." I tossed the manila envelope on the bed beside her.

"What's that?" she asked.

"The money I promised," I answered.

She was silent for a moment, then handed the envelope to me. "You don't have to do it," she said. "I don't need the money."

"I made a promise," I said, returning it to her.

"But we were different then," she said. "Now we are friends and lovers."

"I want you to keep the money," I said. "More now than before, because of the way we feel about each other."

She rose from the bed and kissed me. "You're a lovely man," she said softly.

I held her for a moment, then let her go. "Thank you."

She took the dress from the bed and slipped it on over her body. "Mamacita!" she called.

The old woman hurried into the bedroom. Alma spoke quickly to her. Mamacita nodded and fastened the snap of the dress near the base of her neck. Then she took the envelope from the bed and left the room.

Alma turned back to me. "How do I look?" she asked.

"Beautiful," I said.

"I'll fix my makeup," she said. "You pack your valise, we'll be leaving for the airport in a few minutes."

"What about the police outside?" I asked.

"There won't be any problems," she said. "I spoke to the captain of police. He'll call them off and take us to the airport in his car."

"He believed your story?"

She nodded. "Of course. It was the truth anyway. But he will want to see your passport before we go. You have your visa, and it wouldn't hurt if you also left a thousand-dollar bill with it."

"I thought he was a friend of yours," I said.

"If he wasn't a friend he wouldn't do this for us," she

answered. "You don't understand. Our officials don't earn much money, they need much help."

"We have the same thing in the States sometimes, but we call it graft," I said.

"You have no right to be sarcastic," she said quietly. "You've been breaking almost every law we have on the books."

I stared at her. She was right. Who was I to cast stones? I took her hand. "I apologize."

She squeezed my hand. "Now hurry. Get packed."

I CLOSED THE valise and locked it, then placed the attaché case on top of it. I left them on the bed and walked out onto the balcony. The small black Volkswagen was still parked across the street. While I was watching, a large four-door Ford Fairlane pulled into the street beside it. I couldn't see the driver, but the two men who had been standing next to the Volks seemed to speak to the driver in the other car; then the Ford moved, and the men got into the Volks and started to drive away. I watched them until they had turned the corner, then went back into the apartment. I took my valise and attaché case and walked into the living room.

Alma was waiting for me. I stared at her. She had a dark mink coat loosely thrown over her shoulders, and on the floor beside her were two large valises, a folded hanging bag, and a small, square jewelry bag. All Louis Vuitton. I smiled at her. "You've got class. Planning a trip?"

She laughed. "I'm going to New York with you."

"Hey," I said. "I don't remember talking about it."

"Don't be stupid," she said. "Do you think he would

have believed me if I hadn't told him that you were taking me to New York with you?"

"It's not that easy," I said. "You need a visa."

She laughed again. "I have a multiple-entry visa to the States. After all, I went to school there."

I was silent.

"I also went to school in Paris for a year," she said.

"Are you planning to go there too?" I asked.

"Maybe. But I won't be any problem to you. My *patrón* left me a small apartment in the Hotel Pierre."

I started to laugh. "Maybe you could take me in. I don't have an apartment in New York."

"You can be my guest as long as you want," she said.

The buzzer rang from the house phone near the door. She pressed a button and spoke into it. House phones always have a tinny sound, and this was no exception. The man's voice sounded thin and excited. She spoke to him. His voice came through again. Finally she nodded and replied with the only word I could understand: "Okay."

"*El capitán* is downstairs in the garage under the apartment house. He has kept the two detectives with him. He says they tell him that there are three suspicious characters waiting in a car just outside the entrance to the garage. He thinks they are *pistoleros* because the car has Colombian license plates. He doesn't want us to open the door to anyone except himself."

"Shit," I said. I took the automatic from my pocket. "Do you have another door to the apartment?"

"Service door through the kitchen," she said.

"We better push a table against it," I said. "We don't want anybody to come in from the back."

She called to Mamacita and I followed them into the kitchen and helped them move a heavy wooden table against the door. Then we walked back into the living room. She turned and spoke to the old woman. The old woman began weeping. She hugged Alma and kissed her. Alma kissed her too, said something else to her in Spanish, and finally Mamacita left the room.

Alma looked up at me. "I told her to go to her room and lock the door behind her. That the police were here and they would take care of everything."

"Good," I said. "Maybe you should go with her."

She shook her head. "I have to be there with you. You wouldn't recognize the captain's voice."

"Why are you doing this for me?" I asked. "I'd feel better if you could be safe."

"I'm with you," she said simply. "You pulled me out of the water from the piranhas. Besides we are friends and lovers."

I didn't speak—just leaned over and kissed her. "Friends and lovers," I said.

9

❖

"TEN MINUTES," I said to her. "He's taking his time."

She looked at me. "He's a very careful man. I'm sure he knows what he is doing."

"Maybe," I said. "But I'm getting nervous." I moved to the front door and peered through the wide-angle tiny glass peephole. I could see down the hallway to the elevator door. There was nothing moving. I turned back to her. "Can you reach him in the garage?"

"No," she answered. "It only works one way. When they call here."

A moment later the tinny sound came through the house phone. The man's voice crackled through the speaker. Alma replied quickly. He spoke again, a nervous urgency in his voice. Alma turned and looked at me. There was a puzzled expression on her face, then she spoke to him again. "Okay."

She let go of the speaker button and the house phone went quiet. "I don't understand it," she said. "He called me Alma. He never called me by my first name before."

"But that is your name," I said.

"Yes," she answered. "But you don't understand. He is a very correct man. And this is not his kind of etiquette."

"Okay," I said. "What else did he say?"

"First he asked if we had our bags packed, and if you had your attaché case. I said we were ready, then he said he's coming up in the elevator." She shook her head. "He didn't seem quite like himself."

"I think he's in trouble. Otherwise he would not have known or even asked about my attaché case," I said. I turned to the peephole in the door and called over my shoulder to her. "You hadn't said anything about the attaché case, had you?"

"Don't be an asshole," she said angrily. "I am not stupid."

I laughed. "I never said that you were stupid. But we better find a quick way out of here."

"This is the only way," she answered. "The kitchen door will only take us down the stairway."

I looked through the peephole. The elevator doors began to open. I gestured to her. "Check. See if it's your friend."

She glanced through the peephole. "It's him. But there is another man behind him."

I looked through again. Her friend was not a tall man. But he wore a police uniform and high-heeled boots that added some height. The flap on his leather holster was snapped open, with no gun in it. There was also no gun in his hand. The man behind him was a head taller than he and his arm seemed to be pushing against the captain's back.

The captain's voice came through the door. "Alma! *Estoy Felipe!*"

"What do we do now?" she whispered.

I slipped the safety from my gun and stepped behind the blind side of the door to hide myself. I held the gun tightly in my clasped hands and nodded, whispering to her, "Let him in."

She turned the knob and stepped back as the door began to open. The captain seemed to be pushed into the apartment. He stumbled against Alma. The other man was still on the other side of the door, and I couldn't see him.

"The Americano!" the man said harshly.

Alma kept silent. She gestured to the bedroom behind her. The man shouted in Spanish at them. I didn't understand what he was saying, but I could understand the tone of his voice. Alma shook her head. The man shouted at her again and started to move into the apartment toward her. Now it was my turn.

I slammed my heavy automatic against his gun hand and wrist. His gun fell to the floor as he turned to me and tried to grab my arm. There were a few things I had learned in the army. I stepped back from him slightly, then kicked him in the balls. He grunted and bent forward; this time I laid the gun over the side of his head. Now he was on the floor. He stared at me, then tried to reach for the gun.

But this time the policeman was fast. He had picked

the gun up from the floor. He looked at me and gestured with the gun. "My revolver," he said.

"Good," I said.

The policeman bent over the man and quickly snapped a pair of handcuffs on his wrists behind his back. He rolled the man over on his back and snapped at him harshly. The man snarled back at him. The policeman smashed his gun against his face. A trickle of blood began to come from his mouth and nose. The policeman began to hit him again.

Alma spoke quickly: "Not on the white rug. It won't clean."

The policeman stared at her, then half smiled and nodded. He wasn't a big man but he was strong. Easily he pulled the man across the floor out to the marble balcony, then he hit him across the face again. This time the blood began flowing freely. The policeman growled at him. The man shook his head silently.

I spoke to the policeman. "Do you know anything about him?"

The policeman answered me in English. "Nothing, only that he's Colombian. We thought there were only three of them. We had watched them in the car. He was hiding in the garage and he got me when I got out of the car."

"Where are your men?" I asked.

"In the street watching the others in the car," he answered. He turned to Alma and spoke in Spanish.

She answered in English. "I don't know anything about why they are after us. Maybe they had the same tip that you had about the other man."

I looked at her admiringly. She didn't use Angelo's name. No reason she should call attention to it.

"But did you ever meet this Angelo Di Stefano?" the captain asked.

"Possibly," she said. "Maybe at one of the discos or a party. I meet many people."

"And this man?" he asked, nodding toward me. "How did you meet him?"

"One of my girlfriends from school in the States. She called me and said that he would be calling on me."

He looked at her. "But you went away for almost two weeks with him. Where were you?"

"I was at my small place in the country," she said.

"And you're going to the States with him? It seems like a quick romance," he said.

"Love comes in mysteriously sudden ways," she said.

He turned to me. "You know about guns?"

"I was in Special Forces in Vietnam," I said.

"Where did you get the gun?" he asked.

Alma answered quickly. "I gave it to him. It was given to me by your general."

He was silent for a moment, then turned back to the Colombian. He spoke quickly to him in Spanish. Again he wouldn't answer.

The captain picked him up and turned him around, pushing his belly into the balcony railing. Holding his revolver against the back of the man's head, with his other hand he unlocked the handcuffs and pulled them off his prisoner's hands. Still holding his revolver to the man's head he again snapped at him in Spanish. The

Colombian snapped angrily back. It sounded to me like he was cursing at the captain.

The captain seemed to be shrugging his shoulders. Then he slammed the revolver against the back of the Colombian's head. He half slumped over the railing. The captain moved gracefully. He shoved his hand between the man's legs and lifted him under his groin. As the captain stepped backward, the Colombian flew up over the railing, and, screaming, he fell down toward the street.

The captain looked over the railing. A faint thump came up from the street. The captain turned to us. His face was expressionless. "Clumsy, stupid son of a bitch," he said noncommittally. "He landed on the roof of a new car and ruined it."

We didn't say anything.

The captain replaced his revolver in his holster. "He would have killed all of us," he said.

"I know," I said.

"Do you want to take a look?" he asked.

I shook my head. "I saw enough of that in Vietnam."

He nodded. "Very well. Let us go back inside. I will call for more men, and while we wait for them, I will check your papers.

THERE IS NOTHING like a police escort to take you to the airport. Two motorcycles with sirens wailing in front of a black-and-white police car, then we, in the captain's car, with another black-and-white behind us. People watched us curiously as we sped through the streets.

Alma and I were in the back seat, a uniformed po-

THE PIRANHAS ❖ 83

liceman drove the car, and Captain Gonzales sat beside him in the passenger seat. The captain turned back to us. "I think we're okay," he said. "There's no sign of the Colombianos."

"I wonder where they went," I said.

"Who knows?" he answered. "My men lost them in traffic when they took off after the accident."

"Accident" was a polite way of expressing it. Especially since he had pushed the bastard over the railing. He checked his watch. "You missed the Braniff flight already," he said. "It took off at two o'clock and their next flight won't be until tomorrow."

"Shit," I said.

"Nothing to worry about," he said comfortably. "Air Peru takes off for New York at four o'clock. I can get you on that."

I looked at Alma. She nodded. "It's a good flight. They have a first-class section. I've taken it a number of times."

"Okay," I said to the captain. "We'll take it."

"You'll have to buy a ticket," he said. He reached his hand back to me. "Give me the money and your papers. I'll arrange everything."

I took my hand out of my inside jacket pocket. I laid two one-thousand dollar bills on him, and with it I gave him my passport and exit visa. "Get a ticket for Alma while you're at it."

"Of course," he said and shoved it into his pocket. "It's three o'clock now. I'll set you up in the VIP lounge."

"Thank you," I said.

He looked at Alma. "When are you expecting to come back?"

"I haven't thought about it," she answered. "I might go over to Paris for a quick visit."

"That's very nice," he said politely. "Send me a telex when you're ready to return. I'll pick you up at the airport."

"You're very kind, Felipe." She smiled. "I'll let you know."

He left us with a detective in the VIP lounge as he went to arrange the formalities for the flight. Alma lit a cigarette and a hostess brought us two glasses of champagne. "Excuse me a moment," I said. "I have to go to the john."

"Hurry back."

I went to the toilet and pressed myself against the urinal as I opened my fly. I was doing real good until I looked in the mirror in front of me; then I almost lost it, narrowly avoiding pissing on my pants. Quickly I zipped up my fly and turned. Vincent was standing behind me, leaning against the door.

"What the hell are you doing here?" I asked. "I thought you would be gone."

"I had to stay over," he said. "Did you talk to your uncle?"

"Yes," I said.

"Good," he said. "Then you told him what I did?"

"Of course," I answered. "He was very pleased."

"Okay," he said. He took an automatic fitted with a silencer from his pocket. "Then you'll never be able to deny that you and Angelo were screwed over the coca, that it was all tobacco leaves."

"You're crazy," I said.

"Twenty million dollars crazy," he said moving toward me.

I saw the door open behind his back. Then there was a cough of another silencer, and I was quick enough to get out of Vincent's way as he pitched forward, his gun falling to the floor, the back of his head torn open, with blood and brains falling into the urinal.

Captain Gonzales was standing in the doorway. "One of the Colombianos," he said.

I couldn't talk. I nodded.

"Now, get out of here," he said. "I'll have one of my men clean this up."

I was still silent.

He half smiled. "You're a lucky man," he said. "It's time for you to board the plane."

10

❖

CAPTAIN GONZALES GESTURED to one of his policemen as we stepped from the men's room. The policeman came toward us. The captain spoke to him quickly in Spanish. The policeman nodded and placed himself in front of the men's room door so that no one could enter.

I looked at Captain Gonzales questioningly.

"I want to get you and Alma on the plane before we have to bring the airport police into this. Once they get here, they'll drag in Immigration, and you'll be tied up in formalities, and it might be two or three days before you could leave. I'm sure you're anxious to get home."

"Thank you," I said.

"You're welcome," he said. "After all, you saved my life back in the apartment."

"And you saved mine," I said.

"That is my duty," he said. "To protect innocent people."

I held my hand out to him. "But thank you again."

We began walking to the lounge where Alma was waiting. "Strange," he said. "I don't understand why the Colombianos followed us."

"They probably had the same information that your department received. The only problem is that I was not the man they were searching for," I answered.

"You didn't recognize the man in the toilet?"

I shook my head. "No."

"But he was going to kill you," he said.

"I don't know why," I answered. "But thanks to you, he didn't."

He nodded solemnly. "I will have two more men with me to take you on the plane. I don't want anything to happen to Alma and you."

"I feel safer already," I replied.

He laughed suddenly. "Do you plan to return to Lima again?"

I laughed with him. "I don't think so. I've had enough excitement with this visit."

He nodded. "I think that is wise of you." He glanced at me as we began to approach Alma. "There is no reason for you to tell her anything about the incident in the bathroom. She has been frightened enough over this affair."

"You're just in time," Alma said. "I just ordered a bottle of champagne."

The captain smiled at her. "You won't have time for it. I arranged to preboard you."

"What's the hurry?" she asked. "We have forty minutes before takeoff."

"I want you on the plane before any other passengers get on. We will escort you aboard the plane. Then I will have my two detectives at the foot of the ramp checking the other passengers boarding. They saw three men in the car with Colombian plates."

"You don't think they would be here?" she asked.

"I don't want to take any chances," he said. He picked up her compact valise and the other small valise that she was carrying on board. "Come," he said.

We left the airport through the employee door. Alma and I walked across the crossway to the plane, the captain leading us, and two detectives, one at our side and one following behind. Silently we climbed the steps into the plane. It took a moment for my eyes to get adjusted to the dark after the bright sunlight outside.

A stewardess smiled at us. *"Bienvenido*, Señorita Vargas and Mr. Stevens. *Estoy* Señorita Marisa."

Alma smiled at her. She spoke in Spanish. The stewardess nodded. Apparently they knew each other. The girl led us forward to our seats. We were seated in the last row of first class with our backs to a bulkhead.

"You should be comfortable," the stewardess said. "There are only two other passengers in first class."

"Thank you," I said.

"May I serve you some champagne?" she asked.

"Yes, *gracias,*" Alma responded. Then she looked up at Captain Gonzales as she slipped into the window seat. "Will you join us, Captain?" she asked.

He shook his head as he placed her valises in the overhead rack. "No, thanks, I'm still working."

"I'm sure that there is nothing to worry about now," she said.

"I'll stop worrying when you've taken off," he said. "Enjoy your champagne. They're starting to board the passengers and I want to check them out with my men. I'll be back in a few minutes."

The stewardess placed a bottle of champagne and glasses before us. Quickly she filled our glasses, then walked out to the entrance to greet the new passengers.

I held my glass to Alma. "We're getting great service," I said. "Gonzales is keeping a close eye on us. I wonder what he knows that we don't."

"He's a policeman," she said. "They like to make themselves important."

"It's more than that," I said, thinking about how quickly he had followed me into the toilet. "But I'm not complaining. If it weren't for him we would be in the shithouse."

"It's over now," she said. "We're on our way to the States."

"Yes," I said, then cursed. "Damn, I didn't have time to call my uncle. He'll be worried."

"You'll be in New York in ten hours," she said. "You can call him from JFK." She refilled our glasses. "Relax. We'll have a pleasant flight. Air Peru's DC 8s are more comfortable than Braniff's 707s, even if they are a little slower. We'll be able to stretch out."

"I've never been able to stretch out on a plane," I said.

She smiled. "That's because you've never flown with me. I'll hold your prick all the way. I'll powder it with a little cocaine and you'll be flying on your own."

"You're a real cunt," I said.

"No." She laughed. "Peruvian pussy."

We touched glasses again. I looked up as another couple were escorted up the aisle to their seats. They were middle-aged, very well dressed. The woman wore a mink coat, and her hands sparkled with diamonds. The man took off his homburg, revealing thin curls of white hair; his eyes were hidden by shaded French-type eyeglasses. I watched as they seated themselves and the stewardess served them champagne.

Captain Gonzales returned. "Everything's in order," he said. "The passengers are all boarded. It's a very light flight. There are only forty-seven passengers in the back."

"Maybe you can now join us in a glass of champagne?" Alma said.

"No, thanks again," he said apologetically. "I will have to fill in papers at headquarters for hours." He held out his hand to me. "Good luck, Mr. Stevens. It is an honor to have met you."

"The honor is all mine, Captain Gonzales," I said, pressing his hand. "Thank you for everything you have done for us."

"*Por nada,*" he said, then reached for Alma's hand and kissed it respectfully. "*Hasta luego*, Señorita Vargas."

Alma nodded to him. "*Mil gracias, Capitán,*" she said. "Is there one more favor I can ask of you?"

"Anything," he said.

"We will arrive between two and three in the morning in New York. Would you be kind enough to send a telex to my hotel and have them send a limousine to the airport?"

"I will attend to it immediately, Señorita Vargas," he said, then, touching his hand to his cap in a half-salute, he turned around and walked off the plane.

I heard the click as the doors closed behind us, and the whine of the jet engines began to whistle in my ears. I turned and watched her. Her face was turned toward the window and she was looking at the ground. I leaned over her shoulder and could see the captain and his men walking back to the terminal. The voice came through the intercom explaining the safety instructions in both Spanish and English as the plane rolled slowly onto the runway.

The plane turned slowly onto the head of the runway. The brakes held the plane, and the jets began to rev up. Suddenly Alma's hand held mine. Her grip tightened as we began to race down the runway. There was a faint whine, and then we were airborne. She turned to me, her face pale. "It always frightens me," she said.

But I wasn't thinking about what she was saying. I was thinking about her asking the captain to telex her hotel. It was just now that I realized she had never told the captain which hotel. She placed her hand on my thigh. "The Hotel Pierre," I said.

She looked at me. "What about it?"

"You never told the captain its name."

She laughed. "I told you that we had been old friends. He knew many years ago that my *partón* had given me an apartment there."

IT WAS SLIGHTLY more than three hours and two bottles of champagne into the flight, and I was dozing, when the stewardess placed her hands on my shoulder. I opened my eyes and looked up at her.

She held a fresh bottle of champagne. "Congratulations," she said. "We are just passing over the equator."

I turned to Alma. "Did you sleep?" I asked.

"A little," she answered as the stewardess poured the champagne and went forward to the other passengers. Alma held her glass to mine and leaned over and kissed me.

"Congratulations to you, too." I smiled and kissed her.

"I have a special present for you," she said laughingly. She pressed something into my hand.

"What is it?" I asked.

"Smell it," she said.

I held it to my nose. "It smells like pussy and perfume."

She laughed. "You guessed right. It's my bikini panties. They are still damp. I slipped them off after you fell asleep. Put them into your breast jacket pocket. Everyone will think you are wearing a handkerchief."

I stuck them in my pocket. "You're crazy," I said.

"Not really," she answered. "I just want to give you something that will remind you of when we crossed the equator at thirty thousand feet."

"You took me higher than that without a plane." I smiled.

The stewardess came back. "Dinner will be served," she said.

11

❖

I FELT HER hand on my shoulder and I rolled over in the comfortable bed and opened my eyes. Daylight poured in through the window. She was already dressed. She looked down at me and smiled. "You were sleeping pretty good," she said.

I shook the cobwebs out of my head. "What time is it?"

"Twelve-thirty," she answered.

I bolted half out of the bed. "I have to call my uncle."

"Don't worry," she said. "I already called him. I told him that you were sleeping. He asked that you call him at two o'clock."

I stared at her. "Where did you get his number?"

"Don't you remember?" she asked. "You had me call him from Lima. I never forget telephone numbers."

"How did he seem?" I asked.

"Okay, I guess," she answered. "Kind of sad though."

"Was he surprised that it was you that called?" I asked.

"No," she answered. She gestured to a table near the bed. "We have orange juice, coffee, and real American Danish."

"I'll have the coffee," I said, swinging my legs off the bed. The coffee felt good. Strong and hot. My head began to clear. "What time did you wake up?"

"Eight," she said.

"Why so early?" I asked. "It had to be after four in the morning before we fell asleep."

"I had some things to do, calls to make," she answered.

A chime rang from the apartment door. "That must be the valet," she said hurriedly. "I have a number of things that need pressing. I'll get that arranged while you grab yourself a shave and shower." She picked up two of her medium-sized valises and took them into the living room, closing the door behind her.

I filled my coffee cup again and took it into the bathroom with me. I drank it as I opened the medicine cabinet for a razor, but couldn't find one. I thought a moment, then wrapped a bath towel around me and walked to the door that led to the living room.

Her back was toward me as I opened the door. Two men were standing across the table from her. There were two leather valises on the table next to her Louis Vuittons. Her valises were open, and she was handing cellophane packages of white powder to the men, who were placing them into their own valises.

"Twenty-two kilos," she said, and then one of the men saw me and took an automatic from his jacket.

She turned to me.

I felt stupid. "I was looking for a razor," I said.

"Put your gun away," she said coolly. "He's Di Stefano's nephew."

The man looked at me. "The one that went with Angelo?"

"Yes," she said, then turned back to me. "The razor is in the drawer at the side of the sink."

I nodded and closed the door behind me. I went back to the bathroom. Suddenly I felt sick and threw up into the toilet. Nothing made sense to me anymore.

I turned to the sink and stared at myself in the mirrored sliding doors of the medicine cabinet. I looked like shit, pale and sweating, and my mouth felt sour. I slid open the mirrored door and took out a bottle of Lavoris I had seen earlier.

I emptied the bottle before I was able to gargle out the taste in my mouth. I found the razor, an old double-edged Gillette, but there was no shaving cream, so I covered my face heavily with the faintly feminine soap on the basin. The razor blade was not too bad, but my hands were a little shaky, so I wound up with a few nicks. I held a hot washcloth against my face to take off the small spots of blood, then placed little pieces of damp toilet paper on the nicks to stop the bleeding.

I sat on the toilet until the toilet paper dried, then went into the shower and hit myself with ice-cold water.

I was shivering when I stepped out and wrapped myself with a heavy Turkish-towel bath sheet. I looked at the mirror again. I didn't look too bad this time. Quickly I combed my hair and opened the door to walk back into the bedroom.

Alma was seated at the edge of the bed, looking up at me. "Are you all right?" she asked.

"Fine," I said, reaching for my clothes from the closet. The only thing I saw in the closet were my suits and shoes. I took my valise out and put it on the bed.

"Your shirts, underwear, and socks are in the bottom drawer there," she said, pointing to the chest of drawers.

I dressed while she sat there watching me silently. I began to throw my clothes into the empty valise. I didn't pack it very neatly, but I managed to close the valise and lock it. I picked it up off the bed and made for the door.

She was still seated at the edge of the bed. "Where are you going?" she asked.

"I can use my father's old apartment," I said.

"Wait. Please. I can explain things to you," she said.

"What more can you explain? With more lies?" I said sarcastically.

"I thought we were friends and lovers," she said.

"The only thing we had between us were friendly fucks," I said.

"We were fighting for our lives," she said.

"But we survived," I said angrily. "And you never told me where you fit into it. I thought you were coming to New York with me, not to carry in twenty-two kilos of cocaine."

"That was delivered to your uncle's associates," she said.

"And, of course, you got nothing for it." I was still angry. "I was a stupid fool."

"No," she said softly. "Your uncle and the general had an agreement for many years. I was part of it. I continued working for your uncle after the general died, how else do you think I could live? The general left me everything but money."

"Where did Angelo fit into it?" I asked.

"He was my contact for that last five years," she answered. "And I was his. He needed someone he could trust who could speak Spanish."

"You were lovers?" I questioned.

"Not really," she said. "I would say that we were more like business associates. We had a fuck once in a while but it meant nothing to either of us."

"My uncle knew about you?"

"Yes," she said. "Since I was seventeen. The first time the general brought me to New York."

"And you've been carrying all that time?"

"It was arranged," she said. "They had everything on both sides, Lima and New York. And I was the perfect courier, first coming in and out for school, then as a model through the biggest agencies."

"Why didn't you tell me?"

"I couldn't," she said. "I didn't know how much you knew, so I had to be quiet. Angelo also never told you anything."

I shook my head. "Jesus," I said, then looked at her again. "The captain, was he in on it too?"

"Yes," she said. "It was one of his jobs to protect

you in the airport. You remember he followed you to the toilet?"

I nodded.

"It's good he did," she said. "I saw Vincent following you there and I told the captain."

"Then you know what happened there?" I asked.

"Yes. Your uncle told me when I spoke to him this morning."

"When you spoke to my uncle this morning, what else did he say?"

"He told me to call the captain and have him send the coca to a man named Ochoa in Medellín. That was the same man that Angelo was taking it to." She took a cigarette from the night table. Slowly she dragged the smoke into her lungs. "I told him that I should tell you. He said nothing. Just that you should call him at two o'clock."

I looked at her. "I don't know whether I want to talk to him."

"But he loves you," she said. "And he needs you. More now since Angelo is gone."

I was silent.

"And what about me?" she asked. "We had something special. I need you too."

I met her eyes and there was a hint of tears in them. "It doesn't make sense to me anymore. You'll get along, you always have. But, I don't know how to live in your world."

"You have to feel something," she said huskily. "If not about me, then your uncle. After all, he's still your family."

"The family has given me nothing but grief," I said.

"Tell my uncle if he wants to talk to me I will be at my father's old apartment."

Then I turned so that she could not see the tears in my eyes, picked up my valise, and walked out the door.

12

❖

MY FATHER'S APARTMENT was only a ten-minute taxi ride from the Pierre. Across Fifty-ninth Street and up Central Park West to Seventieth Street. It was in an old-fashioned apartment house, nothing like the new apartments that were being built on the East Side. It was a comfortable apartment on the eleventh floor, with high ceilings, two bedrooms, a living room, a dining room, a kitchen, and two bathrooms. My father had bought it after my mother had died. He couldn't live in the house in which he had spent his life with her. When he moved to the apartment, however, he did get the second bedroom for me, even though most of the time I would be away at boarding school.

Barney, the doorman, greeted me as I stepped out of the taxi. He took my valise. "Welcome home, Mr. Jed," he said, smiling.

I paid the driver and turned to him. He had called me "Mr. Jed" ever since we'd moved in when I was twelve years old. "How are you, Barney," I said.

"Getting on, Mr. Jed," he said, leading me through the lobby to the elevator. "The arthritis is still bothering me. But I can handle it."

"Good," I said, slipping a ten-dollar bill into his hand.

He put the valise down in the elevator beside me and pressed the button to my floor. "The apartment should be nice," he said. "The cleaning girl was just there yesterday."

"Thank you," I said as the doors began to close.

I dropped the valise in the entry hall as I entered the apartment. Barney was right. The apartment was neat and clean, though close. I walked into the living room and opened the windows. The fresh air coming in from Central Park helped. I took my valise and went into my bedroom. I opened the bedroom windows and looked out across the park. I could see the towers of the Sherry Netherland and the top of the Pierre next to it on Fifth Avenue.

It didn't make me feel that good. I unpacked my valise. Then I threw it on the floor of the closet, took my jacket off, and left it on a chair. I picked up the attaché case, went into the dining room, and opened it on the table.

I checked to see that the money was still there. Seventeen thousand dollars. Inside the flap I took out Angelo's passport and his wallet with his credit cards and driver's license. I lifted the Rolex from the zippered slot. I looked at it for a moment. It had a dark-blue face with diamonds at one, six, and nine; the calendar date was at three o'clock. I turned it over. It was engraved in thin script: "To my beloved son, Angelo. On his 21st Birthday, from Papa."

I put the watch back into the slot. I was still angry with my uncle because he was a part of all those playing games with me. But he was my father's brother, and Angelo had been my cousin. And whether I liked it or not, they were family.

I closed the attaché case, took it into the living room and placed it on my father's desk. At the end of the desk was a double silver frame, one side containing a picture of my father, the other of my mother. I stared at them. I was nine when my mother had died. I always felt guilty because I couldn't remember much about her. Then I looked at the picture of my father. I felt strange. For the first time I realized how much he looked like my uncle.

I took a deep breath, went into the kitchen, took down a bottle of Courvoisier from a shelf, and poured myself a good shot. The cognac burned down to my stomach. I began to feel warm. But not better.

I sat down at the desk and swallowed another mouthful of cognac, then picked up the telephone. I didn't know Alma's private number so I called the Pierre.

The operator's voice was professionally cheerful. "Miss Vargas is out."

"Did she say what time she would return?" I asked.

"No, sir," she answered.

"Then would you leave a message, please, that Mr. Stevens called. My number is—"

The operator interrupted me. "She left a message for you, sir. She wanted to let you know that she was leaving for France this afternoon."

"Thank you," I said and put down the telephone. I thought for a moment, then looked up at my father's photograph. "What do I do now, Father?"

But photographs don't answer questions. My father just smiled and looked wise. I took another sip of the cognac and stared at the photograph. Maybe I was getting drunk, but I thought he looked even more like his brother than he had before. The house phone rang, and I picked it up. "Hello."

"Mr. Jed, this is Barney," he said. "Your uncle, Mr. Di Stefano is here."

"Okay, Barney," I said. "Send him up."

I left my glass of cognac on the desk and went to the entry hall and opened the door. I waited until he came out of the elevator. His two bodyguards were right behind him. They started toward me. I held up one hand. "Not them," I said. "I want to talk to you alone."

He motioned to them, and they stayed in the corridor. I stepped back and let him into the apartment and closed the door.

My uncle was a big man. Before I could turn, he put his arms around me in an embrace. Then he kissed me on both cheeks. "My son," he said.

"My uncle," I said stiffly.

He sniffed. "You've been drinking."

"Just a cognac," I said. "Would you like one?"

"No," he said. "You know I hardly ever drink before six."

"I forgot," I said. I led him into the living room and opened the attaché case. "This was Angelo's."

He looked down at it silently.

"Everything in it belongs to Angelo," I said. "There is seventeen thousand dollars left." I opened the flap. "Here are his driver's license, passport, and credit cards." Then I unzipped the slot and took out Angelo's Rolex.

Slowly he took it in his hand and turned to the engraving on the back. Then he began to cry. Hard, dry, heaving sobs, the tears falling from his eyes down his cheek.

I put my arm around his shaking shoulders and guided him into the chair beside the desk. My own voice was choking. "I'm sorry, Uncle Rocco. I'm really sorry."

He held his face in his hands. "I really didn't believe it. I couldn't. Not until now."

"Please, Uncle Rocco," I said. "You have to be strong."

He shook his head, his face still in his hands. "My beautiful son is lost. He is gone. And now I have no son. No heir who came forth from my loins. What have I done to him?"

"You have done nothing to him. All you did was to always love him," I said.

He looked up at me. "I should have stopped him. I told him not to go. I told him I didn't want you to go. But he had to do it his own way. He said if he didn't go, no one would ever respect him, he would always live in my shadow."

I was silent. I didn't know what to say.

He looked at me. "Was he in very much pain?"

"There was no pain. It was over in a second," I said.

He nodded slowly. "I thank God for that," he said. "And I also thank God that you were there with him. At least he had his family around him."

I remembered holding his head in my arms. "Family," I said. Then I killed him. I looked at my uncle. "His family was with him," I said.

My uncle was quiet now. "I will arrange for a mass."

"Yes," I said.

"You will be there?"

"Yes," I answered.

"And you will be my son, my heir," he said, taking my hand.

I held his hand. "But I am not Angelo," I said. "I am not like him. I would not know how to live in his world."

"But you will be rich," my uncle said. "More rich than you ever dreamed. Already you will receive twenty million from Angelo. He left it to you in his will. You were his only heir."

"My father left me all I need. I do not want to be rich. We can give Angelo's gift to the poor."

He looked at me. "You are as crazy as your father. You come with me and a whole world will open up for you. In twenty years cocaine will make you a billionaire."

"Or dead," I said. "The only thing I learned in all of this is that we cannot control this world. The South Americans in time will take over that business. They grow it, they manufacture it, soon they will want to distribute it. Then we will all be out of it or dead."

He stared at me. "Maybe you are not as crazy as I thought. Then what do you want to do?"

"My father had a good business. He rented automobiles. I have another ambition. Airlines are becoming greater each year. But they need capital to own the planes. And capital is difficult to get. I got the idea while traveling on TWA, and I began to notice that behind each cockpit there was a metal sign. 'This plane is the property of Hughes Aircraft Corp. and leased from H.A.C.'"

My uncle shook his head. "I don't understand."

"Hughes owns only TWA. I'm sure that many other airlines would like the same kind of deal," I said.

"Aircraft leasing! But that would take a great deal of money," my uncle said.

"I'm sure that you have the connections to find the money. I think we can begin with two hundred million." I laughed.

"I have to think about it," he said.

"Forget it," I said. "You can't even get into this business. There are seven government agencies keeping close check on the airlines. I think you would have to retire before you get into anything like this."

"Maybe you are really crazy after all," my uncle said. "Money has no name on where it comes from."

"But people do," I said.

My uncle rose to his feet. "I will call you when I have the mass arranged."

"I will be there," I said.

He started to the door, then turned back to me. "You know the girl has gone to France?"

"I know," I said.

"She was a nice girl but not for you," he said.

"What kind of a girl would you like me to marry?" I asked.

"Angelo had a nice girl, from a nice Sicilian family. I think he was thinking of marrying her in time."

"A nice Sicilian family?"

"A very nice Sicilian family. Maybe sometime I can arrange for you to meet them," he said.

"Thank you, Uncle Rocco," I said. "Maybe in time."

Then we embraced, and this time I kissed him also. I opened the door and watched as he walked to the elevator and his two bodyguards waiting out in the hall joined him.

Capo Di Tutti Capi Emeritus I

THERE WAS NO way they could kill Uncle Rocco. Not that they hadn't tried. Knives, guns, and car bombs. Uncle Rocco had a sixth sense. He had made up his mind: that was not the way he was going to die. "I'm getting old," he told me. "And now that Angelo is gone and you don't want to come into the business with me, I have no one to leave it to. So why should I have to fight anymore?"

I stared at him. We were seated in a small booth at the back of the Palm on Second Avenue. We sat alone, his bodyguards seated at another table nearby. Uncle Rocco still wore his black mourning band for Angelo on the sleeve of his jacket. "I don't know, Uncle Rocco," I said. "My father told me a long time ago that you never really get out of the business."

"What did your father know?" he growled, rolling a

large forkful of pasta from his plate. "This is not the old days. This is the seventies. We're civilized, more businesslike. I've already made my agreement with the five families."

"What does that mean?" I asked. "They're not going to kill you?"

"You've been seeing too many movies," Uncle Rocco said.

I cut into my sirloin. It was bloody rare, exactly the way I like it. "You still haven't told me anything."

"I'm moving to Atlantic City," he said.

"Why Atlantic City?" I asked. "I thought you always wanted to retire in Miami."

"It doesn't work that way," Uncle Rocco answered. "Miami is controlled out of Chicago. Bonanno worked it out for me to take care of the hotel and restaurant unions in Atlantic City. It's a simple operation, enough for me. I don't want to work hard anymore."

I slowly chewed another piece of my steak. "And what did you give them for it?"

"They're taking over my operations here. But that's okay. I'll have peace and quiet."

"That's a lot of money," I said.

"I have a lot of money." He smiled. "Maybe a half a billion dollars."

I was silent. I could hardly believe it was that much. But I knew it had to be true. My uncle wouldn't lie to me about that. "What else are you going to do?"

"I'll take care of my investments," he said. "Everything I have is clean money now, I can do whatever I want." He finished his pasta and emptied his glass of red wine. He pointed his finger at me. "You're not eating," he said.

I sliced another piece of my steak. "I don't understand. If you can do whatever you want, why do you stick yourself in a shithouse like Atlantic City and watch a couple of nickel-and-dime unions for them?"

He shook his head. "You don't understand," he said as if he were explaining to a child. "I've spent my life with these people. I can't walk away when they ask me to help them."

"You can be nailed for a small operation just as much as a big deal, maybe more. Why take the chance?" I said.

My uncle refilled his wineglass. "I know what I'm doing," he said testily. "I have connections better than the Bonanno and the other New York families. Ten years from now Atlantic City will be big business."

I looked at him. "Then you're really not retiring."

He smiled. "I'm retiring."

I watched him sip his wine. I had no idea what he had in his mind, but I knew my uncle. In his own way he was a genius. He knew exactly where he was going.

He looked over at me. "How are you doing?"

"Fair," I answered. "I have five of the big banks ready to lend me ten million each. That, with my own twenty, makes me seventy million up."

"Pretty good," he said. "Is that enough?"

"No," I answered. "I need a minimum of a quarter billion."

"Where are you going to get that kind of money?" he asked.

"You," I said.

He stared at me. "Are you crazy?"

I laughed. "You told me you have the money. And you want to use it legitimate. I'm legitimate."

"I'm not crazy," he growled. "If I wanted to piss away my money, I'd throw it in the gutter."

"You'll make ten percent interest on your money and fifteen percent of the profits. All in all you might wind up with forty million a year before taxes. Legitimate."

"You gotta prove it," he said.

"I'll bring you the papers tomorrow morning," I said. "You'll see it then."

"I don't know," he said.

"Check it out," I said. "You can always keep your money in the banks and live comfortably in Atlantic Shitty."

"You're a little prick," he said.

"Family," I said.

He dropped a hundred-dollar bill on the table. "Let's go," he said.

I looked for his bodyguards. Their table was empty. I gestured. "Where are your friends, Uncle Rocco?"

He glanced at the table. "They're probably getting the car."

I felt a knot gathering in my gut. "Wait a minute," I said. "Did you tell them to go out?"

"No," he said. "Why should I? They always get the car for me."

"They know you are out of the business?" I asked.

"Of course," he said gruffly. "Everybody in the world knows that now."

"And nobody complained?" I asked.

My uncle thought for a moment. "Maybe only one. 'Lilo' Galante, one of the underbosses of the Bonanno family. He never liked me. But there is nothing he can do. He is in jail."

"Does he still have connections in the family?"

"Many," my uncle answered. "Many of them want him to be the Capo when he gets out." He thought a moment. "I heard he didn't want to give me any part of Atlantic City. He's a greedy bastard."

I looked at Uncle Rocco. "Are you thinking what I'm thinking?"

He nodded. "We'll go out through the kitchen, then into the hallway and up the staircase. We'll go over the roof to the next building."

The hallway was dimly lit and we hurried up the old rickety staircase and onto the roof. I looked at Uncle Rocco. He was breathing heavily. "Are you okay?" I asked.

"I'm not in condition," he growled. He reached into his jacket and came up with two silver automatics. He held one out to me. "You know how to use this?"

"Yes," I said.

It was a dark night, and we had to walk carefully across the roofs between the other buildings. Fortunately they were all old tenements, and there was little space between them. We began trying to open the roof doors of three of the buildings. It wasn't until the fourth building that the door pulled open.

We stepped onto a completely black staircase. The moment we landed on the fifth floor, we realized that the building was deserted. No lights flickered under doorways, and I heard the scamper of rats or mice as we slowly made our way down the steps. By the time we hit the top of the third staircase a pungent odor of Chinese food came to our nostrils.

"There is a Chinese restaurant on the first floor," I said.

He grunted. "And mice on the staircase. That's why I never eat Chinese."

"It doesn't make sense to me," I said. "The building is closed, but they still allow a restaurant to stay there."

"That's normal," my uncle said. "Half the buildings down here are like this. For money you can do anything."

There was a flickering light on the ceiling as we came down the first landing. Quietly we slipped through the opened door leading toward the Chinese kitchen. I looked into the kitchen; there were several men working. They didn't see us. We walked out the hall door into the street.

"Don't step out too far," my uncle said. "Just see if my boys are out there."

I peered around the corner of the building. There were a number of cars and limousines piled in front of the Palm and McCarthy's restaurant on the corner of Second and Forty-fifth Street. "I don't see them," I said.

"What about my car?" he asked.

"There are a few black limos," I said. "But they all look alike to me. I don't know which one is yours."

"I'll look," he said and peeked over my shoulder. He moved back. "My car is there. Parked right on the corner under the streetlight." He cursed. "The sons of bitches are setting me up. They know better than to park my car under a streetlight."

"What do we do now?" I asked.

"Fuck'em," he said. "I still have some friends in town. We'll go into the Chink's and I'll make a few phone calls."

I followed him back into the hallway, and we went into the Chinese restaurant through the kitchen. A few Chinese looked surprised to see us but did not say anything. We sat ourselves at the bar and ordered a couple of scotches, and my uncle went to the telephone. I watched him make two calls; then he came back to the bar and drank his scotch and ordered another. "We wait now," he said quietly. "They'll let me know when everything is straightened out."

I stared at him. "Just like that?"

"It's just business," he said.

"But they were going to have you killed," I said.

"That's one of the hazards of this business." He smiled. "I've been through it before. I'm still here."

I finished my scotch and ordered another. "What about your bodyguards?" I asked.

"They've lost their jobs," he said.

"You're going to fire them?"

"I don't have to," he said. "Their new boss will take care of that. They quit the job with me the moment they walked out of the restaurant. They're not my problem anymore."

I shook my head. "I don't get it."

My uncle smiled at me without humor. "You don't need to," he said. "Now tell me more about your proposition."

"It can keep," I said. "You have enough problems of your own just now."

"Don't be stupid," my uncle said harshly. "I said it would all be straightened out. You tell me about your great idea."

"It's simple," I said. "I have an arrangement with eleven small countries right now. They all want their own airlines but they don't have the money to pay for them. Still they feel it is important for their prestige. I rent them planes almost like my father leased automobiles."

"How do you know you can get the planes?" he asked.

"I'll pay cash. Money talks. Besides, I hired General Haven Carter as the president of my company. He's a heavyweight, former head of the Air Force."

"He's gotta cost you a bundle," Uncle Rocco said.

"Two hundred thousand a year," I said. "And that's cheap. I would have given a half a million if he asked."

It was a big, deep voice that came from behind us. "Mr. Di Stefano."

Uncle Rocco and I turned on our bar stools. The big voice came from a big man. Black, six four, and four feet wide, a banker's gray suit, a white shirt, and a thin black tie. A dark gray snap-brim fedora was tilted back on his shining black head as he smiled, showing large white teeth.

Uncle Rocco smiled back at him. "Joe," he said. Then he turned to me. "Sergeant Joe Hamilton, my nephew, Jed."

The man's hand was the size of a catcher's mitt. "Nice

to meet you, sir." He turned to my uncle. "We located your boys," he said.

"Where?" my uncle asked.

"Down the block, in a car between Forty-third and Forty-fourth. They have two other men in the car with them. They were double-parked on the other side of Second so they could see your car parked on the corner."

"Damn," Uncle Rocco said. He looked up at the policeman again. "Do you recognize those men?"

"Out of town," he said. "Contract men. I figure that because we never saw either of them before."

Uncle Rocco nodded. "What did you do with them?"

"Nothing," Hamilton answered. "I didn't know what you had in mind. I just have them under watch."

Rocco turned to me. "There's always a greedy pig. I offered everyone a fair deal."

"I learned something in business school. There's no such thing as a fair deal. Someone always wins, and someone else always thinks he's losing."

"So where do we stand?" my uncle said.

I shrugged my shoulders. "Somebody thinks you were screwing them."

"What do you think?" he asked.

"It's your business," I said. "I don't know anything about it. All I know is that someone was going to kill you."

"Then what would you do?" He met my eyes.

"You're my uncle," I said. "And I love you. And I don't want anyone to ever hurt you. But these assholes are only errand boys. If they don't get you, somebody else will be sent after you. You have to get to the head of the snake and straighten him out."

"It's not that easy," Uncle Rocco said. "Lilo is in jail. I can't talk to him there."

"Somebody can, I'm sure," I said.

"Meanwhile what do I do with these assholes, just let them off?" he said sarcastically.

"That could be the first step," I said. "Then you can find someone who can reach him."

The black policeman turned to Uncle Rocco. "I can talk to him. I can tell him that life is simple. There's eight blacks to two whites in that jail, and if he doesn't behave he goes out in a box."

Uncle Rocco thought silently for a moment. "Okay," he said finally. "We'll go that way."

"Good," I said. "I feel that your other friends would approve of what you're doing. No one wants to start another war."

My uncle smiled. "Frank Costello just died. After Lucky, he took the job of being the judge. He kept things quiet for a very long while."

"Maybe they'll give you that job." I grinned. *"Capo di Tutti Capi Emeritus I."*

My uncle stared at me. "That's stupid," he said, but I saw he liked the idea.

He turned to the policeman. "Can you get to Lilo?"

"Easy," he said. "I own that can."

"Okay, it's done," my uncle said.

Sergeant Joe Hamilton nodded and asked one more question. "What do you want us to do about the four guys out there?"

Uncle Rocco lifted his glass. "Beat the shit out of those bastards and leave them in the gutter."

We watched the policeman leave the restaurant, and my uncle turned back to the bar and ordered us another round. "You have a proposition for me, now I have one for you."

"What?" I asked.

"You buy my brownstone on Sixtieth Street. It's a great house and the right location for you. It's big enough for you to have office space as well as living space, and in the upper class that you're going into, living on the West Side isn't the image you should have."

"That's expensive," I said. "I haven't got my business organized yet."

"You've got it organized," he said. "You meet me at my place tomorrow morning. Bring your lawyer and accountant and I'll have mine. I'll give you the money you need and you buy my house."

I stared at him. "Do you think I can afford it?"

"Three hundred thousand, fair enough? In fifteen years it will be worth two million."

I reached for his hand. He pulled me to him and hugged me. "I love you," he said.

"And I love you, Uncle Rocco," I said and kissed his hand.

He took his hand away. "No," he said quietly. "We're family. We kiss on the cheek."

Book Two

❖

LOVE, MURDER, AND THE RICO ACT

1

❖

THE HUM OF the twin-engined four-passenger Beech-craft came softly into the cabin. Daniel Peachtree, president of Millennium Films Corporation, sat comfortably at the controls. He glanced down at the vector dial, then at the Sat-Nav indicator. "We should be there in about twenty minutes," he announced with satisfaction.

"I think you're a fuckin' nut," Neal snapped.

"What a bitch," Daniel said to himself. "Always complaining. Besides I'll get more publicity out of this than anyone else." He turned to the beautifully gowned MTV rock stars seated behind him. "How are you both doin'?"

"Scared shitless, darling," Thyme replied, her voice sounding nothing like her video that had made the top of the hits list. "Shouldn't you be looking out the window or something, darling, instead of looking back at us like a Roman taxi driver?"

Daniel smiled. "We're on automatic right now. I have nothing to do until we begin to land."

"Then get us down, darling," Thyme said. She opened her purse, took out a vial of coke, and turned to her girlfriend. "Here, Methanie, a couple of snorts of this will straighten you out."

Methanie nodded and snorted quickly. "You're saving my life, baby."

Thyme helped herself and then slipped the vial back into her purse. "That really do help."

Daniel looked at her. "Don't get too stoned. We're having reporters and photographers at the airport, and remember this is zero tolerance time."

"Fuck'em, they won't know the difference, darling," Thyme replied. "I've been stoned all my life, no one ever saw me any other way." She leaned forward toward him. "You sure Donald Trump will be there?"

"If you have the hots for him, forget it." Daniel laughed. "He's got a Czech wife. But maybe he'll give you a gig at his hotel in Atlantic City."

"I can live without him or his hotel," she snapped. "I want him to get me next to Mike Tyson."

Daniel stared at her. "What makes you think Tyson will want to meet you?"

"I heard he was playing my albums all the time at his training camp," she replied. "He may be the champ, but he's nothing but an overgrown pussy-whipped baby to me."

"I never knew you really went for men anyway."

"Never men." She laughed. "Only boys. They bring out the mother in me."

"You're a real bitch," Daniel remarked as a buzzer sounded above his head. He pressed a button and reached for an earphone clip. "We're coming in, kids. Remember, keep cool."

"We cool," Thyme said, with a smile. "A little pale but cool." She opened the coke vial again. This time she pinched Methanie's nipples, then her own. "This'll stick them out a little bit, baby. Looks dynamite on black-and-white newspaper photos."

BRADLEY SHEPHERD SQUEEZED himself into the chair behind the small desk in his wife's bedroom and held the telephone to his ear. The music from the orchestra came up from downstairs so he covered his other ear against the noise of the voice in the telephone. "The bank said they wouldn't advance us over twelve dollars a barrel for our crude." Chuck Smith's voice was nervous. As Shepherd's business associate, it was his responsibility to make sure all details were taken care of. "They also want us to make a six million payment against our loan because they have the federal and state auditors up their ass."

"The fucking world is getting crazy," Bradley said. "This value is only temporary, oil will go up. It's the fucking Arabs blowing us out of the market."

Chuck was silent.

Bradley spoke into the telephone again. "Do we make any profit on the fifteen dollars a barrel we get?"

"Our own cost analysis brings it up to eleven dollars

forty, that leaves us three dollars and forty cents. One hundred thousand barrels a month brings us only three hundred sixty thousand."

"We can ship out ten times more than that," Bradley said.

"Sure we can," Chuck said. "But we have no one to buy it. You've been away from Oklahoma a long time. You don't realize what has been going on. All the high rollers have been wiped out and more than seventy banks have folded this year. There's no money around, not even with the shylocks."

"Fuck the Ayatollah," Bradley swore. "I told Jimmy Carter that he would screw us. At least the Shah was on our side. He would have kept OPEC in line."

"You better get back here," Chuck said. "You're the only man who could keep our setup from going down the tube. In Oklahoma you're still the king."

"I'm in the shit up to my ass right here. When I gave four hundred million to the Swissman, I had to take Jarvis into the package. He paid off the Swissman. Now he's pushing me. I have to drop another eighty-five million into the pot for my share of the new movie and TV production."

"Do you have that?"

"I got shit," he said.

"Do you have to pay it?" Chuck said.

"It's in the contract."

"And if you don't pay it?"

"Then he has the right to buy me out," Bradley answered.

"For how much?" Chuck asked.

"My half. Four hundred million."

"Does he have that kind of money?" Chuck questioned.

"He's got more money than God," Bradley said.

Chuck was silent for a moment. "Then you haven't any choice. You're between the devil and the deep blue sea."

"Don't tell me," Bradley said gruffly. "Give me some time, I'll call you back in a half hour. Tell them to hold their balls." He lit a cigar and stared angrily across the room.

His wife's bedroom suite was beautiful, as was the entire house. But for fifteen million dollars in cash, it should be. He shook his head angrily. How could he ever have become so stupid? And in the movie business especially.

Charlene came in from her dressing room. Thirty years married, and she still looked like the best lady in town. Five six, long, light brown hair in formal chignon, a diamond-and-emerald necklace around her throat, with a matching bracelet on her left wrist, the simple gold wedding ring she had worn at their marriage on her finger, and on her other hand a large twenty-five-carat pure white diamond. She looked down at him. "We better start going down to the party. About a hundred of our guests are already here."

"How many are we expecting?" he asked in a hoarse voice.

"Close to five hundred," she answered.

"Shit," he exclaimed.

"What's wrong?" she asked, her eyes searching the lines on his face.

"How much money have you stashed in the kitchen box?" he asked.

She knew what he meant. When they were first married and had very little, they used to hide the money in a box on a shelf behind the dishes in the kitchen. "About twenty million," she said quietly. "Is it that bad?"

"Worse," he said. "The roof is falling down. Where do you have it?"

"Chase Manhattan in New York," she said.

"I'll need ten million of it tomorrow," he said.

She didn't ask any questions. "You can have it all if you want."

He managed a wry smile. "I'll try to manage with that, Mama."

"It's our money," she said. "I always said that."

"I know, Mama, but I was hoping to make it better for you," he said, and rose from the desk and kissed her on the cheek. "Thank you, Mama," he said. "Now we can go down to the fucking party."

THE LONG DRIVEWAY leading to the expansive veranda entrance to the house was jammed with limousines—Rollses and occasionally a Mercedes. The press and the photographers were exploding the flashes on their cameras and screaming to their favorite stars and actors to get answers to their unheard questions as they swept through the double doors and handed their guest cards to the burly tuxedoed security guards standing there.

Reed Jarvis and Sherman Siddely, his personal attorney, attempted to walk by the guards without turning in guest cards. One of the guards stopped them. "Can't enter without a card, gentlemen," he said politely.

"This gentleman is Reed Jarvis," Sherman explained. "We don't have any cards."

"Sorry," the guard said with half a smile. "No tickee, no shirtee. Out."

"This is stupid," Sherman said angrily. "Mr. Jarvis is Shepherd's partner."

"I have my orders," the guard said. "No one without the fancy gold card can enter."

Jarvis was relaxed. Suddenly in his hand appeared a thousand-dollar bill. "If I can have a word with Mr. Shepherd, I'm sure you'll find everything in order."

The guard glanced at the bill. Quickly it disappeared into his own hand. "Wait a moment, sir," he said. "I'll find Mr. Shepherd for you."

"That was a thousand-dollar bill you gave him," Sherman said.

"That will be the most expensive dollar that prick ever made," Jarvis said softly. "He's going to be out of a job tomorrow morning."

The guard earned his money. Bradley was right behind him. He held out his hand. "Reed, I'm so glad you could make it. Come on in."

He led Jarvis and Sherman into the giant party room. At the far end was an orchestra; along the side of the inside room was a long table covered with a massive display of hors d'oeuvres and hot food. On the other side, the large French doors opened onto a tented area completely covering the Olympic-size swimming pool, with beautiful tables decorated with gold and silver arranged on either side of the pool. Bradley smiled. "Nobody would believe a redneck from Oklahoma can throw a party like this. It's putting them all away."

"It's big," Reed replied without enthusiasm.

Bradley stared at him. "Something's bothering you," he said shrewdly.

"We have the directors' meeting tomorrow," Reed said.

"I know that," Bradley said.

"I've heard some rumors that your oil companies are going down the tube. No money," Jarvis said.

"Where did you hear that?" Bradley asked.

"Reliable sources."

Bradley stared at him. "What are you getting at?"

"You have to come up with eighty-five million tomorrow for the new production fund," Reed answered.

"I haven't got it, I need time," Bradley said.

"Sorry," Jarvis said smoothly. "We made a deal. But I don't want to embarrass you in front of the other directors. You simply sell your share of the controlling stock for four hundred million. Then you can go back to your own business and straighten out your oil company."

"And if I don't want to do that?" Bradley asked.

"You don't have any choice that I can see." Jarvis's voice was cold.

Bradley's face was impassive. "Let me think on it a bit, Reed," he said. "I'll let you know before the party is over."

"Fair enough," Jarvis said.

Bradley waved his hand to the now crowded room. "Enjoy yourselves. I have some other guests I have to greet."

• • •

THE LONG BAR at the far end of the ballroom was five deep with people getting a drink. Reed stared at it distastefully. "I hate that. There has to be somewhere we can find a table with service."

"From what I see, all the tables are already taken up," Sherman said.

Daniel Peachtree came up behind them. "I heard you." He smiled. "Follow me, I know about these affairs. If you don't get a table, you're screwed."

Silently they followed him through the large French doors leading outside to the pool area which was covered by a giant circus tent. Daniel had a large table overlooking the stage built at one end of the pool, on which a sixteen-piece orchestra was playing; a dance floor was built across half the pool, leaving the remainder open for the inevitable plunge by a starlet. Colored lights and Japanese lanterns hung from wires strung tautly from tent pole to tent pole, making a strangely pleasant light.

Daniel made the introductions. "You know Neal." He gestured to the others. "Reed Jarvis, Sherman Siddely. This is Thyme and Methanie." He waited until the two men were seated. "We have scotch, vodka, and champagne, ice is on the table. If there is anything more you need, I'll call a waiter."

"Scotch will do for me," Reed said, sitting next to Thyme. "You look very familiar to me," he said. "Have we met before?"

"I don't think so." She poured a scotch on the rocks for him and lifted her champagne glass. "Cheers."

"Cheers," Reed said, sipping his drink. "You're quite beautiful. Are you an actress?"

She laughed again, teasing him. "No."

"What do you do then?" he asked.

"I make records," she answered. "I also like to party. What do you do?"

"I make money."

"That's lovely," she said. "I like money. Maybe we can party sometime."

Reed turned to Daniel. "This girl is delicious. Where did you ever find her?"

Daniel smiled. "You really don't know her?"

Reed shook his head.

"She has the number one MTV video and record in the country. Her album has just gone platinum."

Reed turned back to her. "I apologize. I'm afraid I haven't much time for radio and TV."

"That's okay," Thyme replied. "You do the important thing. Make money." She rose to her feet. "Could you all excuse me? I have to powder my nose."

"You look perfect to me." Reed nodded.

She kissed his cheek lightly. "Silly boy." She laughed, then, turning to Methanie, "Want to join me?"

Reed watched the girls as they walked away, then said to Daniel, "I want to fuck her."

Daniel shook his head. "She's trouble. Completely crazy."

"I like trouble. I can handle a woman like that," Reed said.

"Besides she's lez. That's her girlfriend with her."

"That makes it better," Reed retorted. "I can take care of both of them. It's only a matter of money."

"Money doesn't mean a damn to her. She's in the two million a year class."

"I'll get her," Reed said flatly. "I saw the glint in her eyes when I told her what I do. You just arrange for me to take her back to the city in my car after the party."

"I'll try, but I can't guarantee anything," he said.

"You'll manage it," Reed said. "After all, you're going to be the CEO of the company when I take over."

"I didn't know that pimping is one of the duties of a CEO," Daniel answered, trying to keep his temper in check.

"Your duties will be what I want you to do," Reed said coldly, reading the anger beneath Daniel's words. "For the three million a year plus stock and bonus I pay you, I have the right."

Daniel was silent for a moment, then glanced at Neal. "Tell Reed and Sherman what we heard this weekend."

Neal was nervous. He stammered, "I noticed that Donald Trump, Marvin Davis, and Jed Stevens are here at the party. And there is a friend of mine, a commercial real estate broker, told me that they'd like to buy the seventy acres that Millennium owns on the far end of the Marina Del Rey."

"Were they here together tonight?" Sherman asked.

"I saw them separately," Daniel said.

"Think they joined forces for this?" Reed asked.

"I don't know," Daniel answered. "But the one thing I do know, none of them likes having partners."

"What's the property worth?" Reed asked.

"Millennium bought the land just after the war for three million five. They were planning to move the studio there. But it never worked out. The latest idea that Shepherd has is to build a Fantasy Land there. Something like a Disneyland, and he's already asked several amusement park builders to develop some plans and costs," Daniel said. "He hasn't brought me into it, so I don't know in which stage the plans are. The latest figure I heard from Arthur Young is that the land is worth ninety million, even though it is still carried on the books at cost."

"That means either of them would easily pay a hundred or more for it. They're accustomed to buying high and selling for even more," Sherman said knowingly.

"I'm not concerned about them. A hundred million isn't enough to get Shepherd out of the bag. I hear he needs two hundred fifty million to get even. He also has problems at his oil companies," Reed said quietly. "But I will still make contact with all of them, and let them know that I will protect them when I make the deal."

"Have you spoken to Bradley yet?" Daniel asked.

"He's still thinking about our offer, but I'm not worried," Reed said confidently. "We'll get it." Then he turned to Daniel with a smile. "The only thing you have to worry about at this moment is that you get that black bitch in my car tonight."

"I'd better get right after her," Daniel said, rising to his feet. "Come on, Neal, I saw her heading to the garden. Let's try to catch her."

2

❖

JED STEVENS LIFTED a flap of the tent over the pool area and stepped outside to the large, manicured garden. The fresh night air came up from the lawn. He breathed deeply, filling his lungs. All L.A. parties were the same, no matter how large or small. They all smelled the same, a mixture of perfume, sweat, cigarettes, and grass. He let the flap fall and walked down the pathway. He had heard the stables were down that way. Even horseshit would smell better than what he'd been breathing at the party. There was no light on the path, and he stumbled over a large bush and then tripped over two people kneeling in front of him. "Oh, shit," he said.

Neal stood up in front of him. "What the hell are you doing over here?" he asked angrily.

"I'm sorry," Jed answered. He could not see Neal's face in the dark. "I didn't know that anyone was here."

Daniel stood up next to Neal. "Get your fucking ass out of here," he said, "or I'll break your goddamn neck."

Then Jed recognized the two men—Daniel Peachtree and his boyfriend, Neal. He tried to make light of the incident. "Sorry, fellows," he said. "I didn't mean to disturb you. I'll go back to the party and we'll all forget about it."

"You're going to forget nothing," Daniel said harshly. "I'm going to beat the shit out of you. I'm gonna make sure you keep your mouth shut."

Jed felt his temper rising. "Before you do anything you two better zip up your pants before your little pricks shrivel up and break off from the cold night air."

Neal moved toward him. "I wouldn't try that if I were you," Jed said quietly.

Neal's voice was flat as he zipped his fly. "We're both black belts."

"Congratulations," Jed said. "But I have something better. Two hundred million dollars in Jarvis's deal."

Both men stared at him in surprise. He stared back coldly for a moment before he spoke. "Just in case you two guys don't know it, we're all kind of partners," he said as he turned and walked back up the path to the tent.

He lifted the tent flap and reentered the party. It wasn't until then he regretted what he had done. "Damn," he said to himself. Probably Uncle Rocco would be upset because he had opened his mouth.

BRADLEY WAS ON the private telephone in his own library. Quickly he punched in the telephone number on the computerized speed dialer on the desk. A moment later Chuck's voice answered.

"I want you out here right away," Bradley said.

"I'll get the first plane in the morning," Chuck said.

"I mean right away. That means tonight."

"How can I get there?" Chuck asked. "You have the Lear in California with you."

"An ordinary jet would never make it fast enough for me," Bradley said. "You call my cousin, Brigadier General Shepherd, at the air base outside of town and tell him that I want him to lend us one of the new F-Zero-60s, four-passenger fighters, to bring you and Judge Gitlin over to me tout suite."

"The judge is around seventy years old," Chuck said. "He's probably in bed."

"Wake him up then," Bradley said. "Besides his being my kin, you tell him that he needs to get out here now if he wants to see the twenty-five million he loaned me. Otherwise, he may never see a penny of it. That'll wake him up."

"And what do I tell the general?" Chuck asked.

"He's got a half million shares of my oil stock, and that'll go down into the shithouse too, if he doesn't help us out. If you put everything together, the F-Zero-60 will bring you all here in a little less than four hours. That baby can go better than Mach Two."

"I'll try," Chuck said.

"You'll be here," Bradley said and put down the phone. He glanced at the desk clock. It was nine-thirty. If all goes well they should make it here by two in the morning, he thought.

He left his library and ran into Daniel Peachtree and Neal Shifrin walking across the landing to the bathroom. He stared at them. Their tuxedos were rumpled. "What the hell happened to you guys?" he asked.

Peachtree looked back at him. "We were walking in the garden," he said. "And we tripped over a low cypress hedge we didn't see in the dark."

"What were you doing out there?" he asked.

"I was on my way to the performers' setup," Daniel said. "I wanted to talk to Rainbeau. We have a problem with his new album."

"Did you find him?" Bradley asked.

"No," Daniel said angrily. "We were too busy trying to brush the grass off our clothes."

"I saw you at the table with Jarvis and his lawyer. What were you talking about?" Bradley asked quietly.

Daniel was so surprised at Bradley's having noticed them in the crowd that he blurted out the truth. "Jarvis is thinking of making me CEO over everything."

"He can't do that," Bradley said calmly. "I still have something to say about it."

Peachtree stared at him, then he backed off. "Maybe I didn't understand."

"Maybe," Bradley said succinctly. "Meanwhile you two better get yourselves straightened up."

Bradley watched them walk to the bathroom, then started down the staircase.

SENATOR PATRICK BEAUFORT of Louisiana was a little high. He reached for his fourth bourbon-and-water. "This is a hell of a party."

Roxane Darrieux, a beautiful Creole girl, who was his executive assistant as well as his mistress, placed a calming hand on his wrist. "Slow down, Senator. It's a strong drink."

He looked at her. She shook her head. He put his drink back on the table. He had learned a long time ago in their relationship that she had good instincts. He smiled at her. "Do you have panties on?" he whispered.

"You know I never wear anything under my dress."

"I want to dip my fingers in your pussy," he said.

"Later," she said, looking past him. "Bradley Shepherd's coming to talk to you."

Senator Beaufort turned and rose as Bradley greeted him. "My host," he said warmly. "I have to say that you throw a hell of a party." He gestured toward Roxane. "You know Ms. Darrieux?"

Bradley took Roxane's hand. "Nice to see you again, Roxane. I'm glad you could make it."

"I wouldn't miss it for the world, Bradley," she answered in a soft voice. "Please join us for a drink."

"For just a quickie," Bradley said and dropped into the chair next to the senator while Roxane quickly poured him a drink. "What's the word from Washington, Senator?"

"Reagan's second term is just starting to set in, but it will take a little while for them to get their bearings," the senator replied.

"What's the attitude on oil? Are the domestic producers going to get any relief?"

"Talk, but no action as yet," the senator said. "Like I said, it will take time. But I'm staying on top of it, and the minute we have a chance to move we'll be on it. Don't forget my state is hurting, too."

"I know, Patrick," Bradley said. "And we all appreciate your concern and are ready to back you on anything you want to do." He paused for a moment. "Right up to the White House."

The senator nodded seriously. "Thanks, Bradley. But it's too early to think about that."

"Just remember, Senator, the independent oil producers are right behind you." Bradley sipped his drink. "Have you heard anything about Reed Jarvis applying for special consideration to become an American citizen?"

"The Canadian?"

Bradley nodded.

"Why are you interested in him?" The senator looked at him curiously.

"He's making an offer for Millennium Films and also the seven TV and radio stations that we own. I remember that Ted Kennedy sponsored a bill to get Murdoch a quick citizenship."

"Are you for or against him?" asked the senator.

Bradley shook his head. "I don't know yet. I have to get more information on his offer."

The senator smiled and held his hand toward Bradley. "Just let me know what you decide. I'll go with you."

Bradley rose to his feet. "Thank you again, Patrick." He bowed to Roxane. "Good to see you again."

Roxane watched him walk away. "I've heard some rumors that Bradley has big money troubles."

Patrick laughed. "So what else is new? Bradley is an old-time wildcatter. He's used to money troubles, but he's always been able to overcome them and come up smelling like roses."

"I don't understand," Roxane said. "If it's true that he is in money trouble, why does he throw a party like this? It has to cost at least two hundred fifty thousand."

"He's wildcatting," Patrick answered. He gestured toward the party crowd. "Look around you. There is enough money here on his guest list to pay off the national debt. Somewhere in this pie he might come up with a plum."

Roxane looked around at the crowd, then back to him. She smiled teasingly. "Would you like some pussy pie? But just remember, you'll have to lick your fingers, it's very, very juicy."

IT WAS DRIZZLING lightly as the limousine entered the Tinker Air Force Base in Midwest City, fifteen minutes from Oklahoma City. An Air Force MP Jeep pulled in front of them and gestured for them to follow. They crossed almost to the far end of the airstrip at the edge of the field.

Before them they could see the plane. "F-Zero-60" was painted on the tail. Around the plane were a number of uniformed ground crewmen, and just as the limousine pulled to a stop, Brigadier General Shepherd, uniformed in a white flight jumpsuit, opened the door. He stuck his head in the back door of the car. "Judge Gitlin, Chuck," he said quietly, shaking their hands. "We're ready to go."

"Thank you, sir," Chuck said.

The judge looked at the airplane. "It doesn't look very big," he said in a nervous voice.

"It's big enough," the general answered reassuringly. "Enough room inside for the four of us."

"You're piloting us?" the judge asked.

"I'm sitting copilot," the general said. "I've got the best pilot on the base with us for this one. Lieutenant Colonel Sharkey. He's already logged two hundred hours on these planes."

"Which one is he?" the judge asked.

The general gestured toward a man also in a flight jumpsuit. He was not very tall, maybe five eight, and very slight.

"He seems like a kid," the judge said. "If he's twenty, that's a lot."

"Twenty-one," the general replied. "That's about the age of kids we want for this plane. Their reflexes have to be fast enough to match the plane. After twenty-four, we move them over to other jobs."

"Then why are you copiloting?" the judge asked dryly. "I was at your baptism—you're fifty if you're anything."

"I figure that I'm going to wind up fired for doing this job as soon as the Pentagon learns about it, so I might as well have some fun with it."

"You ever fly one of these bastards?" asked the judge.

"Five times, Judge," the general said. "Don't worry, I know how to handle it if I have to."

"I'm seventy-three years old," the judge said. "Are you sure this is a good idea for me?"

The general laughed. "Better late than never, Judge. Let's go."

The pilot was already in his seat, and he turned around to shake their hands. "Judge Gitlin, Mr. Smith."

They both greeted Lieutenant Colonel Sharkey. A

ground crewman climbed inside the plane and strapped the two passengers into their seats. He removed the judge's white felt hat and fitted him with a flight helmet, then did the same for Chuck. The general slipped into his seat. "Don't worry about the helmets," he said. "Sometimes it gets a little rocky taking off and landing, and I don't want you to bump your heads."

"It's not my head I'm worried about," the judge said sardonically. The swing-out doors closed. "How long will this flight take?" he asked.

"Between an hour fifteen to an hour thirty," the pilot said. "Depends on the weather conditions at the landing point."

"How many miles?" the judge asked.

"Eleven hundred and seventy miles."

"Jesus," the judge said. "That's almost a thousand miles an hour."

"About," the pilot said. He began turning on switches. A humming noise filled the cabin. Slowly the plane began to roll along to the head of the landing strip, then he turned into it; ahead was a soft blue-lit path of landing lights outlining the strip. The plane stopped and waited like a bird ready to fly.

A hollow voice echoed from the overhead speakers. "F-Zero-60. Hold position for five minutes. Two commercial flights are on your flight path."

"Roger, tower, I read you," the pilot answered.

"How do you control where you're going?" the judge asked, his voice echoing in his helmet earphones.

"I don't have to do anything beyond entering the flight data," the pilot said. "I just take it up and put it down. The minute I reach my altitude for the flight, automatically the plane takes over. When we're about one hundred miles over the Pacific below Los Angeles, then it comes back to me and I start taking it down."

"Jesus Christ!" the judge said. "I guess the only thing we have left to figure out is how to stick a rocket up our asses and point us in the right direction."

The hollow tower voice spoke to them. "Clear for takeoff, F-Zero-60. Good flight."

As the plane took off, a loud pop echoed behind them as the airplane sped down the runway, and it seemed like only a second before it was climbing straight up into the night sky.

3

❖

THE GIANT GAME room was situated about a half-floor below the ballroom. Beyond that was the large rolling glass door that enclosed a complete gym loaded with the latest Nautilus equipment as well as mirrored walls in which aerobic dancers and exercisers could watch themselves in the height or depth of their glories. Outside the windows was a large path that led the way to the swimming pool. As big as the game room was, it was packed with the performers whom the Shepherds had hired for their party. The room was filled with the odor of grass being smoked down to the fingertips. More than half the performers were not only stoned, but drinking champagne as if it were tap water, and snorting coke, their noses burning with the ice-blue Peruvian being passed around.

Rainbeau sat in a corner of the room, which his two

giant black bodyguards had taken as his private territory. Next to Rainbeau was a beautiful black girl whose long, wild, frizzed blond wig almost covered her face. She accompanied Rainbeau on the electric mandolin. Her sister, almost a carbon copy of her, played the bass guitar.

Beside them was Jaxon, the drummer, his pale white face frozen in ecstasy with the rush of cocaine, and Blue Boy, the piano player, who looked like a black version of the Gainsborough painting. The group kept to themselves, neither talking to nor looking at anyone else in the room. With three videos on the top ten, they didn't have to bother. Besides, Rainbeau was angry that he was hired for the party and not invited to it as a guest. He was also angry that he had had no choice in the matter. The deal he had made with Daniel Peachtree gave him the right to do the song he wanted, and they'd paid for the full cost of the video—and that came to a lot of money, almost as much as making a motion picture.

He heard her voice before he saw her. No one had a voice like hers. Pure cunt. He looked up. She was standing outside his circle. "Thyme," he said, "come on over here."

The bodyguards made room for her to move closer. "What are you doing down here?" she asked.

"Doin' a gig," he said. "You too?"

She seemed puzzled. "Not really, I came up with Peachtree on his private plane."

"You're a guest?" he asked.

"I guess so," she answered. "It doesn't make sense. I saw Michael and Brooke Shields up there."

"Michael doesn't work for Peachtree." He looked at her. "Neither do you, right?"

"Check," she said.

Rainbeau said, "He laid a hundred grand on us for this gig."

"It still ain't right," she said. "Probably you would do it for nothin' if he asked like a gentleman."

Rainbeau nodded. "Some people don't have no class," he agreed. He changed the subject. "What would be your pleasure? We have it all."

"I want to sing with you," she said, looking into his eyes.

"We got no song together, no rehearsal. Besides, you're a guest and I'm just a hired hand."

"Horseshit," she said. "We can put something together that'll work for us in five minutes."

"You'd do that for me?" he asked, slight surprise in his voice.

"We're the same kind of people, aren't we? Maybe I'm black and you're Puerto Rican but we come from the same street."

He stared at her silently for a moment, then, "How did you find us down here?"

"One of the asshole security men thought I was one of the entertainers, he shoved me down the steps."

"Balls," he said. "Where was Peachtree?"

"Probably somewhere getting his boyfriend to give him head," she answered.

His eyes met hers. "You mean it? What you said earlier?"

"Anytime, anyplace," she said. 'We'll be great together."

"I have an idea," he said.

"Tell me."

"You know my song, the first one I hit, 'I'm Just a Boy'?"

"Every word," she said.

"Okay, you sing, but instead of boy you say girl. Then I'll do your song, 'The Boy I Love.' Only I sing it the 'girl.' We know the music, the arrangements should be a piece of cake."

She hugged him close to her. "Oh, baby. I love you. Really I do."

He kissed her cheek. "Now, let's try to get it together."

AT EXACTLY THE stroke of midnight, a drum roll brought Bradley and Charlene to the center of the stage. The room was silent as Bradley took the microphone.

"Friends and honored guests," he began, his faint mid-western drawl enhanced by the sound system. "For many years in Oklahoma, Charlene and I had an annual party in honor of our firstborn. On this day in 1955, Charlene and I stood on the ground beneath the derrick, Shepherd Oil Well Number One, our firstborn, as the gusher shot up into the sky, then fell, covering us completely with black gold. We were holding each other, screaming to each other, but the only thing I could remember about what Charlene said to me was, 'Now, Bradley, you can finally get a store-bought suit.'"

A wave of laughter and applause filled the tent as guests rose from their seats. Bradley held his hands up, and slowly the guests returned to their seats.

Bradley, holding Charlene's hand in a gesture of acknowledgment, smiled. "To cap the story: I finally got my store-bought suit two years later, after Shepherd Oil Company Well Number One Hundred came through and I needed a suit to go to the bank, because now that I had money I had to borrow money to pay my taxes."

Again the crowd laughed and applauded. "Thank you all for coming, and now you can relax, have a good time, and enjoy the show and dinner." Charlene and Brad held up their hands and waved warmly to their guests.

The music started and the stage began to turn as if on a disk, and Bradley and Charlene, together with the orchestra that had been seated on the stage, gradually disappeared from view as the lights dimmed, and finally there was total darkness.

WHEN THE LIGHTS came on again, there was a completely new stage set and rock and roll music was blasting away. Then the spotlight picked out a young man in midair landing in front of the group, his half-naked body painted in colors and sparkling with sequins, a microphone in his hand. There was a roar of applause as the crowd recognized the exciting showmanship style of Rainbeau. A moment later, another singer appeared, to the delighted surprise of the guests. Thyme stood beside him, in white floating chiffon that silhouetted her beautiful dark nudity beneath the costume.

Reed Jarvis, leaning against a marble column, whispered almost to himself as they began their song and dance. He felt a numbness in his stomach. "That's almost pornographic. I can't believe it at a party like this."

Daniel Peachtree appeared beside him. "Reed," he said, "this is Hollywood, not Winnipeg, Ontario."

Reed turned to him. "You don't look so good. What happened, you fall down a flight of steps?"

Daniel shook his head. "I tripped over a cypress in the garden while I was looking for your girlfriend." Then he looked at Reed. "Who's that Jed Stevens? He says he's got two hundred million in with you."

"He has the money if he wants in," Reed answered. "But it's not his money that's in my deal. He's just checking it out for his uncle."

"Then he's not a partner with you?"

"Hell, no," answered Reed, watching Thyme as she went into her solo number. "I don't have partners, and he won't be a part of us after tomorrow."

"That easy?" Daniel said sarcastically. "I hear Bradley has no intention of bowing out tomorrow. At least, he doesn't sound like it to me."

Reed shrugged and glanced again at Thyme onstage, then back to Peachtree. "I still want to fuck that girl," he said. "Have you talked to her yet?"

"I was trying to find her when I ran into the fucking cypress hedge in the garden. The first time I've seen her is right now, onstage."

Reed looked at him. "All I want to know is, can you arrange for me to fuck her or not?"

Daniel didn't smile. "I don't know," he said. "The name of the game is money. If money doesn't tempt her, she won't be a player."

"I don't care what it costs, you just get her," Reed said flatly.

• • •

JUDGE GITLIN SANK tiredly into the easy chair in the upstairs library and looked up at Bradley. "It's only two in the morning for you here in California but it's five in the morning for me."

Bradley handed the judge a four-finger shot of corn whiskey. "This will wake you up."

The judge nodded. He emptied the glass. "Another taste," he said.

Bradley nodded and refilled the glass. This time the judge sipped it slowly. He looked up at Bradley. "That's a big do you're having down there."

"Hollywood bullshit," Bradley said. "It's something you have to do."

"Costs a penny," the judge said. "You have the money to pay for it?"

"That's up to you." Bradley poured a drink for himself. "I'm not only drowning in oil, but the piranhas are eating on my flesh."

"What about the money you owe to the bank already. Twelve million? And twenty-five million to me personally?"

"Down for a penny, down for a dollar," Bradley said wryly.

The judge stared at him. "I know you. You come from a long line of Indian traders. How can I get you the money when the federal and state auditors are climbing up my ass?"

"Fantasy Land. The eight acres I bought at the far end of the marina I had you hold in trust for me. It was never turned over to the studio. As a matter of fact, Jarvis and I never even discussed bringing Fantasy Land into the studio-and-television deal. At the time he wasn't interested. It was not until Disney said they were opening in France that he even talked to me about it."

The judge looked at him shrewdly. "You never used any money from the picture company to develop it?"

"No. I never did anything with it. Just left it there lying fallow."

The judge thought for a moment. "So maybe it's worth fifty or sixty million. The way I see it you have no choice. Take his four hundred million and run. Take the option he offered you, that costs you nothing. If things look good, pick it up. If it looks bad, let him shove it up his ass."

"I feel like an asshole," Bradley said. "I was going to show the movie business how to do it."

"There are others who went for worse. You'll still get four hundred million out of it. You could have lost the whole damn pot. Sit tight. Oil will straighten up sooner or later, the real estate you own around the marina for Fantasy Land will do nothing but go up. All you hurt is your pride."

Bradley looked down at the judge. "Is that it? Just pride?"

"Our family has never been known for being humble." The judge smiled. "Jes' tell that Jarvis feller you'll take his money an' wish him luck. You stay in the neck of the woods you know best. Oil and land."

"I guess you're right," Bradley admitted. "But, man, this business is real fun."

"You'll have another shot," the judge said wisely. "Who says that Jarvis fellow is any smarter than you were? He can go on his ass just as easy. Then maybe you'll be able to get back in."

"Okay." Bradley nodded. "I guess I'll catch up with Jarvis and tell him what I decided."

"Tell him shit," the judge said, annoyed. "Let him wait until the directors' meeting tomorrow. Meanwhile, give me another drink."

4

❖

THE CENTURY CITY Hospital was almost hidden at the end of the Century City Building complex in a quiet corner of the Avenue of the Stars and Pico Boulevard. There were eleven stories comprising the hospital. The other floors were occupied by various medical doctors, dentists, and medical laboratories.

Dr. Fergus Maubusson, one of the most successful and well-known cosmetic surgeons, had an imposing suite consisting of two complete operating rooms, one recovery room, two private consultation rooms—one for himself and the other for his assistant and associate, Dr. Jon Takashima—another business office for the receptionist and bookkeeper, as well as for his three nurses, one of whom was in his office twenty-four hours around the clock. Beyond that door was the small, quiet, softly lit entrance room. Appointments were very carefully policed so that no patients would ever meet.

But this day was special. All morning appointments had been rearranged because at five o'clock in the morning Mr. Reed Jarvis had requested an emergency appointment with the doctor. When the night nurse had awakened the doctor, while holding Jarvis on the line, the answer came without hesitation. What Mr. Jarvis wanted, Mr. Jarvis would get.

Dr. Fergus Maubusson, born Fred Markovits on the Lower East Side of New York, had long ago decided that if he wanted to be successful in Beverly Hills, the name was the key to success in a town that was built of names and bullshit. And he chose his name carefully—Fergus, because it was Scottish and the Scots were long known for conservatism, and Maubusson, because it was French and would suggest a Gallic taste for cosmetics and beauty. And he topped off his qualifications with many genuine medical degrees, along with two years in the famed hospital specializing in cosmetic surgery in Lyon, France. The only photograph of importance in his reception room was of himself with Dr. Ives Pitanguy, who was usually considered the most important cosmetic surgeon in the world.

At the moment, he was seated on a high stool at the foot of his specially built operating table looking down at his patient, whose knees were held by stirrups much like those used by a gyn-ob to examine his patients. He spoke without reflection. "I've never seen a girl who could do a circumcision as surgically precise as this. She had to be Jewish."

Reed stared across and up at the doctor, squinting at

the blue halo from the light behind the surgeon. Reed was angry.

"It's nothing to laugh about, Doctor. What can we do about it?"

Dr. Maubusson was direct. "First, we have to give you a tetanus shot. That might prevent any infection. Second, I would like you to bring in the girl that gave you this treatment. I want to check her out just in case; we need to be aware if we might expect other complications."

"Shit, Doctor," Reed snapped. "Isn't it bad enough that I ran into a vampire instead of a fucking cocksucker?"

"There could be, well . . ." the doctor said flatly . . . "AIDS, for example. There have been many cases traced to prostitutes."

Reed felt a chill running through him. "Could that be possible?"

The doctor opened his hands expressively. "Who knows? We don't even know how it happens. But whores could be carriers without even knowing that they have it."

Reed looked at him. "I don't know if I can get her to come in. She's a very well-known lady."

"You can tell her the visit will be completely confidential," Maubusson said.

"She won't come," Reed said flatly.

"Maybe you should have her see her own doctor?"

"I don't think she would do that either," Reed said. "We haven't parted in a friendly manner."

"Tell her that you had a checkup this morning and

that you tested a possible positive. That she should check herself for her own sake."

Reed nodded silently, then looked up at him. "Meanwhile, what can we do about this?"

"Two things for the moment," said the doctor. "We load you with penicillin after we clean up the wound and bandage it. Then shoot you with a series of tetanus shots. It will be a series of about six shots. It will be uncomfortable for you. Fever and aches."

"The hell with that," Reed said sharply. "What will it do to my prick?"

"It may look a little different," Maubusson said. "But it will function normally."

"What do you mean, look a little different?" Reed asked.

"You've seen Japanese penises," Dr. Maubusson said. "Sort of slanted on the underside of the head and a little shorter."

"Jesus!" Reed exclaimed. "The damn thing is small enough. Is there anything you can do about that?"

"Sure," Dr. Maubusson said, smiling. "I can build it up to any size you want. But first we have to get you over this."

Reed leaned back. "Okay, let's go on with it. How much time will it take?"

"The procedure won't take very long, but we have to keep you here for at least three hours in case you have any reactions to the tetanus shots."

"Do I have to?" Reed asked. "I have some very important meetings this morning."

"If you're not carefully watched you could wind up

with some very bad consequences. Possibly even a seizure."

Reed thought for a moment. "I'll arrange to hold off on the meetings until later in the day."

"That makes sense, Mr. Jarvis," the doctor said.

"I'll have to use your telephone," Jarvis said. "I'll have to get in touch with a number of people."

"You can use my private office." Dr. Maubusson nodded. "No one will interrupt you."

IT WAS SIX o'clock in the morning and Daniel was having his morning coffee and getting ready for his usual morning call to the East Coast when the telephone rang. He picked it up. "Peachtree."

Jarvis's voice was harsh. He dispensed with greetings: "I'll be a little bit late; I should be able to make it by noon."

Daniel was worried. "Is there anything wrong?"

"Not with the deal," Jarvis said. "I have a personal problem that I can't delay."

"Any way I can help?" Daniel asked.

"No," Jarvis said abruptly, then quickly changed his mind. "Can you get in touch with that nigger?"

"Thyme?" Peachtree asked.

"What other nigger did we talk about last night?" Jarvis said, annoyed. "I want to talk to her."

"I'll get her to call you," Daniel said.

"No," Jarvis said. "Just give me her number and I'll talk to her."

"Hang on," Daniel said, putting him on hold while he searched his computer file for the number. A moment later he was back on the line. "Here it is. If she doesn't answer, call me back and I'll chase her down."

"Okay," Jarvis said shortly.

Peachtree paused, then spoke with concern. "Look, if there is a real problem, I can straighten her out."

"It's my problem," Jarvis said.

"What if Shepherd is pissed off when you're late? We've pushed him into the meeting for this morning," Peachtree said.

"Tell him nothing. They can just wait for me," Jarvis snapped. "I'm only being polite to him about this deal. If he gives me any trouble I'll cut his balls off. He's out of money, no one else to go to except us."

"I'll be in the office by eight o'clock if you want to reach me," Peachtree said.

"Good," Jarvis said and put down the telephone without a parting word.

Daniel continued to hold the phone long after Jarvis had hung up. This was not going to be easy. Reestablishing a dial tone, he called Thyme's number.

Her husky voice echoed in the receiver. "Hello."

"It's Daniel," he said. "Did Jarvis call you?"

"I just spoke to him," she said angrily. "That man's crazy."

"What happened?"

"He started to beat up on me when I didn't want to fuck him."

"Then what did you do?"

"What the hell do you think I did?" she said. Then she began to laugh. "You should have seen his fucking face when I bit his goddamn cock."

"Jesus!" Daniel exclaimed. "You hurt him?"

"Just a little," she said, still laughing. "I think I bit his foreskin off. He was bleeding like a pig when he left."

"Now we're both in trouble," Daniel said. "He's going to blow off your contract."

"I won't be in any trouble," she said. "I already called Jimmy Blue Eyes. He told me if the asshole bothers me, he'll take care of him."

"Just keep everything cool," Daniel said placatingly. "I'll get things straightened out."

"You better," she said flatly and hung up.

5

❖

IT WAS 1 P.M. and the sleeting rain slammed against the penthouse thermopane windows in the World Resort and Casino in Atlantic City. In the large living room an old man leaned back, comfortably wrapped in his blankets, in a specially built Barcalounger. Around him were several assistants. The old man looked at his watch and then up at them. "Get my nephew in California."

"Yes, Don Rocco," answered his secretary from her desk.

Jed was on the line in less than a minute. "Weren't they supposed to close the deal by now?" Rocco growled, glancing at his wristwatch again. "It's after ten o'clock in the morning there."

"We've heard no word," Jed said.

The old man sounded annoyed. "The fucking Canadian is screwing us."

"How can he, Uncle Rocco?" Jed asked. "Without our money he can't swing the deal."

"I heard that Milken got him four hundred million from the Japs," Rocco said.

"Want me to talk to Jarvis?" Jed asked.

"No. If he's trying to screw us there's only one thing to do," the old man said. "We screw him first."

Jed held the telephone without speaking.

"I knew we should have put a blanket on the son of a bitch," said Rocco. "The way this deal was set up, we don't know what the hell he's been doing; we might have four hundred million vanish into this goddamn thing before we know it."

"Who do you want me to talk to?" Jed asked.

"They're having a directors' meeting at noon at the studio. I want you to talk to Shepherd; don't talk to Jarvis. Shepherd has to come up with eighty-five million for a production fund. If he doesn't make it, Jarvis has the right to pay him off in full. You tell Shepherd that you'll back him."

"What makes you think that he'll believe me?" Jed asked. "He doesn't know enough about me to be willing to trust my word."

"He knows money," Uncle Rocco said. "You bring a bank check for the eighty-five million. He'll believe money."

"Then where do we go after that?"

"We screw Jarvis. You talk to Milken. He'll listen to you. After all, you're a good customer. You've already placed four billion in bonds through him."

"And what are you going to do?" Jed asked.

"I'll get my money back from him. After all, it's my bank who loaned him the money," Rocco said.

"But you gave the money to a Canadian company."

"It was the Canadian bank that gave him the loan," Rocco countered. "We'll work it out or he'll lose his ass."

"Okay," Jed said. "I'll get over to the meeting. Anything else?"

"Yes," Rocco said. "You tell Shepherd that under no circumstances does he make any further deals with Jarvis. We'll stay behind him all the way."

"All right, Uncle Rocco," Jed said.

Rocco suddenly changed the subject. "What's the weather like out there?"

"Beautiful," Jed said. "Sunny and warm."

"Damn," Rocco complained. He got out of the Barcalounger, walked over to the thermopane windows, and looked down through the sleeting rain toward the boardwalk and the ocean. He still had the telephone in his hand. He mumbled complainingly to his nephew, "There's no fucking luck. Here I am freezing my ass in the East while you're out there in sunshine and orange country getting fat and happy. We Sicilians have no luck."

"You can move out here, Uncle Rocco," Jed said. "You can live like a king."

"No," Rocco said. "I made my deal. I agreed to stay here. I move out there and it would be like Bonanno. Everybody agreed that he could move out there. His business would be protected. He'd have no problems. Then a few years later, he started his car in his driveway and that was all. Boom! I feel safer in my own territory. At least I know what's going on here."

THE FOURTEENTH STORY of the high-rise building just inside the studio gate was known as the Gates of Heaven. The top floor was reserved exclusively for Bradley Shepherd. The other executives were placed on the floors below in accordance with their importance—the higher the position, the higher the floor. But everyone knew that below the ninth floor there were flunkies with titles instead of money and power, even though their large windows looked down on the sound stages and other offices of Millennium Films.

It was already eleven-thirty in the morning. Jed parked his customized Chevy Blazer where the guard at the studio gate had indicated. Somehow it didn't look out of place among the splendors of the stretch limos, the Rollses, Mercedeses, European sports cars, and their American cousins, the Cadillacs and Lincolns.

The guard, sitting importantly behind the massive desk in the large pink marble lobby, looked at him with a surly expression. He asked Jed's business, then whispered into the telephone, and finally pointed to the first bank of elevators. "First door, Mr. Stevens. That's the private elevator express to Mr. Shepherd's office."

Jed stepped into the elevator. There were no buttons to press. The doors closed automatically, and the touch of his weight on the elevator floor sped it up to the fourteenth floor. He stepped out of the elevator. A receptionist, who could have been a clone of Meryl Streep, nodded to him coolly. "Mr. Stevens?"

He nodded.

She pointed an elegantly manicured finger. "Door one."

"Thank you." He walked to door one and opened it. Behind the door, three secretaries sat at their desks. One rose from her chair and came toward him. "Mr. Stevens?"

He nodded.

"I'm Sherry," she said in a soft voice. "I'm Mr. Shepherd's personal secretary. He's in the directors' meeting at the moment, but he asked if you would make yourself comfortable in his office until he returns. In the meantime, may I offer you some coffee, tea?"

"Nothing, thank you," he said. "I have time, I can wait." When she left the office, he walked over to the window. To the south and west he could look out over the studio, and to the north and east were the seventy acres of bleak land beyond the marina that were planned for Fantasy Land. He took a cigarette from his pocket and lit it. "Shit," he said to himself, thinking about the eighty-five-million-dollar cashier's check in his pocket. "There has to be a lot of money out there somehow."

He turned from the windows and looked down at Shepherd's desk. It was completely bare: not a piece of paper, not even a telephone. He wondered how the man got his telephone calls. Maybe he had an Austin hearing aid stuck into his earlobe with a button dial stuck in his pocket. Then he laughed aloud. "Sherry," he called out to the empty room.

The secretary's voice came from hidden speakers in the ceiling and walls. "Yes, Mr. Stevens?"

"Could you come in for a moment?" he asked.

She appeared immediately. "What can I do for you?"

"Is there any way you can get Mr. Shepherd out of his meeting for a few minutes?"

"It's an important meeting," she answered.

"Then it's even more important that you have him speak to me."

She hesitated. "How important?"

"I have an eighty-five-million-dollar cashier's check made out in his name," he answered.

Sherry was bright. "I'll get the message to him."

"Thank you. And meanwhile, could you have one of your assistants bring me a cup of black coffee with two sugars?"

BRADLEY SAT AT the head of the large oval director's table. Silently he glanced around the group. The only director absent was Jarvis. Brad spoke to Siddely, Jarvis's attorney. "Where the hell is Jarvis?"

Siddely was nervous. "I don't know," he said anxiously. "I've called everywhere I thought I might be able to reach him but no answer. The last I saw of him was when he left the party. That was about two in the morning."

"Reed said he would have a check for me," Brad said. He turned to Daniel Peachtree. "Have you heard from him, Daniel?"

"Reed has never been late to an appointment," Peachtree answered. "Maybe he had a problem with his car."

Sherry came into the boardroom and pressed a note into Bradley's hand. She waited a moment until he had scanned it. "Any answer, sir?"

Bradley nodded to her silently. After she had left the

room, he turned to Judge Gitlin, who was seated beside him. "Guess we might wait a bit more," he said. "Gentlemen, the bar will be open in the dining room next door for coffee and drinks. Judge Gitlin and I will be in my office. Just give me a call as soon as Jarvis shows up," he said, addressing the table at large.

6

❖

THE GIANT SIGN spread across the two-lane entrance-
way. Between the lanes was a two-man guard shack,
above it a sign that read MILLENNIUM FILMS CORP. INC.

Reed Jarvis gazed at the sign as he sat back in his
white, bulletproof, specially built stretch limousine,
complete with blackout windows in the rear-seat compartment. He spoke softly into his scrambler telephone
to Peachtree. "I'm on the way," he said.

Despite his physical discomfort, he felt good. The
company he was just entering represented three billion
dollars of newly invested American money. It was not
only the film company—it was twelve television stations, thirty radio stations, and real estate that already
consisted of thirty-four high-rise office buildings, apartments, and hotels. There were also the cable company
and the video film rental and sales, sold in more than

twenty thousand retail stores across the country. And he had control of all of it for only 200 million of his own and 800 million of syndicate money. All he had left to do was to spin off the real estate, and he would have more than enough to take the syndicate out, and Milken and Drexel Burnham Lambert had agreed to guarantee his money.

They were all assholes, he thought to himself. It was not important to him that they had lost more than a half billion dollars in the last two years. There were assets to make all that back and even more. Little did they know what was on the horizon. He would show them how to make this business work. He glanced toward his chauffeur's compartment as the driver spoke to the uniformed guard who had come out from the guard shack to check them. Reed smiled to himself. This was only the first day—after today they would all know his car.

The guard nodded at the chauffeur, and, holding a plastic card in his hand, went behind the car and placed the card under the rear axle of the limousine. He nodded back to the chauffeur, and waved to him to proceed.

The guard stood outside the small shack until the limousine turned and then stepped back into the guard shack and looked down at the two guards he had tied securely on the floor. Coolly he removed his gun from his holster and carefully attached the silencer to his automatic; then he shot each of the guards in the forehead. Calmly he walked out of the guard shack and onto the street outside the studio gate.

Quickly he slipped behind the wheel of an inconspicuous dark green Ford and turned on the motor. Then he glanced back at the studio gate, checking the second sweep of his watch. At exactly the moment when the second hand reached twelve, he drove his car into the traffic as the deafening roar of the exploding bomb came to his ears from the studio behind him.

DANIEL PEACHTREE WALKED into the boardroom where the other directors were sitting. "I've just heard from Jarvis. He's in his car, on the way here. It should only be a few more minutes."

Siddely smiled, relieved. "Good. I never knew him to miss a meeting."

The moment the words had fallen from his lips, the noise of the explosion echoed through the room, rocking the building.

Siddely was pale. "What the hell is that? An earthquake?" His hands gripped the table tightly.

"No way," Daniel said. "I'm a Californian. I've been in a few earthquakes, they're not anything like that. Let's go out on the balcony and see what's happening down there."

The other directors quickly followed. They looked over the steel railing and down at the front of the office building. There was a large white stretch limousine spread and twisted on the roadway below them. Smoke poured from inside the car, but it still held together like a swollen, spoiled can of sardines. Around the roadway shattered glass was scattered from both the windows of the car and the windows of the office entrances. The noise of a fire alarm screamed into the air, and men in uniforms came running from the office building staring at the car.

"What the fuck happened?" one of the directors asked.

Daniel looked down at the mess below them, then turned to the directors, who were staring at him. His voice was as pale as his face. "I guess we just lost Reed Jarvis. That was his limo. I recognize it."

"That had to be a car bomb," said McManus, Bank of America's representative on the board. "I spent two years in Beirut and I've heard a few of them. I wonder who the hell could have done it."

"I haven't the faintest idea," Peachtree said. "But that's not my job—that belongs to the police. I still have business to take care of."

He walked back into the boardroom and picked up the first telephone. Quickly he tapped out a combination of internal numbers.

A girl's voice answered. "KFAN-TV."

"News desk. Emergency," he said shortly.

Siddely came up behind him. "Aren't you going downstairs to see what's happened?"

"In a moment," Daniel said. "I want the TV crew outside before any of the other stations get out here to cover it." He turned and spoke into the telephone. "This is Peachtree. A limo just blew up on the lot, in front of the Gates of Heaven. If we don't have our TV crew on this and on the air before any other station has it, I'll have a whole new staff running this news department tomorrow." He waited a moment, listening. "I know nothing other than what I told you," he said finally.

He hung up and turned to the other directors. "I just

thought, since it was our own story, we should at least be the ones who get the scoop before anyone else."

They stared at him. Sherman Siddely, who had put the whole deal together for Jarvis, lit a cigarette with a shaking hand. "If it's really Jarvis inside that car, we're all in a lot of trouble."

Bradley appeared in the doorway. "It was Jarvis in the car," he said, moving into the boardroom, Judge Gitlin and Jed Stevens following behind him. "I just came from downstairs. The whole lobby is a mess, but fortunately no one has been hurt there. The guard down there told me it was Jarvis's limo that had just stopped in front of the building."

"Jesus." Siddely paled. "I can't believe it."

"You need a drink," Bradley said. He turned to the others. "We all need a drink."

Daniel went back to the bar and took out several bottles. He placed a tray of glasses on the bar and began pouring whiskey into each. Silently they began swallowing their drinks. He sipped his own slowly and watched Bradley.

Bradley held his glass in his hand without drinking. He met Daniel's eyes and nodded. "I saw the TV crew moving on the scene. I figured that you called them."

Daniel nodded. "I hate to appear callous, but why should another station beat us on our own story?"

"Good thinking," Bradley said approvingly. "What was it that you told me at the party? That Jarvis was going to appoint you CEO?"

"That was what he was thinking about," Daniel answered nervously.

Bradley nodded. "It was a good thought. You have the job."

Daniel's mouth was agape. "I—I don't understand. I thought—"

Bradley interrupted. "Don't look a gift horse in the mouth. Obviously you can handle this business better than I can. You just proved it under fire. You know how to take advantage of every opportunity."

Siddely flushed. "But now we have problems. Without Jarvis, where are we going to get the money to continue operating?"

"We'll manage," Bradley said calmly. "The main thing is not to panic. Let's adjourn this meeting until five this afternoon. I have a feeling we're going to be crawling with cops and press for a few hours." He turned to Daniel. "You're the CEO, so you're stuck with having to deal with this."

"I'll call the PR boys in on it," Daniel said.

"Good." He turned to the others. "We'll meet here again at five."

DANIEL CAME INTO Bradley's office, his face drawn and tired. "The police want to talk to all the directors. I told them that we were all in a state of shock, and they agreed they would wait and talk to us tomorrow."

"Okay," Bradley said.

Judge Gitlin looked at Daniel. "Do the police have any idea as to who might have done it?"

Daniel shook his head. "They just feel that it was a professional hit. The killer also shot the two guards at the entrance shack. He took no chances that he could be identified."

"I wonder if the killer was in the shack when I came in. I got here only about a half an hour before Jarvis," Jed said.

"Did you get parking instructions?" Daniel asked.

"Yes. He stuck a sticker on my windshield."

"Then you saw one of our own men. Maybe one of those who were killed. Meanwhile the police are going to check on what Jarvis has been doing in the last few days. Maybe they'll learn something more about him that will give them a clue about this."

"This publicity isn't going to help us. Our stock hasn't been doing that great in the market as it is. Now it will really go into the shithouse," Brad said. "Let's get back to the directors and see if we can find some way to counter it. Mr. Stevens, please excuse me for just a few minutes."

Silently they filed into the boardroom. The other directors were already there. Quickly Bradley went to the head of the table. He remained standing as they took their seats. Briefly he told them what Daniel knew about the police investigation. "We're all in shock, gentlemen, so I think this meeting should be brief and to the point. There are two important problems facing us right now. The first problem is money to continue operating. Fortunately I have been able to arrange a short-term loan of eighty-five million dollars. I think that can hold us for the moment. The second problem is up to all of us. We have to marshal our friends in the market to rally round us. I will ask each of you to help in this matter."

A general assent came from the directors.

Bradley said to Siddely, "Sherman, we have to know as soon as possible who will control Jarvis's stock, and their intentions about it."

Sherman looked at him, then at the other directors. "As far as I know, Jarvis had bought this stock in his name personally. I don't know the details of his will, but I do know his wife will be his only heir."

"Can you talk to her and find out what she has in mind?"

"I can try," Sherman said. "But one thing I do know, she hated him. They stayed married only because of the financial problems that would be created had they gotten a divorce. She's in Toronto, and I'll get up there to see her."

"Good enough. Thank you," Bradley said. "Now for other important business. As you all may know, I have to devote more time to my own oil company, and I feel that it would be unfair to Millennium if I continue in the day-to-day operation of the studio. Therefore, I ask you to agree with me that Daniel Peachtree should be elected to the position of President and CEO of the company and I will move to the position of Chairman of the Board."

There was a moment's silence as the directors looked at each other. Then Sherman Siddely spoke up. "I'm concerned only about the public relations of this change in management at this particular moment. I am afraid that the public might feel that you are running away from this situation and the difficulties that now face the company."

"That's a crock of shit, Sherman," Bradley said evenly. "I know that you and Jarvis had already spoken to the directors about Peachtree's position. The only difference in this proposal that I'm bringing to the table is that I become the Chairman instead of Jarvis. Daniel will do a good job, and I will be behind him and continue to support the company throughout its financial problems."

Siddely's face flushed. "Jarvis had a plan to refinance the company."

"It might sound a little cold, Siddely," Bradley said, "but dead men don't make plans. All I can suggest is that you stay on top of his estate and make sure that we don't have any flap in that area." He turned to the others. "Now I will entertain a motion for the promotion of Peachtree and for me to become Chairman."

It took only moments for the motion to be made, seconded, and approved. Bradley smiled. "Congratulations, Daniel. Now your work really is cut out for you. You'll have to send out press releases about the reorganization, and also about the sorrow we all feel concerning the Jarvis tragedy."

Daniel glanced around at the directors. "I already have the public relations people working on a statement to go out tomorrow."

"Good," Bradley answered.

"I'll send the releases out about the changes in our positions the following day," Daniel said. He looked at Bradley. "The eighty-five-million fund is firm?"

"I have it in the bank, we'll transfer it to the company as soon as we complete the paperwork," Bradley confirmed.

"That will help me a great deal," Daniel said. "I have several good opportunities for production in film and TV, but the big problem is that the major agencies want to see our money."

Bradley turned back to the board of directors. "I suggest that we adjourn and let Daniel do his work. As for the rest of us, I have a feeling we're going to be driven crazy by the media and the police. There's no way we'll be able to avoid them. My advice to you is to relax, tell them what you know, and it will be over soon enough."

Siddely shook his head. "I still can't believe it. I don't know who would want to have him killed."

"I do," Bradley said. "Me."

7

❖

"CONGRATULATIONS, MR. PEACHTREE." His secretary greeted him as he returned to his office directly from the board meeting.

"Thank you, Gladys. How did you find out?"

Gladys laughed. "The studio tom-toms are faster than you realize." She picked up a sheaf of telephone messages from her desk as she rose to follow him into his office. "Thyme has called twice. She said it's very important."

"I'll call her," he answered. "Ask Mr. Shifrin to come to my office."

"Yes, sir," she said. She started to walk away, then turned back to him. "Jack Reilly wanted to know if you would like him to have Mr. Jarvis's office redecorated for you before you moved in."

Daniel looked at her. *The king is dead. Really dead.*

Long live the king. "I haven't really thought about it yet. Tell him I will let him know."

"Yes, Mr. Peachtree," she said. "I'll get Mr. Shifrin for you."

He waited until the door had closed behind her, then picked up the phone and dialed Thyme's private line. "Thyme?"

"Yes?" She sounded nervous.

"Daniel." He spoke in a low voice. "I wanted to talk to you but I was tied up. You know about Jarvis?"

"I couldn't miss it. It's been all over TV. He must have been a real mess. Christ, and how he was pissed off when I only bit off a little piece of his cock. I wonder what he's thinking about now?"

"Be serious, Thyme," he said. "The cops are going to find out that you saw him last night."

"The cops were already here," she said. "That's why I called you."

"What did you tell them?"

"The truth," she said flatly. "He took me home from the party and I invited him up for a nightcap. He got too aggressive, tried to deep-throat me, and I bit his cock. Then he called me some names and went away mad."

"You told that to the police?" he asked incredulously.

"I learned a long time ago, you don't lie to the police. They always find out if you do."

"Did you tell them that I brought you to the party in my plane?" he asked.

"They already knew that."

"What else did they ask?"

"Nothing much," she answered. "They asked if I knew of anyone who would do him in, and I told them nobody except me. So they laughed and went away."

"I hope you were straight when you talked to them. I don't think they would like it if you were high," he said.

"Don't be an asshole, Daniel. They're homicide, not narcs."

"You're going to show up in the papers," he said.

"There's no such thing as bad publicity. Especially if there's a smell of scandal attached."

"You're a real bitch," he said in an admiring tone. "There's nothing sacred to you."

"You're no better," she said. "I don't hear you crying."

"We don't have any choices, do we?" he answered. "We have to play the cards they deal us." He glanced up as a knock came from the door and Neal poked his head in. He gestured to Neal to enter. "Okay, Thyme, thanks for the call, and keep in touch if there is anything I can do for you."

"I'm cool," she said. "Rainbeau has invited me to spend a week with him at his home in Puerto Rico. Methanie and I are leaving tomorrow morning in his private jet."

"You should have fun," he said. "I hear he has a fabulous place there."

"It won't be just fun. We're planning an album and a video together. He has a number of songs that we can work on," she said.

"That makes it even better," he said. "Rainbeau is signed to our label."

She laughed. "But I'm not. You'll have to deal with my people."

"Smartass." He chuckled. "But I'm not worried about it. We'll work it out."

"I'm sure you will," she said flatly. "Especially after all we've been through together."

"Bitch." He laughed.

"'Bye, baby," she said and hung up.

Daniel looked at Neal. "That was Thyme," he explained. "Everything is okay with her. We'll not have any trouble. The police have already spoken to her."

"She didn't tell them that you arranged the date?" Neal was still anxious.

"She's a smart bitch," Daniel answered. "Always thinking, but a little blackmail goes a long way."

Neal smiled. "I feel better already. It could have been very embarrassing for us." He was still standing in front of the desk. "Congratulations, Daniel. You've made it. I don't know whether to kiss you or shake your hand."

Daniel laughed. "For now, you can shake my hand. I don't know who will be popping into the office."

"The power trip gave me a hard-on that won't quit," Neal said, rubbing his crotch.

Daniel stared at the bulge in Neal's pants. His mouth went dry. "Take it out," he said hoarsely. "I want to see it."

Neal quickly opened the zipper and his erect penis sprang, swollen, before him. Without touching himself, he met Daniel's eyes. "Say the word," he whispered, "and I'll come all over your desk."

Daniel took a deep breath, his face flushed. "Put it away," he said nervously. "This is no time to get crazy."

"But I love you," Neal said.

"Wait until we get home," Daniel said. "Right now, we have work to do."

Quickly Neal straightened his clothes and stretched back into the chair in front of Daniel's desk. "Okay." He smiled. "I'm ready."

"Is the presentation we prepared for Jarvis about changes in the company still at the printer's?"

"Yes."

"Get all the papers back and take them home. Make sure you have all of them and then put all except two into the shredder. Any asshole who might get a copy could blow us out of the water."

"You mean all the work we put into it goes down the toilet?" Neal asked.

"Not really," Daniel said. "We'll simply rewrite it from Shepherd's point of view instead of Jarvis's. The program is just as good for one as the other."

"But Jarvis had the money to carry it off. How do we know how much Shepherd has left?"

"I figure that he has the money," Daniel said. "He was too quick to move in during the meeting."

Neal stared at him. "Do you think Shepherd had anything to do with Jarvis's death?"

"I don't think so," Daniel answered. "I had a feeling that Bradley was ready to take Jarvis on at the meeting. The rest was coincidental." He rose from behind his desk. "Now get on your horse, you can make the printer before he closes at eight o'clock."

He waited until Neal had closed the door behind him; then he asked his secretary to find Siddely for him. He was located in Jarvis's office, and Daniel reached him there by phone. "Sherman," he said, "I think we have to talk."

"I was thinking the same thing," Sherman answered. "I'll be right down to your office."

The attorney seemed to have regained his composure after the shock of the afternoon. He held his hand out to Daniel. "Congratulations," he said effusively. "I am glad that Bradley has made the right choice."

"Thanks, Sherman." Daniel gestured toward a chair. "We still have some problems. The most important is if there will be any flap from Jarvis's company or heirs."

Sherman shook his head. "I've already been trying to get in touch with Mrs. Jarvis, but she's traveling in South America, and nobody seems to know exactly where she is."

"That doesn't make me feel any better," Daniel said.

"But there is another problem," Sherman added. "Jarvis had two hundred million of his own, but it wasn't enough, so he took an under-the-table partner to advance him another two hundred million to begin the deal with Bradley. He was also expecting another four hundred million to buy Bradley out. I don't know where he was going to get that money."

"That's a lot of money. How could he hide it?" Daniel said.

Sherman looked at him. "Jarvis was a strange man. He kept things to himself. Even I don't know who he was doing business with for that money."

"Dirty money," Daniel said flatly.

"Maybe," Sherman said, holding up his hands. "But we don't know."

They sat silently for a moment; then Daniel said, "All

I can think is that we have to sit tight." He reached for his first cigarette in six months. Deeply he sucked in the smoke, then coughed and choked. Quickly he put it out. "Shit," he said. He looked across the desk at Sherman. "Do you think that Bradley might have been tied into it?"

"I don't think so," Sherman said. "Bradley was tapped out."

"Bradley seemed very sure of himself. Even before the explosion," Daniel said quietly. "But there are two things I still don't understand. Why were Judge Gitlin and Jed Stevens meeting with him?"

"Judge Gitlin is Bradley's attorney from Oklahoma. Jed Stevens I know nothing about."

"I know about Stevens. He's the CEO of General Avionics Leasing Corporation," Daniel said. "He must be sitting on top of at least six billion. He leases commercial airplanes to half the airlines in the world."

"Do you think Bradley brought him in?"

"Anything's possible," Daniel said. "That's just another thing we have to find out."

8

❖

BRADLEY SANK INTO the oversized chair behind his desk and looked across at Judge Gitlin and Jed, who sat in comfortable chairs opposite him. He pulled the white handkerchief from his breast pocket and wiped the sweat from his brow. "Jesus," he said. "Jesus."

Judge Gitlin looked at him. "We could use another drink."

"Sherry—" Bradley spoke into his intercom—"the judge will have a shot of CC straight up. I'll have a Glenmorangie on the rocks." He turned to Jed. "And what will be your pleasure?"

"Coffee, black, with sugar," Jed answered.

A moment later Sherry came into the office and placed the drinks before them.

"Hold all calls," Bradley said, as she turned to leave. She nodded and closed the door behind her.

Bradley lifted his drink. "Cheers."

The judge nodded and swallowed half his drink. Bradley spoke into the intercom again. "I forgot, Sherry," he said. "The judge never takes one shot, he needs the bottle."

Sherry returned quickly with the bottle of Canadian Club, placed it on the desk in front of Judge Gitlin, then left again.

Bradley sat there silently for a moment, then said to Jed, "I'm puzzled. You came in out of left field. What brought you into this game?"

"I was at your party last night," Jed answered.

"So were almost five hundred others. But none of them came in with eighty-five million dollars."

"That's another thing I'm curious about," Judge Gitlin said. "It's the exact amount that was needed to keep Bradley in the company. How did you know about that?"

Jed smiled. "You have friends. I have friends. Friends talk. And I'm a gambler."

"That's high stakes," the judge said.

"You don't win with nickel bets," Jed said.

"What do you expect to get out of it?" Brad asked.

"I don't know yet," Jed answered. "That's what we have to talk about."

"Even with the eighty-five behind me, it would still have been tough with Jarvis in the deal. But you came in with the money before anything happened to him," Bradley said. "I still don't know why."

Jed smiled. "Maybe I like your style. You throw a great party."

The judge refilled his glass. "You're a young man," he said. "Where do you get that kind of money?"

"I'm holding sixty percent of the stock of a company that I started: General Avionics Leasing Corporation, which has six billion in assets." Jed looked at them. "So, gentlemen, you can see I can afford the game. Now, you just relax, I'm not going to take anything away from you. Maybe we'll be lucky and make a lot of money together."

Bradley turned to the judge. "What do you think?"

"You have no choice," the old man said. "Besides, he reminds me of you. You're both crazy."

"Jarvis's stake in this still worries me, now that his estate still has an option of forty percent of Millennium's stock. How do we know what they'll do?" Bradley said.

The judge spoke in a cold steely voice: "You got yourself into that problem. You'll have to get yourself out of it."

Jed turned to the judge. "Brad will work his way out of it," he said. "I have faith."

"Thank you," Bradley said. "But we'll have to talk some more after we have more facts in hand."

"We will," Jed said. "But right now I have to get back to my office." He rose to his feet and placed several business cards on the desk in front of Bradley. "You call me or I'll call you. We'll set up some proper meetings. Lawyers, accountants, the works."

Bradley looked up at him. "But meanwhile don't you want a note for the eighty-five?"

Jed met his eyes. "Do you have the money to cover it?"

"No," Bradley said.

"Then what difference will it make?" Jed smiled. "We'll work it all out later." He shook Bradley's hand, then the judge's. "Gentlemen, until later," he said and left the office.

Judge Gitlin stared at the closed door. He turned to Bradley. "We better get a line on that boy. He's too relaxed for my taste. Also, it's hard to trust a man who don't drink."

Bradley shook his head. He called Sherry on the intercom. "Get me McManus at the Bank of America." He nodded to the judge. "You met McManus at the directors' meeting. He's been on our board since I got into Millennium. He'll check Stevens out for us."

"When can we go home?" the judge said. "Don't forget I'm an old man. I need some rest."

Bradley laughed. "Then I'll tell Charlene to cancel your dinner date."

"A dinner date?" the judge exclaimed. "With who?"

"Zsa Zsa Gabor," Bradley answered. "She likes older men."

"I don't want to change Charlene's plans," the judge said quickly. "I'll be okay for dinner."

JED TURNED INTO the parking garage on the street level of the ten-story green-mirrored glass building on Century Boulevard opposite the air-freight area at LAX. He left his Chevy Blazer with the valet and walked toward the elevators. He pressed the button for the seventh floor, which would take him to his office.

Kim Latimer, the attractive VP of Corporate Relations, and Jim Handley, the always worried-looking VP and Treasurer of G.A.L.C., were always waiting at the elevator door. It was crazy, but he could never get into his office without one or the other waiting at the elevator door. He was sure that they had paid off the parking valet.

"You've had a busy day," Kim said.

"Kind of," he answered as he started toward his office.

"What did you do with eighty-five million?" Jim asked. "It left us short on the payment to Boeing."

"It's safe," he said. "Pay Boeing out of the Rental Reserve Account."

They followed him into his office. He looked down at the messages on his desk. He shook his head. Uncle Rocco was always the same. He never left any messages.

Handley looked at him. "What happened to Jarvis?"

"He blew his top," he answered wryly.

"Not funny," the treasurer said. "Does it affect us?"

"I don't think so," Jed said. "I'm dealing with Bradley."

"How do we fit into this?" Jim asked.

Jed shrugged his shoulders. "I'm not quite sure. I'm playing this one personally. I'll repay the company from my own account tomorrow."

"Okay," Jim said. "I just want to protect you and us."

"We'll be okay," Jed said. "Thanks."

Jim left the office. Kim stood in front of his desk. "Are you all right?" she asked.

"I'm okay," he answered. He slid into his chair. "This has turned into a rough day," he said. "I'm tired."

She came around behind him. "Let me rub your neck and shoulders. It'll ease the tension."

"Good," he said. Her hands were gentle and warm. He turned his head. "That's like magic. It really helps."

"Your Uncle Rocco called me on my private line," she said.

He turned to her quickly. "Why didn't you tell me before?"

She shook her head. "Not in front of Jim."

"What did he say?"

"He said that he will call you at home at midnight, your time," she said.

"What else did he say?"

"'Rico,'" she said. "They couldn't get him in New York; now they're putting together a grand jury to nail him in New Jersey." She looked at him. "He wants you to have your phones debugged. And to sweep your apartment as well."

"Get John Scanlon in Security and have him take care of it."

"Are you in trouble?" she asked in a concerned voice.

"Not me," he answered. "But I am worried for my uncle." He watched as she called Security, then looked down at his messages. There was only one that was important. He picked up another phone. "Let me talk to Rudy Mayer in Purchasing," he said to one of the secretaries in his outer office.

Rudy came on the line. "Yes, Boss."

"What kind of deal does Aerospatiale want to give us on the A 300s?"

"It's their new model. A 300-200. Stretchouts. It carries four hundred passengers. You order ten and place them on U.S. airlines, they'll give you a twenty percent discount and a twenty-year finance plan."

"They give you any idea of the figures?"

"No," Rudy said. "They won't give any numbers until you tell them that you're interested."

"Usually domestic airlines are cautious about foreign planes. But there is a market for them. Vacation season. Florida. Mexico. They're always short of space."

"What do you want me to tell them?"

"Tell them I'm interested. I'll start talking to Eastern, American, Western, and Mexicana," he said.

"Mexicana isn't a U.S. line," Rudy said. "Maybe they will be selling to them direct."

Jed laughed. "The Mexicans have no money. I can guarantee Aerospatiale."

"Okay, Boss," Rudy said. "I'll get on it. Just one question. What do you do if Boeing is pissed off because you short them on 727-200s?"

"It all comes down to money," Jed said. "The A 300 has a better payload and uses thirty percent less fuel than the B 727. Maybe it's time Boeing stopped believing they're the only airplane in the world."

He put down the phone and looked up at Kim.

Kim nodded. "Scanlon said he would get on it right away."

"Good." He smiled at her. "Come home, I'll shower and dress up. Then I'll take you out to dinner."

"You have a deal," she said. "With one exception."

"What's that?" he asked.

"I won't ride in that pickup truck."

"Okay. We'll take the Corniche."

"Lovely." She picked up the telephone.

"Who are you calling?" he asked.

"Chasen's," she said. "Where else do you go in a Rolls?"

9

❖

"WHY DON'T YOU come to bed?" Kim asked. "It's almost two in the morning and you better get some sleep."

"Uncle Rocco said he would call, and he will," Jed replied.

"It's five in the morning in the East," Kim said. "He's not a young man, he's probably gone to bed. He'll call you in the morning."

"You don't know anything about my family," Jed said. "Uncle Rocco will call. He's not called the *Capo* for nothing."

"Okay," she said. "Maybe he got tied up with something."

The telephone rang. Jed looked at it in surprise. It wasn't his private phone—it was the hotel switchboard. Slowly he picked up the receiver. "Stevens."

The desk clerk sounded apologetic. "Your uncle is here to see you, Mr. Stevens. He didn't give me his name."

"My uncle doesn't need a name. He's my uncle." Jed laughed. "He's alone?"

"No, Mr. Stevens. He has two gentlemen with him."

"Have one of the bellmen lead them to my bungalow." He put the phone down and looked at Kim. "Uncle Rocco is here."

"I'd better put something on," she said.

"Take your time," Jed said. "I'll meet them in the living room. My uncle isn't alone," he added. "He's with his secretary and his bodyguards."

"Uncle Rocco must be quite a man," she said.

"He's old-fashioned," Jed said. "The Godfather never goes out without his staff."

"If he's old-fashioned, what will he think about me?" she said stepping into a pair of slacks.

"He called you, didn't he?" Jed asked.

"Yes," she answered, slipping on a blouse. "He wanted to talk to you."

"He wouldn't have called you if he didn't believe you were okay." Jed smiled. The door chime rang. "I'll get it," he said.

He crossed to the entrance hall and opened the door. He slipped the bellman a fiver and led his uncle into the bungalow. They looked at each other for a moment, then hugged and kissed each other on the cheek. His uncle was wearing a cashmere winter coat. "Welcome to California, Uncle Rocco," he said. "Let me take your coat. It's warm here."

His uncle agreed. "I'm sweating," he said as he

slipped out of his coat. Then he gestured to the men with him. "You remember Danny and Samuel?"

Jed nodded and shook hands with the men. At that moment Kim came into the living room.

His uncle smiled at her. "You're Kim, Jed's girl. I've spoken to you on the phone several times." He took her hand and kissed it as an old-fashioned courtier might.

He turned to Jed. "She's very pretty," he said, and then in Italian, "Siciliana?"

Kim laughed and answered him in Italian. "No, I'm sorry, my parents were Scotch and Irish."

"That's not too bad," Uncle Rocco said.

"You must be exhausted," she said. "Can I get you some coffee and sandwiches?"

"Just coffee, black and strong," Uncle Rocco said.

"Right away." She turned and went to the kitchen.

"You're looking good, Uncle Rocco," Jed said.

"At my age you have to watch your diet. Less pasta, less meat, more fish and green vegetables."

"Vino?" Jed asked.

"Maybe later. You are surprised to see me?"

"Yes," Jed answered.

"It's family business," Uncle Rocco said. "We couldn't talk about this over the phone, so I chartered a plane."

Jed looked at him silently.

"Do we have a place where we can talk alone?" his uncle asked.

"The den. No one can hear us in there," Jed said.

Kim left two pots of coffee for them and closed the door behind her. Jed filled both cups and leaned back in the chair. "Okay?" he asked.

"She makes good coffee," Uncle Rocco said.

Jed nodded. "You didn't come here for coffee."

"That's right." He took another sip. "The Canadian got whacked," he said.

"I know," Jed said. "I was there."

"He was a bad man," Uncle Rocco said.

"No worse than the others," Jed said. "Everybody gets greedy when it comes to money."

"It's not only money," Rocco said. "He turned on his friends. That's against the rules."

"I don't understand," Jed said.

"Rico," he said. "He went to New York and told Giuliani where I get all the money I loaned him. Now Giuliani is getting the U.S. District Attorney in New Jersey to prepare another case against me. They tried to get me in Manhattan, then in Brooklyn, and lost. Now they're trying again."

"What is that law about double jeopardy?" Jed asked.

Rocco laughed. "Don't be stupid. Each case is different. They're digging up other charges. The latest I hear from the grapevine, they're trying to tie me into the unions and the corruption in Atlantic City."

"Can they make it stick?" Jed asked.

"I don't think they can. When I was offered Atlantic City unions, I turned it all down and gave it to the Scarfo family from Philadelphia. They wanted it, so I told them they could have them all. I was not interested in the day-to-day bullshit. I wanted to be like Frank Costello. An elder statesman."

"Then what do you have to worry about?"

"Nothing, I hope," he said. "The only hard information they have was from Jarvis. But he can't go in front of the grand jury now. Dead men can't give testimony."

Jed stared at his uncle in surprise. "Don't tell me you had him whacked?"

Uncle Rocco was indignant. "Do you think I'm stupid? Then Giuliani would really crawl up my ass."

"He'll still try to nail you," Jed said.

"Trying and getting are two different things," Uncle Rocco retorted. "Not that I wouldn't have liked to get the son of a bitch, but somebody beat me to it."

"I need a drink," Jed said, getting up. He looked down at his uncle. "Would you like something?"

The old man nodded. "Do you have any *vino rosso?*"

"Bolla Chianti," he said.

"Vintage?" his uncle asked.

"Of course. I learned something from you."

He walked into the living room. Uncle Rocco's men were sitting on the couch, a pot of coffee on the small table before them. He went into his bedroom.

Kim was sitting on the bed, a newspaper spread out in front of her. She looked at him. "Are you all right?"

"Fine. How about you?"

"I'm okay," she said. "A little bit nervous but okay."

"Relax," he said. "Uncle Rocco wants *vino rosso* and I need a drink, too. I just came out to get it."

"Want me to help?" she asked.

"No, I can handle it." He went back through the living room to the kitchen. He opened a bottle of wine. Then he went to the bar in the corner of the living room and picked up a bottle of Glenlivet, glasses, and a bucket of ice, put them on a tray, and went back to the den.

His uncle picked up the wine and checked the label.

"Eighty-two," he said in a satisfied voice. "A very good year. You really learned something."

Jed smiled and helped himself to scotch on the rocks while his uncle poured himself a glass of wine. He held up his glass. *"Salute."*

"Salute." Jed sipped at his drink. He waited until his uncle finished his wine and refilled the glass. He met his uncle's eyes. "Do you have any idea who did it?"

"I have an idea," Uncle Rocco answered. "The hit was ordered out of Canada. The hit man was a French Canadian who works both sides of the border."

"It ought to be easy for the police to pick him up then," Jed said.

Uncle Rocco smiled. "They'll never come near him. He's a real pro. By now he's probably on his way to Europe or South America."

"You seem sure of that," Jed said.

"That's where he'll be paid. France or Peru." His uncle drank more of his wine. "If he's really smart he'll go to France. If he winds up in Peru, he'll be finished. He'll get whacked."

"You know something that I don't?" Jed asked.

His uncle nodded. "Alma Vargas."

"The Peruvian girl?" Jed said in surprise. "Where did she get into this?"

"She had married Jarvis in France three years ago. He was getting ready to divorce her. She didn't like it. Jarvis was a very rich man. Now she's a very rich *putana*." Uncle Rocco chuckled. "You don't know how difficult it was for me to get her out of the country when you came back with her. She wanted to marry you."

"Jesus," Jed said. He poured himself another scotch. "There goes your money."

"Maybe not." Uncle Rocco smiled. "She still likes you."

"Wait a minute," Jed said. "She's not going to give you back the money."

"I know that," Uncle Rocco said. "All I want you to do is arrange for her to put Jarvis's interest in support of Shepherd."

"Does she know that you gave Jarvis the money?"

"She introduced me to Jarvis. I thought he had a great plan." He stared into his wineglass. "Maybe I wasn't so smart, but neither was Jarvis. That Peruvian *putana* was smarter than all of us."

"Peruvian pussy." Jed laughed.

"I don't understand," his uncle said.

Jed looked at him. "One day, many years ago, when I was young, she stood naked on the deck of the boat in the Amazon, and she told me about Peruvian pussy. It was the best in the world, she said. But she never told me as well that it was the smartest."

"What do you think?" Uncle Rocco asked. "Will you talk to her?"

"Of course I will," Jed replied. "But we don't have to do anything. The money is already in the company and there's no way she can get it out. Believe me, Uncle Rocco, this is something I really know about. By the time I'm finished, Shepherd and I will control it all, and she will have only a minority interest."

The old man stared at him. "You mean that?"

"That's my kind of business," Jed answered.

Uncle Rocco sat there silently for a while, then he

sighed. "I'm getting old," he said. "Ten years ago I would never have gone for a scam like this. It was too legal for me."

"Legal or illegal—it's where they draw the lines. They're the same thing."

"No," the old man said. "I'm too old. I've lost my smarts."

"You're the same as you always were, Uncle Rocco," Jed said gently. "It's just a different game."

Uncle Rocco shook his head slowly. "I want you to come back to the family."

"I've never left the family, Uncle Rocco," Jed said. "What is it that you want me to do?"

"I am getting old," Rocco said in a weary voice. "I want you to help me."

Jed took the old man's hand. He felt it trembling. "Tell me, Uncle Rocco."

"Get me out of the battlefield," Uncle Rocco said. "I want to die in bed."

The Last Man of Honor

SALTWATER TAFFY. THE Steel Pier. The auction houses that filled every other store on the boardwalk with phony antiques. The two-passenger rolling chairs pushed back and forth along the boardwalk by a smiling black man who also acted as a tour guide for seventy-five cents an hour. The white sand covered with picnicking families. The vendors, mostly teenage kids, selling candy apples, Eskimo pies, and popsicles. That was the Atlantic City I remembered when I was eight years old and spent two weeks at Aunt Rosa's in the small house she had rented at the far end of the boardwalk.

It was not anything like the monster hotels and casinos I looked down on from Uncle Rocco's penthouse that turned the million lights into Las Vegas-on-the-boardwalk. I moved away from the windows and went back to Uncle Rocco's large mahogany desk. On the corner of the desk was a large candy dish of saltwater taffy. I gestured toward it. "I never knew that you liked that."

"Why not? The President has a jar of jelly beans on his desk."

I laughed. "Okay. But I remember when I stayed at Aunt Rosa's she wouldn't let me have any. She said it would make cavities in all my teeth."

"All women had funny ideas in those times. Did it ever give you any cavities?"

"I had a few when I was a kid," I said. "But I don't know whether it was from saltwater taffy. I never got to eat that much."

"I eat it all the time and I don't have any cavities. All it does is stick to my choppers and I have to take them out and clean them."

"I never knew you had false teeth."

"I've had them a long time," he answered. "When I was young some son of a bitch hit me in the face with a baseball bat."

"What did you do?" I asked.

"Nothing," he replied. "I was going to blow the bastard away but your grandfather stopped me. He was a Genovese, and it would have started a war. That would have been really crazy because they would have wiped us out. At that time the Genovese was the biggest family in New York. So my father sent me to the best orthodontist in Manhattan and I wound up with the greatest-looking choppers in the world."

I laughed. "They're still pretty good."

He nodded. "This is about the fifth pair."

I looked at him. "We have some things to talk about."

"That's right," he said. The telephone rang and he picked it up. He listened for a moment, then answered, "Send him in." He looked up at me. "I have to talk to this man. It won't take too long."

"I can wait," I said. "Do you want me to leave the room?"

"No," he answered. "You can stand near the windows." He opened a drawer from his desk and handed a Luger automatic to me. "I know you know how to work one of these."

I stared at him. "You're expecting trouble?"

"Not really," he said. "But in my business—" He shrugged his shoulders.

I walked over to the windows as I slipped the gun into my jacket pocket. From the corner of my eyes I saw the man come through the door—a swarthy man of medium height wearing a tight-fitting suit and sporting a dark and angry face.

My uncle rose from his desk and held out his hand. "Nico," he said smoothly, "good to see you."

The man ignored my uncle's hand. "You screwed me out of three hundred grand," he said harshly.

My uncle was unruffled. "You're a fool," he said. "If I wanted to screw you I would have taken you for three million."

Nico seemed to get angrier. "It isn't the money," he snapped. "It's the principle."

"What do you know about principle, you asshole?" Uncle Rocco's voice grew cold. "You screwed your father before he was cold on his deathbed. What happened to the money your father wanted to divide between you and your uncle?"

"My uncle disappeared," Nico said. "We never could find him."

"You made sure that nobody would look for him," Uncle Rocco said, his voice still cold. "Especially in the pig farm you owned in Secaucus."

"That's all horseshit," Nico said angrily. "That has nothing to do with this. You still owe me three hundred grand."

Uncle Rocco stood up behind his desk. "I am a man of honor," he said quietly. "I made an agreement with your father when I came down here. He took over the unions and he gave me five thousand a month for expenses. After your father died I never asked for the money. It was sent each month to me by messenger just as it came from your father."

Nico stared at him. "Nobody was authorized to do that."

"That's your problem," my uncle said flatly. "Maybe nobody in your organization likes you."

"I'll get rid of the son of a bitch," Nico said.

"Still your problem," Uncle Rocco said. "You make sure that the five grand comes to me every month. Just as your father and I had agreed."

"And if I don't?"

Uncle Rocco smiled and again sat back in his chair. "As I said, I am a man of honor. I keep my word, and I believe you will honor your father's word." He paused a moment, then smiled gently. "Or you will find yourself joining your uncle in the pig farm."

Nico stared at him. "You're crazy, old man. I can hit you right here."

I started to take the Luger from my pocket, but Uncle Rocco, who was watching from the corner of his eye, shook his head. I let the gun stay in my pocket.

"Then you're more of a fool than I thought," Uncle Rocco said easily. "You'd never get out of here alive." He laughed. "I'm seventy-two, you're only forty-seven. You're getting lousy odds. Insurance companies give me four years, they give you twenty-seven."

Nico sat quietly for a moment. Finally he nodded. "Don Rocco," he said in a respectful voice, "I apologize. I was angry."

"It is nothing, my son," Uncle Rocco said quietly. "Just think before you act. You will find that life will be easier."

"Yes, Don Rocco," Nico said, rising from his chair. "I apologize again."

"Goodbye, my son," Uncle Rocco said. He watched Nico leave the room, then turned around to me. "Now you know why I want you to get me out. I'm tired of dealing with these crazies."

"Do you really think he would have done anything?" I asked.

"Who knows?" Uncle Rocco asked. "But he won't get another chance. I have his first underboss already talking to the Feds. They'll get him."

"You deal with the FBI?"

"No," he answered.

"But you had his man talk to the Feds."

"That man came to me for advice. He knew I was a man of honor with much experience," he said quietly. "All I told him is that the Feds would not kill him, and Nico would. What he decided to do was his own choice." He held out his hand. "Give me the gun."

I placed the Luger on the desk in front of him. He placed it in the desk drawer, but not before he polished it with a soft rag. "I don't want any of your fingerprints on it."

"Thank you," I said. "And why did you leave it unloaded? I might have been killed."

Uncle Rocco smiled. "No way. I have a sawed-off shotgun built into the desk aimed at the chair he was sitting in. He would have been blown across the Atlantic Ocean."

I stared at him. "You lie a lot, Uncle Rocco. What else have you lied to me about?"

He shook his head sadly. "You're family. I am a man of honor. Whatever I tell you is for your own protection."

"What protection do I need?" I asked. "I live a straight life. General Avionics is a respected company. All we do is buy airplanes and lease them to airlines. Everything is legitimate."

My uncle looked up at me sadly. "A Di Stefano is a Di Stefano even if his legal name is Stevens. Maybe the world you live in doesn't know that, but the world that you were born into knows who you are. Even back in Sicily. That's why your father went off the mountain in Trapani. Old worlds don't die, their hatreds and vendettas live on."

I stared at him. "You haven't retired, have you?"

He didn't answer.

"My father said that," I said bitterly. "Not to trust your word."

Uncle Rocco looked straight into my eyes. "You have to believe me. I have never betrayed my family."

"A man of honor," I said sarcastically. "I haven't heard that before. Where did you pick that up?"

His voice was cold. "The five biggest families are in New York. They respect me. The Sicilian commission, composed of the most important families, including the Corleones and the Borgettos, honor me as the only American who is their equal. I have never betrayed their trust and respect."

"If that is true," I asked, "why are you concerned that someone would kill you?"

"The older men are gone. The young are taking over and they're all greedy. They can't wait."

"What do they want from you?" I asked. "You tell me you're out of the business."

Uncle Rocco shook his head. He tapped his temple with a forefinger. "This is what they want. I am the only one left who can communicate between the old world and the new. They know that one word from me, and they would be cut off from the old country."

"Why should that bother them?"

"Ten to fifteen billion a year," he said.

"The Sicilians have that much power?"

"They have a worldwide army. They have made deals with the Chinese triads and the Colombian cartels. That gives them thousands of soldiers." He took a deep breath. "But here in America, it's not like it used to be. Once we were kings, now we're scrambling for crumbs. The Americans are getting weaker, each family is becoming smaller and smaller, what with the American government nailing them from all sides with the Rico Act."

I was silent for a moment. "I still don't know what you want me to do."

He stared at me. "How much do you think your business is worth?"

"Maybe two or three billion," I said.

"How much do you get out of it?"

"Over a million a year."

He laughed. "Chicken shit."

I just looked at him.

"What if I could put you into a legitimate investment company with over twenty billion in cash and assets that you would own forty percent of, and earn you more than five million a year?" His voice was dripping honey.

"And who would own the other sixty percent?" I asked.

He nodded. "Other men of honor?"

I shook my head. "Uncle Rocco, Uncle Rocco," I said, laughing, "that's too rich for my blood. I'm happy in my own little store."

"You're getting more and more like your father," Uncle Rocco grumbled. "I could have made him into a multimillionaire. But he went his own way."

"He did all right," I said. "He had a good business and a good life. What more can any man want?"

Uncle Rocco shrugged. "Maybe you're right."

"He didn't need anyone's permission to retire." I watched my uncle silently for a moment, then asked, "Now, how can I help you?"

"First, you take my offer to head up the investment company. After that we begin to buy companies with profit potential. Your company, Millennium Films Corporation, then Shepherd's oil companies, Jarvis's Canadian holdings. Outside of your own company, they're all cash short and losing their asses, but they can be brought up. Then there is a list of other companies we have looked at. It will be up to you to get them all together. It could be like RJR and Nabisco, but cash rich, not on borrowed moneys." He watched me intently, as if wanting to see my decision before I spoke.

"What do you think the government will do when they find out all of your 'men of honor' are in a business like this?" I asked.

"They are not in the company. The company is nothing but legitimate businessmen, Japanese, Europeans, Arabic. The banks are all the big banks. Citicorp, Morgan Stanley, Chase. Stockbrokers, Merrill Lynch, Hutton, Goldman Sachs. Everyone completely straight and blue ribbon."

"And what do you get out of it?" I asked.

"Out of this," he said, "I retire completely legit."

I took a deep breath. "Do you know that I love you, Uncle Rocco?"

"I know," he said quietly.

"But it won't work. It's like a daydream."

"They are all men of honor. We made an agreement. We have all the money we need. Twenty billion clean. The government has no strings on it, all the taxes have been paid. We will have a legitimate business. For us, the Mafia is over."

"For you old men it may be over, but the Mafia will never be finished. It's like the Leaning Tower of Pisa. It leans a little more each year, but it never falls."

Uncle Rocco stared at me. "What are you trying to tell me?"

"You have no choice, Uncle Rocco," I answered. "You have to stay here. You know too much. You have too much in your head to walk away from them." I met his eyes. "How long do you think you would last?"

"Your father told me that same thing fifty years ago," Uncle Rocco said.

"My father was right then," I said. "And his advice is just as good now."

Uncle Rocco sighed. "Then what do I do?"

"You seem to have everything under control here," I said. "Just do what you always did. Fuck all of them."

"I still want to get Jarvis's piece back. It's a big number and I have some partners who want their shares back."

"I told you I would help you with that," I said.

"Good." He smiled suddenly. "Let's go down to the dining room. I have a surprise for you."

UNCLE ROCCO LOVED surprises. This was a big one. There stood Alma Vargas with her eleven-year-old daughter, Angela—named after her father.

Book Three

❖

THERE ARE NO MORE
GODFATHERS

1

❖

KIM WAS ANGRY. "You're an asshole," she said. "What the hell do you care if your uncle loses two hundred or four hundred million? He has so much money that he won't even miss it."

"He asked me to help," I said. "After all, he is family."

"That's his con," she said. "He doesn't give a damn what happens to you. All he wants to do is get you into his spiderweb. You can take care of *his* business, he doesn't care what happens to the business you built and developed over the years. And you have enough money, you don't even need his help."

"Calm down and come to bed, Kim," I said. "Everything will work out all right."

"Sure," she said sarcastically. "You'll either wind up in jail or in the ground with the others."

"I'm staying in my own business," I said. "All I'm doing is straightening things out. Then I'm out of there."

"Meanwhile, you're out eighty-five million," she said bitterly. "I don't see where he's going to return the money to you."

"He'll return it," I said stubbornly. "It's a matter of honor."

"But you have already signed the agreement with Bradley. You've guaranteed him another four hundred million, and his shrewd old lawyer set it up so that you don't get any stock in the company until all the money is paid in." She stared at me. "Where did your brains go? You don't work like that with General Avionics. You make sure that all the t's are crossed and the i's are dotted when you make any deal."

"What are you getting pissed about?" I snapped. "It's my problem, not yours."

She turned away from the bed. "And why are you talking to Senator Beaufort to work out a U.S. citizenship for that cunt?" she asked in a strained voice.

"Jarvis was going to get it before he got whacked. Now she has to get the citizenship or the FCC won't allow her to buy a share in the company, because only Americans can own television or radio stations. They'd never okay my uncle with his record. Rupert Murdoch did it that way, and that was a bigger deal than this," I answered.

"And if it doesn't work?" she asked, not looking at me.

"Then Uncle Rocco winds up with the short end of the stick," I said.

She turned to me. "No, he doesn't."

"What do you mean?" I asked.

"He's very smart. He's already got you on the hook," she said. "For almost five hundred million dollars. You'll have to sell General Avionics to pay that off."

"He'll come up with the money," I said.

She met my eyes. "Like he came up with Angelo's kid. A child with sandy-brown hair and green eyes like yours. Did Angelo look like that?"

I was silent. Angelo had black hair and dark brown eyes.

"Your uncle paid her to get out of the country when she wanted to marry you. You told me that," she said.

I shook my head. "I have a big mouth."

"You were both fucking her," she said.

"Not at the same time," I said.

"Close enough," she said. "The kid could be yours."

"Crazy," I said.

Then I saw the tears on her cheeks. "Men are so stupid."

I reached for her hand. "I'm not that stupid," I said. "I have you."

She buried her face in my chest. "I'm afraid," she whispered, "that you're going to lose everything you worked for."

"No way," I said. I turned her face up to me and kissed her.

"She's a bitch," she said. "She's been completely done over with plastic surgery. Eyes, face, tits, tummy tuck, asslift, liposuction."

I was surprised. "How do you know?"

"You told me," she said. "You said she looked like

she did twelve years ago. It doesn't work like that. Not for any woman. Especially after she's had a child."

I started to laugh. "I wonder if she had her cunt done too."

"It's possible," she said seriously. "Would you like to check on it?"

"Not me," I said quickly. "I'm not interested in time travel."

She reached down to hold me. "You have a hard-on," she said. "She's turning you on."

"Bitch!" I kissed her and pulled her on top of me. "And you think your hands all over me don't turn me on?"

"You're so bad," she said.

"You're angry," I said. "Come sit on my face. I'll suck all the anger out of you."

IT WAS ABOUT three months ago when I saw Uncle Rocco in Atlantic City and we had dinner with Alma and her daughter. The dining room was on the lower floor of Uncle Rocco's duplex penthouse. Alma was already there, seated at the small bar in the corner, looking out onto the ocean. She turned and rose as she heard us enter.

She smiled and held both hands out to me. "Jed," she said warmly.

I held her hands and kissed her on both cheeks. "Alma," I said, "it's a real surprise."

"Not really," she said. "I always knew that we would see each other again sometime."

"I can't believe it," I said. "You look just as lovely as you did when we first met. Really even more beautiful."

She laughed. "French makeup. It does wonders for one."

"It takes more than that," I said. "I got older and heavier, but you have found the fountain of youth."

"Don't be silly." She laughed. "Then you were a boy; now you're a man. You look marvelous."

"Thank you," I said. "Uncle Rocco told me you have a daughter."

A faint shadow crossed her face. "Yes," she answered. "I never knew that I was pregnant with Angelo's child."

I met her eyes. "Life is strange."

"True," she answered. "The way we meet again. All because my husband dies."

I still held her eyes. "I don't know whether to offer you congratulations or condolences."

She didn't turn away from me. "Maybe a little of both."

A white-jacketed houseman came from behind the bar. He refilled her drink and looked at me.

"Scotch on the rocks," I said.

He placed the drink on the bar in front of me and left the room. I held the glass up to her. "Cheers," I said.

"Salúd." We sipped our drinks. "My husband was a shit," she said.

I was silent for a moment. "But you married him," I said. "Why?"

"There were three reasons. One, he was rich; two, he had the hardest prick I ever felt; three, he asked me." She laughed. "He was crazy about my Peruvian pussy. He used to say my clit was almost as big and hard as his prick."

"That sounds romantic," I said.

"It was romance for him," she said. "But he was crazy. He really hated women. He wanted to destroy me. When he found he couldn't do that, he decided to divorce me."

I was silent.

"I signed a prenuptial agreement. A million for each year we were married, but then at the end he also wanted to screw me out of that."

"It doesn't make any difference now," I said. "You're his widow, you'll get everything."

"It won't be that easy," she said. "He has two sons from a previous marriage. One is thirty-two and the other thirty. They're both officers in his corporation and the only inheritors of his estate."

"How did you learn that?" I asked. "Sherman Siddely told me that you were the only heir."

"Well Siddely was wrong. I've heard from his Canadian attorneys. He made his will seven years ago. If I cooperate, they said, they would see to it that I would get something out of the estate."

"You're going to cooperate with them?" I asked.

"I'll break their asses," she said angrily. "I'll get my share." She took a deep breath. "It might have been better if he had not been killed."

"It doesn't make sense," I said. "I thought you went after him."

A genuine look of surprise crossed her face. "Why should I do a thing like that? I knew that his sons were going to get all of it. It would have been easier for me to fight with him than with his estate."

"Then who killed him?" I asked.

"You don't know?" she asked.

I shook my head.

"Your uncle," she said quietly. "When he found out that Jarvis was going to screw him, he went into a rage." She was silent for a moment. "Godfathers don't forgive."

UNCLE ROCCO HAD dinner at seven o'clock each night. Tonight the table was set for four people. It was beautiful. I'd never thought the old man cared about things like that. Candles. Tall-stemmed glassware. English Coalport dishes and lovely French silverware.

He nodded as he came into the room and looked at Alma. "Where's the baby?"

"She'll be here in a moment," she answered.

"I arranged a special treat for her," he said. "Hamburgers from McDonald's."

He turned to me. "Have you seen the baby yet?"

Alma laughed. "She's not a baby anymore. She's eleven years old."

"She's still a baby," he said. He turned to the door as the child entered. "Angela." He bent down to kiss her.

"Grandpa," she giggled. "Your whiskers tickled me."

"The better to eat you with, my dear."

"You're not the big bad wolf," she said. She looked at me. "Are you my uncle?" she asked.

She had green eyes and blondish-brown hair like my mother's. She was tall for her age, and I was curious about her accent. She sounded British. "I don't think so," I said. "Probably your cousin."

"Grandpa is not your daddy?"

"No," I answered. "He is my uncle. Your father was his son."

She turned to her mother. "You said he was my uncle," she said accusingly.

"In a kind of way, he is," she explained. "Your father and he were like brothers."

She thought for a moment then looked up at me. "May I call you Uncle?"

"Of course," I said.

"You have a funny name," she said. "Jed. None of the boys in my school have that name. Is that your real name?"

"Jed is an abbreviation," I said. "The full name is actually Jedediah."

"That sounds like a biblical name," she said. "The pastor in Sunday school always told us about names like that when he read to us from the Old Testament."

Alma cut into the conversation. "Angela goes to school in England," she said. "There are many things that puzzle her about Americans."

But the child was stubborn. "I've seen pictures of my daddy. He had black hair like yours," she said, looking at her mother. "Uncle Jed looks more like me than either of you." She was silent for a moment, then turned to me. "Did you ever fuck Mommy?"

None of us could find an answer for that. Her voice was sweet and innocent. "Mommy went to bed with a lot of my uncles," she said. She looked up at me again. "There were sometimes she even went to bed with Grandpa."

I glanced at Uncle Rocco. His face was flushed. I laughed and reached down for the child's hand. "Forget about all this nonsense and let's have dinner."

Dinner was perfect. The child had McDonald's hamburgers and we had *spaghettini al pomodoro al dente* and rare sirloin steak Sinatra with green and red peppers and onions.

2

❖

UNCLE ROCCO LOOKED at me quizzically as we
walked up the staircase after dinner to the living room.
Alma was taking the child to bed. "What do you think
of the baby?" he asked gruffly.

"She's pretty," I said. "And bright, too."

"She's a Di Stefano," he said.

"I'm sure," I said.

"I gave her a trust fund for a million dollars," he
said.

I smiled at him. "Fair enough. After all, she is your
granddaughter."

"Maybe," he answered. "But it doesn't matter. She is
a Di Stefano. And I know Angelo would have liked it."

He watched me again as we reached the landing. I
met his eyes. "Uncle Rocco," I said, "you did the right
thing. Angelo deserved it."

"I had nothing left of him," he said heavily.

I pressed his hand gently. "You have now," I said quietly.

I followed him into the living room and we sat down at a square glass card table. Next to his chair there was a wooden chest with three hand-painted, decorated drawers. He took a key from his pocket and opened the top drawer. Carefully he lifted out a black enameled box. He placed it on the table and opened it.

"What's that?" I asked.

"Just a moment," he said. Quickly he took out a number of glassine bags. He spread them out in front of him. "This is the biggest business in the United States. More than GM and American Express combined. Over three hundred billion dollars retail."

I watched him silently.

He tapped the small glassine bags and a little powder came from each. He pointed to the first powder. It was yellowish brown. "This is Southeastern Asian heroin." The next was pure white. "This is Pakistani-Afghanistan heroin." Following that was a blue-white crystal-like substance. "South American cocaine." The next bag held a small amount of shredded marijuana. "This is from Colombia and Mexico." The last bag he opened had a number of variously colored pills and tablets that he spread onto the table. "This is new," he said. "We call it 'designer drugs.'"

"Okay," I said. "What has this got to do with me?"

"All of this is processed in Sicily. The families used to control the streets, but now they are upset because there are many small dealers bringing in their own material and selling it on the street for less than the families."

"How did that happen?" I asked.

"Men became greedy. The agreement with the families fell apart and war came. Many died and the government took advantage of the situation and moved right in. Now life is very different for the families."

"You're retired, Uncle Rocco," I said. "You have nothing to do with it."

He looked at me. "I thought that. But now they have other ideas."

I looked at him without speaking.

"Many years ago," he said, "after the war, Luciano arranged that there would be a commission. Nothing could be done without the agreement of the commission. No territories could be invaded, no businesses could be taken out, and most of all, no killing of capos or heads of families unless agreed to by the commission." He took a deep breath. "For years, everything was quiet, we all did well and profited. And then everything fell apart."

"Why was that?" I asked.

"Luciano died. Costello became the judge, but he wasn't Lucky; he was good but he couldn't hold the line. Gambling, unions, street banking, business-protection service—he could handle that. But then there were drugs. That was a new business. More money than anyone could ever imagine. And everyone became greedy and tore at each other like animals." He fell silent.

"What do they want from you, Uncle Rocco?" I asked.

My uncle was quiet. "The Sicilian commission knows that I am a man of honor. And so do the Americans. They both agree that they want me to be head of the commission. They say I would be the Capo di Tutti Capi, and whatever I would say would go."

"Jesus," I said. "What kind of money would you get for that?"

"More millions than you can ever imagine," he said. "But that doesn't matter. I don't want it. I told you before that I wanted to die in bed. If I do this I will die in a year. In the street. Like Castellano, Bonanno, Galante."

"What can I do to help, Uncle?" I asked.

"You talk to them," he said quietly. "You tell them that I am an old man. I have problems with my head. I forget things. That I can't handle the complications of a responsibility like that. Tell them I am now getting ready to go into a rest home."

"And they'll believe me?" I asked incredulously.

"Maybe," he said shrugging.

"But they don't even know me," I said.

"They know," he said confidently. "They knew your father. They knew that he was straight and honest. And they know that you are your father's son."

"Oh, God," I said. "And when am I supposed to do this?"

"You have some time," he said easily. "After you straighten up the business with the film company."

"I don't know when I'll get that finished. Jarvis's sons won't even acknowledge my offer for their stock."

Uncle Rocco smiled. "We'll get the stock," he said confidently. "They took my money for that stock. The money came from my Canadian bank. The bank has asked them to pay the money back. That's four hundred million plus interest, and the Jarvis Corporation hasn't got it. They have agreed to turn over the stock to the bank in return for cancellation of the loan without penalties."

Alma's voice came from behind us. I hadn't heard her come into the room. "I also waived my suit against the Jarvis estate. They insisted on that."

Uncle Rocco looked at her. "You will still get three million from the estate. And if this all works out, you'll get a good commission."

"I want five million dollars," she said.

He laughed. "You're nothing but a Peruvian *putana*."

She laughed with him. "I'm also the mother of your grandchild."

I turned to my uncle. "You're both having fun," I said. "But I'm the only one who is short on this deal so far. I laid out eighty-five million cash and went on the line for four hundred million; so far I haven't received a penny back."

Uncle Rocco met my eyes. "If you're worried, I'll give you the money the first thing in the morning."

"Uncle Rocco," I said, shaking my head, "you know I won't be here in the morning. I have to leave at five A.M. to be back at eight o'clock in the morning for meetings."

"Then I'll send you the money when you return to L.A.," he said.

"Sure," I said. I knew he wouldn't send me the money tomorrow. That wasn't his way.

"I am a man of honor," he said quietly. "When you wanted to get money to start your business, I gave it to you. You will get this money too."

"Fuck it," I said. "I really don't give a shit whether I get the money or not. After all, it's family."

He nodded. "Family. That is all that really matters." He looked at his watch. "It's ten o'clock," he said. "We can pick up the news on the Philadelphia station."

He turned in his chair and clicked on the remote. The large television lit up. The announcer's voice could not hide his excitement. "Less than twenty minutes before coming on the air tonight, we learned that one of Philadelphia's gang lords was shot and killed as he stepped out of his limousine on his way to dinner at his favorite restaurant." The picture suddenly changed from the face of the anchorman to the face of the man who had been murdered. The announcer was speaking over it, but Uncle Rocco was no longer interested. He turned off the set.

I looked at him. He knew I had recognized the man. He had been in Uncle Rocco's office earlier today. "What happened?" I asked.

My uncle shrugged his shoulders. "I told you that he was a shit. Nobody liked him. Sooner or later somebody was going to whack him."

I was silent for a moment. "And this is the world they want you to control?"

"I said I couldn't handle it," he said. "That's why I want out."

I got out of my chair. "I'd better get to bed," I said. "I have to wake up very early tomorrow."

Alma smiled at me. "I thought we'd have some time to talk a little."

"We will," I said. "But tomorrow I have to meet with Senator Beaufort about your citizenship application."

I bent over and kissed Uncle Rocco's cheek. His fingers brushed my cheek lightly. "Sleep well," he said. "I love you."

"I love you," I said to him. And I know he believed it.

I kissed Alma's cheek, too. "Goodnight, dear," I said. "And your daughter is beautiful."

"Thank you," she said, and I left them in the living room while I went down the steps where the guest bedrooms were located.

THERE WERE FOUR guest bedrooms, and mine was the last at the end of the hall. In a way it was the best room of all: large and at the corner of the hall. There were French windows on the far side of the room that opened onto a long terrace that reached along the building past each of the other bedrooms. I stretched out on the bed in nothing but my jockey shorts and turned off the light. I cursed silently. Despite the blackout curtains over the windows, light still came in from the cracks between the curtains. There was too much Las Vegas on the boardwalk outside. I turned on my side, facing the wall with my back to the windows. After a while I fell asleep.

I don't know how long I had been asleep, but suddenly I felt a blast of cold night air and sensed a flash of light coming from the drapes. I rolled quickly to face the windows. The drapes had already fallen closed.

Alma's voice came to me. "Are you awake?"

"I am now," I said.

"Let me get under the covers," she said. "I'm freezing."

"Stupid," I said. "Why didn't you come through the door?"

"One of your uncle's guards is sitting in the hall," she said. "Come on. Let me in, I'm freezing."

I moved over and she got into bed and pulled the blankets over herself. She took my hand. "Feel," she said. "I'm really cold."

She guided my hand over her breasts. She *was* cold. Then she placed my hand over her belly and down to her fur. "But my pussy is warm. It's always hot."

"Great," I said. "So what else is new?"

"Do you have a hard-on?" she asked.

"No," I said.

"I can fix that," she said.

"Wait a minute," I said. "What have you come over here for?"

"I wanted you to know," she said, "Angela is your child, not your cousin's."

"No big deal," I said. "I'm sure Uncle Rocco figured that out."

"I don't give a damn what Uncle Rocco thought," she said, her voice quiet but angry. "Don't you feel anything about your own daughter?"

I looked at her. "She's not my child," I said flatly. "You made a good deal with Uncle Rocco, don't fuck it up."

Her open hand stung my face. "You cold-ass son of a bitch!" she snapped.

I shook my head to clear it, then turned on the dim bedside light and smiled at her. "I'm disappointed. I thought you just came here for an auld lang syne fuck."

"Fuck yourself!" she answered angrily and started to swing at me again.

This time I caught her arm. She tried to hit me with her other hand. Now she was overdoing it. I had a temper of my own. I belted her on the jaw. She tumbled backward off the bed, falling face down across the chaise, her naked buttocks and legs hanging out of her silk robe.

I stood over her as she stared up at me. "You have a hard-on," she said huskily.

"I have to take a piss," I said.

A faint smile began to appear on her face. "Piss on me," she said.

"You're crazy," I said. "Go back to your room."

She turned quickly. Pulling down my shorts, she cupped my testicles in her hand. "Your balls are heavy with come," she said.

"Get out," I said angrily, "or I'll fuck you in the ass."

She rose on the chaise and got on her knees, her ass in the air dog-fashion. Quickly she wet her fingers with her cunt juices and spread the moisture over her anus. "Do it," she said. "I love it."

I stood there for a moment. Then she grasped my prick with her hand and pushed it inside her. I grabbed her by the sides of her buttocks to pull her to me.

Suddenly there was a noise, and the bedroom door opened. Angela stood in the doorway far across the room, the light from the hallway framing her. "Is my mother here?" she asked in a soft voice.

3

❖

ALMA QUICKLY ROLLED from the chaise to the floor, and when she came to her feet her robe completely covered her. I still had half a hard-on so I turned my back to the child and grabbed for my pants. Alma spoke to her daughter angrily. "I told you never to follow me!"

"I didn't follow you, Mama," Angela said quietly. "I just wanted to tell you that the guard in the hall is dead."

"You were watching television again," Alma snapped.

The child was still calm. Quietly she opened the door wide. "Look," she said.

Angela was right. It wasn't television. The guard was still sitting in his chair, a look of surprise on his face, a neat bullet hole in the center of his forehead, his gun lying on the floor underneath his outstretched hand.

"What else did you see?" I whispered to Angela, quickly crossing the room and pulling her inside.

"I peeked through my door. There were two men. They ran up the steps toward Grandpa's," she answered.

"Take her with you to my bathroom and lock the door," I said to Alma.

"What are you going to do?" she asked.

"First I'm going to get the guard's gun. Then I'll figure out something. You get into the bathroom. Now."

I watched them go into the bathroom and heard the lock click shut. Then I went to my bedroom door and looked out into the hallway. It was empty except for the dead guard. I stood silently, listening for any sound. There was none. Quickly I ran across the hall to the dead guard, grabbed his gun, ran back to my bedroom, and closed the door behind me.

I checked the gun. It was a Beretta .380 automatic with an eleven-cartridge clip. The clip was full—not a cartridge had been used. I locked the clip tight and opened the safety. Then I looked down at the telephone next to the bed. There were six intercom buttons. One was listed "Mr. Di Stefano's Bedroom." I picked up the receiver and pressed the button.

There were three slow buzzes, and just as my heart sank, Uncle Rocco's voice came on. "What the hell do you want?" he asked gruffly.

"Are you okay?" I asked.

"I'm fine," he said irritably. "Now what the hell do you want?"

"I want you to know that the guard down here has been killed," I said. "And two gunmen have gone up the stairs."

"I haven't heard anything," he said. "Certainly I would have heard shots from the bodyguards outside my room."

"Maybe they've been whacked, too," I said. "I heard nothing from the hall when they killed the guard. They must have used silencers."

"Shit," Uncle Rocco complained. "Nobody fights fair anymore."

"They'll be going into your room after you," I said.

"No way," he said. "They can't get in. My bedroom is a safe room. Steel door under the wooden panel and steel panels in the walls. And all the windows are presidential bulletproof glass."

"What if they have plastic explosives to blow the door?" I asked.

"That would be embarrassing," Uncle Rocco said calmly. "But for them, not me. Once they get through the door, I have two Uzis and a double sawed-off shotgun aimed right at them."

"In Nam, they threw in tear gas before going in," I said. "You can't see to shoot anything when you're blind and choking."

"Where's the *putana* and my granddaughter?" he asked.

"They're safe," I said. "I have them locked in my bathroom."

"That don't mean shit if those assholes come after you," he said. "Get them to the fire stairs and have them go all the way to the main floor. The security men will take care of them."

"But what about you?" I asked.

"Get them on the steps; then, if you want to be a hero, come after me," he said.

"Don't be sarcastic," I said. "I promised to help you die in bed, and not with bullets. How do I get to you?"

"There's an outside staircase between the terrace on your floor up to mine. It comes up to the back of my office French doors. Do you have a gun?"

"I grabbed the guard's gun," I said.

"That's a Beretta special," he said. "Do you know how to use it?"

"Of course," I said.

"Okay," he said quietly. "When you get up there, just shoot the sons of bitches in the back. Give them no warning or they'll blow you away."

"Gotcha," I said.

"Now put a sweater on when you go out on the terrace, it's freezing out there, and I don't want you catching a cold," he said.

"I have a sweater," I said.

"Good," he said. "Now check your watch. You come in my terrace doors in seven minutes exactly and start blasting. At the same time I'll come out of my door with the shotgun. If you don't get them, I will."

"I want you to stay in your room," I said.

"Don't be stupid," he said. "This is family."

The phone clicked off. I knocked on the bathroom door. "Come on," I said.

Alma opened the door. She was clutching the child beside her. "What's going on?"

"Rocco said to get you off this floor." I pulled on my sweater. "Now follow me."

It took me two minutes to find the fire staircase. I opened the door. "Now get down to the main floor. Rocco said that the security men down there will take care of you."

"And what about you?" Alma asked.

"Uncle Rocco and I have a plan. Now, get going."

Angela looked up at me. "Uncle Jed," she said, "you're a real hero."

I laughed. "Get going, honey."

Two and a half minutes had elapsed by the time I got to the terrace doors. I opened the door, and the icy blast from the ocean almost took my breath away. My chest was screaming in pain as I slipped and slid up the ice-covered terrace steps. My hands felt almost frozen to the iron railing along the staircase. I don't know how I got there, but my watch showed six and a half minutes as I crouched near the upper terrace doors.

Damn, I cursed to myself. Uncle Rocco said seven minutes. I still had thirty seconds to wait. Thirty seconds in windy, icy hell. The Beretta turned into pure ice in my hands as I clasped it. I prayed to Jesus that I could squeeze my fingers to make the damn thing shoot. Fifteen seconds later, I rose from my crouch. As Uncle Rocco had predicted, I could see the two gunmen inside. I leaned quietly against the terrace door and turned the doorknob, but it was frozen and wouldn't open. I tried to kick the door. It still wouldn't move.

By this time the two bastards had their guns on me. I didn't know which prayers would give me the most protection: my mother's Adonai or my father's Blessed Mary, Mother of God. I saw the blue-white flashes from their guns, but I heard no sounds. Maybe I was already dead. But then I heard the faint ping of the bullets hitting the terrace windows. They never touched me.

Then, behind them, I saw Uncle Rocco come through his bedroom door, his shotgun in his arm. The sound of the two blasts could be heard even through the windows. Uncle Rocco caught both men in their backs as they turned to shoot at me through the window. They never knew what hit them. They fell on their faces, and Uncle Rocco stepped carefully around them. He dangled a large key in his hand, then opened the terrace door.

"Get inside," he said. "It's freezing out there."

"You bastard!" I said through chattering teeth. "You could have got me killed."

"Impossible," he said. "I told you that it was presidential bulletproof glass."

"What about pneumonia?" I asked, still shivering.

"Wait a moment," he said. "I have the best Sicilian grappa. One shot of this, you'll be as good as new."

He crossed to the bar and poured me a shot and one for himself. *"Salute,"* he said.

"Salute," I answered. The grappa burned into my gut. I turned and looked at the two men on the floor, then looked around the room. "Where are your bodyguards?" I asked. "I don't see them anywhere around."

Uncle Rocco gestured to the two dead men. "There they are."

"I don't get it," I said.

"They've been reached," he said. "Money is the root of all evil and it destroyed them."

I stared at him. "Who paid them off?"

He shrugged. "Probably Nico. But I guess they didn't know that Nico was already gone. If they did, they wouldn't have tried it, because there was no place to get the money for it."

"Did you get Nico whacked?" I asked.

"No," he answered. "I am way above all those things."

"The bodyguards," I said. "It doesn't make sense."

"It made sense," he said. "They didn't have to do anything tonight. They could have whacked me in the morning when I came out for breakfast. They knew that nobody could have gotten into my bedroom."

"What do you really need me for, Uncle Rocco?" I asked. "It seems to me you do pretty good on your own."

"I don't agree with that. If you stay in the business, sooner or later they'll get you. I can't handle this excitement anymore, I'm too old for it." He looked at me. "You're family. Look down at the floor. Is this any way to live? You're going to have to get me out."

I stared at him. "I'll have another grappa."

We both put away another shot. Finally I felt warm again. "How do we get this thing cleaned up?"

"I have connections downstairs. There'll be no word." He looked down at the two men on the floor.

"There is only one thing that I feel badly about. That Oriental rug on the floor cost me a hundred and fifty grand. It was one of only two in the world. And these two bastards have ruined it."

4

❖

THERE WAS ONE thing about grappa: maybe it burned your guts out, but it also blew the cobwebs from your brain. It turned my head into a 64K computer. I sat on the bar stool and watched Uncle Rocco talking on the telephone. Around us in the room, cleaning men were working and straightening, getting everything back to normal.

Uncle Rocco was speaking in Italian. I didn't understand Italian all that well, but my mental computer enabled me to know exactly what he was saying. He told whoever he was talking to that they were assholes, and none of them could follow the rules. And if they didn't obey the rules they would all wind up in the shithouse. Then he smiled, said *"Ciao,"* and put down the telephone.

"Alma and the child are on their way up," he said to me.

"Good. I have to get some sleep. I have to catch a shuttle to New York for an L.A. flight."

"You're not going," he said firmly. "We have a more important meeting here tomorrow."

"I've made arrangements to conclude the contract with Aerospatiale at my office tomorrow," I said. "I have a half billion on deposit with them, and if I don't sign, I can blow it all."

"You won't blow it," he said confidently. "But if you don't make this meeting tomorrow you *will* blow it."

The 64K grappa computer clicked in. "Uncle Rocco," I said, "I thought you asked me to be here for family business, but that wasn't it, was it?"

Silently he poured more grappa into our glasses. "Drink," he said.

"You're my uncle," I said angrily. "I came up here tonight ready to die for you if I had to. But you're not being honest with me. You're just playing Godfather."

"There are no more Godfathers," he said quietly. "We are all nothing but honest businessmen."

"What is the business then?" I asked sarcastically. "Death?"

"I didn't look for it," he said. "These men were children playing games. They saw too many movies."

I stared at him for a moment. "I don't get it. What does your meeting tomorrow have to do with my agreement with Aerospatiale?"

"The meeting is with Europeans," he said. "They have more influence with Aerospatiale than you have as an American. And your biggest competitor is a Dutch company that is bidding on the same deal."

"I know that," I said shortly. "Tell me something I don't know."

"The Dutch company will buy you out for three billion," he said. "Cash."

"Two years from now," I said, "my business will be worth five billion."

"The magic word 'deregulation' has doubled the number of airlines of three years ago. You did well because they needed you. But now labor, maintenance, and fuel costs are beginning to rocket," Uncle Rocco said seriously. "Seventy percent of the new airlines are underfinanced and loaded with junk bonds, shylock-interest payments. The industry is already discounting fares like crazy just to keep their heads above water. A small recession, and you'll wind up with more repossessed aircraft than you can stick up your ass."

"It's not going to happen," I said. "The market is still climbing, and all the business forecasts are upbeat."

"I've been around a long time," he said quietly. "And there's one thing I've learned. Life is a roller coaster. Everything that goes up comes down."

"But sooner or later it goes up again," I said. "History taught me that."

"Right," he agreed. "But you have to be careful that you don't get castrated in the downslide." He gulped his grappa. "If you get three billion for your company, how much do you net?"

I rolled the numbers over in my head. "Between six hundred and six hundred fifty million after taxes."

A new respect came into his face. "You're rich."

"I'm not in your class, Uncle Rocco," I said.

"But you did better," he said heavily. "You never had to shovel society's shit since you were fifteen, you never had to do hard time for eleven years of your life, or murder to save your life or to gain respect from the society. And you never had the dead imprinted on your eyelids when you went to sleep."

I placed a hand on his arm. "It was many years ago, Uncle Rocco," I said. "It was another time, another world."

"But I'm still alive," he said quietly. "And for me it's still the same world. That's why I want to get out of it."

It was my turn to fill the glasses with grappa. *"Salute,"* I said. We gulped our drinks. The door opened and four men in overalls carried in another large rug and placed it on the floor, replacing the bloody one that had been removed.

I stared down at the rug, then turned to Uncle Rocco. "I thought you said that there were only two rugs of this kind in the world."

He smiled and nodded. "That's true. But I wasn't going to take any chances if anything should happen to mine. So I bought both of them."

"What are you going to do with the other one?"

"I'm shipping it to Pakistan. It was made there over two hundred years ago, but the Pakistani are still the only ones who can clean and repair it."

I got down from the bar stool. My legs were a little wobbly. "I'm going to bed," I said.

Alma appeared, fully dressed now. She crossed to Uncle Rocco. "Are you all right?" she asked.

He nodded "Everything's okay."

She turned to me. "Angela is already asleep."

"Good," I said.

"She adores you," she said. "She thinks you're a hero."

I laughed. "She's a child. When she grows up she'll think I am stupid."

It was Uncle Rocco who interrupted. "You are a hero. You came to save my life."

"I was stupid," I said. "You didn't need any help." My head was beginning to hurt. "I'd better get to bed, I'm getting dizzy."

"I'll help you downstairs," Alma said quickly.

"No, thanks," I replied. "I'll manage."

She turned to Uncle Rocco. "Did you tell him that I was going to Los Angeles?"

I stared at Uncle Rocco. "You didn't tell me."

He held his hands outstretched. "I forgot."

"Oh, shit." I said. Then I weaved out of the room and managed almost to fall down the staircase. The three security men that were posted on the floor helped me tumble into bed. The ceiling spun around and I passed out. Grappa. I couldn't believe it. I didn't wake up until noon the next day.

Uncle Rocco was sitting on the edge of my bed when I opened my eyes. "How do you feel?" he asked.

I squinted at the light. My head felt like it was exploding. My mouth felt like it was stuffed with cotton. "Awful," I mumbled.

He reached to the night table and picked up an empty glass and a pitcher filled with a reddish-brown drink loaded with ice cubes. He filled the glass and handed it to me. "Drink it. You'll feel better."

I held it to my mouth. A terrible smell hit my nose. "What the hell is it?" I asked.

"Bloody Mary and Fernet Branca," he said. "Swallow it."

I drank it quickly. I began to feel nauseous. "It tastes like shit," I said.

Quickly he refilled the glass. "Again," he ordered.

Automatically I did as he said. Suddenly I could breathe again, my eyes cleared, and my headache disappeared. "Jesus," I said. "Who gave you that formula?"

He laughed. "It was my mother's anti-grappa medicine."

"It works," I said. "I'll grab a shower and get dressed. What time did you say that we'd have a meeting?"

"I've already had the meeting. There was no way I could wake you up," he said.

"Then what the hell happened?"

"Everything is all right." He smiled. "I told them that you said you would take care of it."

"Take care of what?" I asked.

He smiled. "Buy control of Millennium Films."

"I don't know anything about that business. What am I going to do with it?" I asked.

"Turn it over to them," he said.

I thought for a moment. "And what happens if I decide to hang onto it?"

"That's what Jarvis wanted to do," he answered.

"Then I have no choice," I said.

"And neither do I," Uncle Rocco said. "I'm the *patrone*. We'll both be dead."

5

❖

I PULLED THE Blazer into the garage of my office building and stopped in front of the parking attendant. He came out of his small booth and smiled at me. "Good morning, Mr. Stevens."

"Good morning, John," I said.

He looked at me. "Miss Latimer is waiting for you in the garage-floor waiting room at the elevator."

"Thank you, John," I said and crossed toward the elevator corridor. I opened the door. She was alone in the small room. She stubbed out a cigarette in the sandbox next to her.

"What's wrong?" I asked. I'd never seen her smoking in the daytime.

"You didn't tell me that cunt was coming to the meeting," she said angrily.

"I told you all of them would be here. She's one of the principals," I said. "I couldn't leave her out."

"I don't trust her."

"You're jealous," I said. "Forget it. It's only business. After today you won't see her anymore."

"Maybe I won't," she said. "But will you?"

"Don't be silly. I won't either."

"I *am* jealous," she admitted. "She really is special."

"Yesterday's style." I laughed.

She looked at me. "You mean that?"

"You're definitely today's style," I said, kissing her. "You're my baby."

"I'm sorry. I got upset."

I started toward the elevator. "Everybody up there?" I asked.

"All there," she said. "And they were early. Shepherd and his attorney, Gitlin; McManus from the B. of A.; Peachtree and his assistant, Shifrin; the cunt and her banker from Canada; the team from D.B.&L.; Siddely; the attorney representing Millennium; then Jim Handley from our office with our accountant, Dave Blitz. I thought I'd fill in as secretary and notary."

I smiled at her as the elevator went up. "Bitch," I said. "I should have known that you'd find a way to get yourself into the meeting."

"I'm not crazy. I wasn't going to leave you alone in the room with that woman."

I COULD SEE the curiosity on their faces as I entered the meeting. I stood at the head of the table, Kim sat to my left, her tape recorder and her stenotype machine in front of her.

"Good morning, Mrs. Jarvis and gentlemen. First, I want to thank you for your attendance at this meeting on such short notice. As you know, for the last few months I have been studying operations and problems of Millennium and I genuinely believe we now have to face the moment of truth. The company is hocked up to its ass and its income cannot support its operation for another two weeks. Under these circumstances even Chapter Eleven won't help us. We have no inventory or assets to live on until we get well. All that faces us is protection under a reorganization plan or a public auction, neither of which will do any of us any good. Everything will be lost."

They all were silent for a moment, then Judge Gitlin spoke quietly. He went right to the heart of the matter. "If the company busts," he said, "there are only two real losers: Mr. Shepherd and Mrs. Jarvis. They each have four hundred million in it."

"True," I said. "But Shepherd owes me eighty-five million. I don't see how he can pay me back, so I lose too."

"You told him that you would support him," the judge said quietly. "You knew that you would be on the line for the four hundred."

"It wasn't on paper," I said. "And you never told me how much the company was in the shithouse."

"We'll sue your ass off," the old man said.

"I have an eighty-five-million-dollar note that Shepherd signed. I have a better lawsuit than you have."

"You're nothing but a crook," the judge said pleasantly.

"*C'est la vie,*" I answered. "Life changes."

Mr. Kinnard, Alma's Canadian banker, looked at me. "How do we fit into this?" he asked.

"I don't know," I said. "That loan was made to the late Mr. Jarvis. I understand that his stock was given to the company as collateral."

"But you tell me that this company is worth nothing," he said.

"All I can give you is my sympathy," I said.

"Jed, you're nothing but a prick!" Alma snapped. "I thought I could depend on you." She started to sob.

"Personally, you can," I said. "But this is not personal, Alma, this is business." I had to admire her. She was giving one of the greatest performances I had ever seen. A woman scorned—not a conspirator from the beginning. I wondered if she had used some of these same wiles in wresting control of the estate from Jarvis's two sons.

"Wait a minute," Shepherd said. He looked shrewdly at me. "You didn't ask us to this meeting just to tell us that the company is broke. We all know that. You have something else in mind."

I smiled at him. "You're guessing right, Brad."

"You want to take the company over," he said.

"No, Brad," I said. "I want to buy it."

"You're crazier than I was," Brad said.

"Maybe I'll be lucky," I said. "I'll give you fifty percent on the dollar for your interest."

"It won't work," Brad said. "My agreement with Jarvis was to pay him off at one hundred percent."

"Jarvis is dead," I said. "Mrs. Jarvis might be agreeable."

Alma looked at me, then at the Canadian banker, Mr. Kinnard. "What do you think?"

"Fifty percent would be better than nothing," Mr. Kinnard said.

Alma nodded to me. "You have a deal."

"You heard her," I told Bradley.

He said to Judge Gitlin, "What do you think, Judge?"

Judge Gitlin smiled wryly. "There's something screwy in this deal, but we fell into a pool of piranhas. Take the money and run."

I rose from the table. "Thank you, gentlemen. Now I'll ask the attorneys to draw up the agreements as quickly as possible. I have the money already in an escrow account for you."

Bradley looked at me, his face flushed and angry. "You screwed us, didn't you?"

I was silent.

"I thought that you had come in to help us," he said.

"I did," I said. "But I didn't know that you were already dead in the water. Jarvis had shoved the harpoon up your ass. If it wasn't for me you would have absolutely nothing. Now you can go back and put your own house together."

Silently Bradley left the room with Judge Gitlin. I turned back to the table. "Alma, you and Mr. Kinnard begin putting your papers together."

Alma nodded. "We'll arrange it."

"Thank you," I said. I watched them leave the conference room. Peachtree and his assistant were staring at me.

"Daniel," I said, "you're still the president of the

company. I have faith in your knowledge and ability even though you are a son of a bitch. I'm transferring one hundred million dollars to the company operating account, and I expect you to keep production moving smoothly. I have also appointed Jim Handley as executive vice-president and chief financial officer of the company. I ask you both to go through the company and clean it up. I expect you both to live up each other's asses."

Peachtree looked at me. "Thank you, Jed. But as you know, I do not have a contract as yet."

"Okay, you'll have one tomorrow morning," I said. I met his eyes. "How much money do you want?"

Daniel shrugged. "I haven't thought about it yet."

"Then think about it," I said. "And we'll sit down and work it out."

"I need ten million dollars tomorrow," he said. "I have the opportunity to take the distribution of *Star Island*. Every studio in town has the hots for it, but the producer is an old lover of mine. He knows we'll give him a fair share."

"That's your job," I said. "Do it."

"What about Jim Handley?" he asked.

"Jim will handle the finances—you both work together."

"Good enough," he said. He rose from his chair. "I have work to do. I'll get back to the studio."

We shook hands. "Have a nice day," I said.

He laughed. "You, too," he said and left the conference room with his boyfriend.

I leaned back in my chair and lit a cigarette. "Jesus,"

I said. I felt as if I had gone through a wringer. I was still waiting for Uncle Rocco's money.

Jim Handley leaned toward me. "What do we do next?"

"Borrow," I said. I turned to Ron Schraft, who headed the three-man delegation from D.B.&L. "Can we market a billion dollars of high-yield bonds?"

Ron was young, but he was bright and very close to the source. He came directly to the point. "No chance," he said. "Mike says the numbers don't work out."

"We have the assets," I said. "Real estate is worth at least four hundred million and earns us forty million a year. One hit movie and we'll be swimming in money."

"Millennium has lost almost two hundred million during the last two years," Ron said. "There was no hit movie. Besides, Mike doesn't have any faith in the movie business."

"I think he's wrong," I said.

"But Mike likes you and wants to do business with you. If you merge Millennium into General Avionics, he thinks he can sell five billion high-yield bonds for you."

I stared at him. "That's shit," I said. "General Avionics doesn't need any money, I'm not going to be put into hock for the picture company."

Ron was calm. "It's just an idea," he said. "Mike just wanted to help."

I rose and held my hand out to him. "Thank him," I said. "This is not the kind of help I need." We shook hands politely and they left the conference room.

"Sons of bitches," Handley said.

"It doesn't mean anything," I said. "It's just business for Mike."

Sherman Siddely turned to me. "I was talking to McManus and we agreed that B. of A. isn't going to help."

I laughed. "When did you ever know of a bank that would lend you money if you really need it?"

McManus said, "You're right. But B. of A. has forty million of negative loans in movies that died."

"Come on, Mac," I said. "B. of A. has blown hundreds of millions in negative loans in the film industry over the years. Forty is a drop in the bucket. Besides the only reason you made the loans to Millennium is because you thought that Shepherd would transfer his oil company's accounts over to you."

McManus grinned. "Smart ass," he said.

"Why don't you be a sport and split the Star Island negative deal with me? Five million isn't that much."

"And what do you give me for it?"

"New business from General Avionics," I said.

"Do you mean that?" he asked.

"I keep my word," I said. "And besides that, I will guarantee you the first money out of the picture if it pays out."

McManus turned to Siddely. "What do you think?"

Siddely nodded. "Peachtree knows what he's doing. I'll put my money on him. If Shepherd ever had production men as good as that fag, he wouldn't have fallen into the shit."

McManus said to me, "I'll check it with my home office. I think it's a deal."

"Thanks," I said. "Every little bit helps."

Siddely turned to me. "Jarvis knew what he was doing. He had Peachtree really checked out."

"Too bad he wasn't smart enough to check out his car," I said.

"Jarvis chased the wrong girl," Siddely said. "She had a Las Vegas gangster boyfriend." He looked at me. "I didn't know that you had known Mrs. Jarvis."

"She was married to a cousin of mine a long time ago," I said.

"I tried to get in touch with her," Siddely said. "But she would never even talk to me."

"I don't know anything about it," I said. "I hadn't even heard from her until she contacted me about this deal."

"That was a stroke of luck," Siddely said

"Not bad," I said.

Siddely looked at me. "Jarvis offered me the job as vice-president and general counsel for Millennium."

I met his eyes. "If you're still interested in it, you've got it."

He hesitated, then held out his hand. "We'll do well," he said.

I smiled. "I know we will."

Finally, the meeting was over, and I went back to my office. I walked over to the small bar in the corner of the room and had myself a scotch on the rocks.

Kim watched me. "How do you feel?"

"Tired," I said. I downed half the drink in one swallow. "Get Uncle Rocco for me."

"What do you want him for?" she asked.

I stared at her. "He promised me five hundred million dollars and I haven't seen a penny of it."

6

❖

HE WAS SITTING in my office when I returned from lunch. He rose from his chair and smiled at me. "Mr. Stevens." He held out a business card.

I read it quickly. It was a European type card, much larger than an American business card.

LEONARDO DA VINCI

Director Financial Transactions

Super-Sattel EuroSky Broadcast Corporation

Canale 2[1]   *Liechtenstein*

I looked puzzled.

"My apologies, Mr. Stevens," he said. "I did not mean to intrude, but Mr. Di Stefano assured your secretary that it would be all right."

Silently I walked to my desk and called Uncle Rocco on the speed dialer. "Congratulations," he said. "I heard that you completed the deal."

"What do you have? Spies in my office?" I snapped. "First, you know about the deal by the time I come back from lunch, then you send an emissary to my office unannounced. I thought we agreed that I was to have some privacy in running the studio."

"It's family," he said. "There is no such thing as privacy with a family. Besides this has nothing to do with privacy. Leonardo is only there to balance our finances."

"Okay," I said. "How?"

"Relax," Uncle Rocco replied. "Just leave it to Leonardo." The receiver clicked off and I put down the telephone.

Da Vinci was a tall man, about six three, broad-shouldered like an athlete, blue-eyed, with black hair and a neatly trimmed beard. He wore a black silk suit, Italian cut, white shirt and black tie. He held out his hand. "Just in case you're wondering," he said, laughing, "I have no talent as an artist."

I laughed with him. "Then how come the name?"

"I thought it would be a more interesting name than Leonard Davidson," he answered. "Something about the name Da Vinci always impresses people."

"It impressed me," I said.

He took an envelope from his inside breast pocket

and gave it to me. I opened the envelope and quickly scanned the accounts listed on the paper it contained. It held all the advances I had made to Shepherd and all the new commitments I'd made for Millennium. The total added up to five hundred and ninety-five million.

He looked at me. "Do you find the figures correct?"

I nodded. "Yes. But I don't understand how you discovered them so quickly."

"It is part of our business," he said. "Now that you have agreed with the amounts, we'll begin to settle our accounts."

"Good," I said. "Then I'll ask Jim Handley, my financial vice-president, to join us. He can help us direct the money into the correct account."

"Excellent," he said.

"By the way," I asked, "will the checks you give us be drawn on U.S. banks or foreign?"

"Checks are old-fashioned," he said. "We'll transfer the money directly into your bank accounts."

Handley came into the office just as Da Vinci opened a thick, clumsy attaché case and placed it on my desk. Quickly Da Vinci set up a lap-top computer and connected it to a ten-inch satellite disk, both powered by four six-volt batteries. He flipped the power switch, and light spilled onto the screen. The screen was blank until he turned the disk direction, and then letters in blue appeared on the screen: EUROSKY CANALE 21.

He turned to me. "We're ready for business."

I introduced the two men. Handley was curious about what was going on, but clever enough not to ask questions. Quickly I told him what was being done.

He turned to Da Vinci. "Isn't this against the law?"

Da Vinci shook his head. "Not if you notify your bank in advance that you will make certain deposits in this fashion. After all, banks transfer and deposit between themselves in that manner all the time."

"What connection does Mr. Di Stefano have with EuroSky? And why does EuroSky want Millennium?" I asked.

"As far as I know," Da Vinci answered, "Mr. Di Stefano is one of the investors in EuroSky. And EuroSky is a new company created for the new open market of international television in Europe. EuroSky has already placed four satellites over Western and Eastern Europe, and they are in direct competition with the British companies of Murdoch and Thames for the continental European market. And Millennium is one of the last companies that has over fifteen hundred feature films plus many other film subjects for distribution."

"Is it clean money?" Handley asked.

"Yes," Da Vinci said. "The money is coming from Lloyd's Bank of London and Crédit Suisse in Geneva." He paused for a moment. "In order to transfer the money to your accounts, I would appreciate it if you gave me the account numbers of each of the banks you want money transferred to."

I looked at Jim. "Okay, give him the numbers."

Jim was still nervous. "If we give you the account numbers, wouldn't it be possible that you could make withdrawals from these accounts without our knowledge?"

Da Vinci smiled. "No, not if you notify your banks that this method is to be used only for deposits into your account."

"Okay," I said. "Let's go."

The whole transaction took only about fifteen minutes, and then Da Vinci said, "You've got your money."

Jim looked at him. "How do we know? I don't have any confirmation."

Da Vinci laughed. "Call your banks, they'll tell you."

"Okay," Jim said and walked over to my desk and picked up the telephone. It took him another twenty minutes to verify the deposits. He looked impressed as each bank confirmed that the money was already deposited into the accounts.

Jim turned to me. "The first eighty-five million dollars you advanced to Shepherd is your own money, and I have authorized that money to be placed in the reserve account."

"Good," I said.

Jim continued, "We will then pay the other sums agreed to at the meeting."

I listed the payments to Jim. "The payments to Mrs. Jarvis and Mr. Shepherd will be paid as their paperwork is completed. As was agreed with Peachtree, one hundred million dollars will be put into the production account and a separate amount will be deposited for the acquisition of distribution rights to *Star Island*."

"Okay," said Jim. "I've got it. Now I'll get back to my office and start getting things organized."

Jim left, and I watched Da Vinci put his computer and his equipment back into his attaché case. He placed the attaché case on the floor and asked, "Are you planning to stay on with the studio?"

"I don't think so," I said. "I know nothing about the entertainment business. It's another world."

Da Vinci commented, "It's no longer an entertainment business. It's now communications. It's becoming a new world."

I looked at him. "General Avionics is a big enough world for me. I'm not greedy."

Da Vinci shrugged his shoulders. "That's up to you." He looked at his watch. "It's late, almost five o'clock. If you don't have any plans tonight, why don't you join me for dinner?"

"I have no plans," I said.

"Good. Suppose we meet at the Palms on Santa Monica Boulevard at eight P.M."

"It's a date. I'll bring a girl."

Da Vinci smiled. "And so will I."

I waited until he had left my office and then called Uncle Rocco again. "It's all finished," I said. "Now what do we do?"

"I still want you to think about my earlier proposition. We have a very big investment corporation and you could do very well with it."

"Is that company invested in EuroSky?" I asked.

"Of course," Uncle Rocco said. "We own it all. We have some of the most important motion-picture and broadcasting people in Europe to operate EuroSky."

"How much did that cost you?" I asked him.

"Not that much," Uncle Rocco said. "Maybe eleven billion dollars, but we will get more than fifty percent of that amount back in the first five years because we are leasing space on our satellites in Europe to telephone and other communication companies. They should give us about a billion a year of income."

I laughed. "I don't know what you need me for. You're doing very well on your own."

THEY WERE STANDING six deep at the bar at the Palms at 8 P.M. I was glad I had asked Kim to call and make a reservation for us. We found Da Vinci at the bar, holding a drink, and with a worried expression on his face.

"Have you spoken to Mr. Di Stefano in the last hour?" he asked.

"No," I said. "I spoke to him earlier this afternoon after we had completed our business. But not since."

"I am a little concerned. I tried to telephone him a few times and there is no answer at his apartment," Da Vinci said.

"That is strange," I said. "There is always someone at his apartment."

"There's been no answer," he said quietly.

"Let me try to get him," I suggested. At the same time, my beeper went off. I looked on the tiny screen and saw a number that was unfamiliar to me.

I turned to Kim. "Have a drink at the bar with Mr. Da Vinci, and I will return this call and then try to locate Uncle Rocco. I'll only be a minute. I'll use the car phone."

I was lucky. The nice thing about having a Corniche is the valet always parks the car in front of the restaurant. I slipped the valet a fiver as he unlocked the door. I got into the car and picked up the telephone. First I called Uncle Rocco's number. The phone rang six times, but there was no answer. Then I dialed the other number. To my surprise, Uncle Rocco answered.

"What took you so long?" he asked gruffly.

"What's happening? Where the hell are you?"

"I'm in the Air France first-class lounge at JFK."

"What the hell are you doing there?" I asked.

"I got word there's a contract out on me," he said.

"Do you know who ordered it?" I asked him.

"I have an idea. But I'll have to clear it in Europe. Meanwhile I've got to stay undercover. So I'm renting a yacht in the South of France. I'll stay on the boat until I get everything straightened out."

"How do I get in touch with you?" I asked.

"I'll let you know where I am and you arrange to meet me there as soon as I call," he said.

"I thought you said you were out of this business."

"I am out of the business," Uncle Rocco said. "The trouble is there's some assholes that won't accept it. That's why I want you to straighten them all out."

I groaned into the telephone. "Okay, Uncle Rocco. Call me. I'll be there. Meanwhile, you take care of yourself."

"I will," Uncle Rocco said.

The phone went dead in my hand and I put it back into its cradle. Then I returned to the restaurant.

Da Vinci looked up at me. "Did you try to reach Di Stefano?"

"I got no answer from him either." I shrugged. "Let's have dinner now. We probably won't hear from him until tomorrow."

"Where do you think he is?"

I began to hear warning bells echoing in my head.

"Mr. Di Stefano loves opera. He probably went into Manhattan to the Metropolitan Opera. He must have let his staff off for a couple of hours until he returns home."

Gigi, the manager of the Palms, led us to a table. We sat down and ordered drinks. "I thought you were bringing a date?"

"I had invited Mrs. Jarvis, but I was stood up," he answered. "I couldn't reach her by telephone either."

7

❖

THE GREAT THING about the Palms is that you can really eat if you have an appetite. The potbellied waiter arrived with our drinks and announced, "We have a special tonight. Loch Ness Monsters. Six-pound lobsters!"

Kim shook her head, smiling. "No way we could ever finish one of those."

I said, "How about splitting a four-pounder and then splitting a rare New York steak, a loaf of fried onion rings, and cottage fries?"

Kim cut in quickly. "We'll start with one of Gigi's salads."

I turned to Da Vinci. "What are you going to have?"

"I'll have a New York steak, medium rare," he said. "And a side of spinach and a baked potato."

"How about a bottle of Chianti?" the waiter suggested.

"Good enough," I said.

The waiter took off, and we sipped at our drinks. "How did you meet Mrs. Jarvis?" I asked Da Vinci.

"I was her account manager at her bank in Paris," he said.

"Was she married to Jarvis at that time?" I asked.

"No," he answered. "About the time she was married, I went to work for EuroSky, and we lost touch."

"How did you tie up with EuroSky?" I asked.

He laughed. "They needed a banker who knew computers. At that time there weren't many of us working in Europe that had a knowledge of computers."

"Didn't EuroSky advance money to Jarvis for Millennium Films?" I questioned.

He looked at me with a completely open expression. "If they did," he said, "I knew nothing about it, because I was just assigned to this project a couple of weeks ago."

The waiter had just brought out our salads when a small group of people passed us on the way to their own table. I recognized Thyme, the exotic black singer whom I had seen at Bradley's party. One of the men with the group paused at our table and spoke to Da Vinci. "I didn't expect you in town this soon."

"I had some special business," Da Vinci said. "But I was planning to get in touch with you first thing in the morning."

The man, who was well-dressed, good-looking, and middle-aged, nodded. "You can reach me at the hotel tomorrow morning; I'm returning to Las Vegas in the afternoon."

Da Vinci said, "I'll be in touch." And the group moved on to their table. I thought it was curious that Da Vinci hadn't introduced us to his friend.

Kim said, "That black girl is Thyme. She has the number one hit on the charts right now. And I've heard that her boyfriend is a Las Vegas gangster."

Da Vinci smiled and continued eating his salad.

Service at the Palms was efficient. Our entrees came through in short order. By 9:30 P.M. we had finished. When the waiter brought the bill, Da Vinci reached for the check. I put up my hand. "No way," I said. "This is my town." And I paid the bill.

We walked outside. Da Vinci asked the valet to call him a cab.

"Don't bother," I said. "I'll drop you off. Where are you staying?"

"I'm at the Beverly Rodeo," he said.

"Jump in," I said, as the valet opened the car door for Kim.

I dropped Da Vinci at the Beverly Rodeo Hotel. His jacket swung open as he stepped out of the car.

"We'll be in touch tomorrow," Da Vinci said.

"Okay," I answered, and watched him as he went into the lobby of the hotel. Then I moved the car away from the curb and into the traffic.

I looked at Kim. "He's got a gun in a shoulder holster."

"How do you know?" she asked.

"I saw it when he got out of the car. It doesn't make

sense to me. Why does a computer banker need a piece?" I shook my head. "Nothing makes sense."

"You're tired," Kim said. "Let's go back to the hotel bungalow and you can relax. Maybe you need a bath in the Jacuzzi. It's been a rough day."

I nodded. I still hadn't told her about Uncle Rocco's leaving the country.

"But first, I need to speak to Alma," I said. "Call her at the hotel, tell her I'm coming over to talk to her."

Kim picked up the car phone and dialed Alma's hotel. She asked for Mrs. Jarvis.

The desk clerk spoke into the phone. Kim hung up the receiver and looked at me. "She's checked out."

"Okay," I said. "I guess there's nothing I can do. Let's go home."

IT WAS ABOUT 11:30 P.M., and Kim and I were sitting in the Jacuzzi. I leaned back into the bubbling water.

Kim looked at me. "I've come to a decision, Jed. I'm quitting my job."

"What the hell for?" I asked her. "You have a great job."

"I don't need a job," she said angrily. "I need a relationship. I thought we had one, but all we have is a fuck every now and then."

"I have many problems," I answered.

"You had more problems when we first started this business," she said. "But you still had time for us."

"We'll have it yet," I said. "I just need a little more time to get through all of this."

"I don't know," she said. "In another year I'll be thirty years old, and my mother always says that if you're not married by the time you're thirty, you're an old maid."

"Oh, Jesus," I said. "You're still a kid."

"You're not that young either," she said. "I think we'd better decide what our future is going to be."

"I know what our future is," I said. "We'll get married, just like everybody else."

"Do you mean that?"

"Of course I mean it," I said. "But don't push me."

She got out of the Jacuzzi.

"Where are you going?" I asked.

"I'm going to shave my pussy," she said. "I want to feel young again."

I stepped out of the Jacuzzi and put on my terry-cloth robe. "Come on to bed," I said. "We'll practice a little."

She looked at me. "Don't you want me to shave my pussy?" she asked.

"It doesn't bother me," I said.

"Then you better shave your beard, or you'll scratch my clit."

"Oh, balls," I said. "Let's go to bed."

The telephone began ringing. She reached for it, listened, and then turned to me, a look of disgust on her face. "There's a limo in front of the hotel," she said. "Your niece, Angela, is waiting to come up."

Kim slipped into a jumpsuit and I changed into jeans and a T-shirt. The doorbell rang and I opened the door. Angela was standing there, and a bellboy stood behind her with a valise.

"Uncle Jed," she said in a small voice.

"Yes, sweetie."

"My mother told me to stay with you for a few days." She looked apprehensively up at me. "Is that okay?" Obviously she didn't know if she was welcome.

"Come on in, honey," I said, taking her hand. "Where is your mother?"

"She had to go on a business trip."

"Where?" I asked.

Angela looked at me. "I think she's going to France." She turned and saw Kim. "Is she your wife?"

I smiled at her. "She's my fiancée," I answered. "We're getting married very soon."

Angela was smart. "She's a very pretty lady," she said.

I introduced them to each other. Kim smiled at Angela. "Have you had dinner?" she asked.

"I haven't had much," she answered.

"C'mon, let's have something to eat," Kim said, and they walked together into the kitchen."

I CALLED PEACHTREE on the telephone while Kim was showing Angela to the guest room. It was near midnight, and I apologized for calling that late.

"I need some information," I said. "I remember that you escorted Thyme to Brad's party."

"That's right," Peachtree answered.

"I also heard somewhere that her boyfriend was a Mafia gangster out of Las Vegas."

"That's right," Daniel said, "although I'm not sure 'boyfriend' is the right term—he's more her protector. His name is Jimmy Pelleggi, and he used to be Sam Giancanna's representative in Las Vegas."

"Does he still have anything to do with the casinos?" I asked.

"I don't think so," Daniel said, "because the gaming commission got all the Mafia out of the gambling operations."

"Then what do you think he's doing in Vegas?" I asked.

"What I hear is that he runs drugs and prostitution. He's a tough man," Daniel added. "They call him Jimmy Blue Eyes because his eyes are blue like ice."

"What does he have to do with Thyme?" I asked.

Daniel laughed. "He follows Giancanna. After all, Giancanna had a singer under his wing for a long time."

"Do you know anything about a man called Leonardo Da Vinci?"

"The artist?" Daniel asked.

"No," I said. "He's a European banker, and I know that he knows Jimmy Pelleggi."

"I don't know anything about that," Daniel answered.

I thanked Daniel and put down the telephone. For the first time I felt frustrated that I couldn't get in touch with Uncle Rocco. There was a peculiar setup going on. I knew now that Jimmy Blue Eyes was in the drug trade. And I remembered that Alma had also been in the drug trade. And I knew that Da Vinci had contact with both of them. Something was going on, but I didn't have the answers.

Kim came into the living room. "Angela has gone to bed."

"Good," I said. "I think that we should do the same. It's been a long day."

Kim looked at me. "Why do you think Alma took off for France in such a hurry?"

"I don't know," I said. "But I have a feeling it has something to do with Uncle Rocco. He's also taken off for France tonight. He may be in real trouble."

8

❖

KIM AND I were having coffee and Danish for breakfast.

Kim said, "We have to get someone to take care of Angela when we go to the office. We can't leave her alone."

"I didn't think about that. Do you know anyone that could do it?" I asked.

"My sister has three kids. She'll know someone who can help."

"Get in touch with her," I said. "We need someone right away."

The telephone rang. Kim answered it. "It's Da Vinci." She handed me the phone.

"Good morning," I said.

"Good morning," he answered. "Have you heard anything from Alma?"

"Not a word," I said.

"Well, I have," he said. "I heard that she left her child with you."

"It was a surprise for me," I said. "She showed up after we came home from dinner."

"Did she say anything about where her mother had gone?" he asked.

"No, she only said that her mother told her to stay with me for a few days," I answered.

Da Vinci was annoyed. "I have two valises of Alma's that I was supposed to give her. Now I don't know what to do with them."

"What's in them?" I questioned.

"I don't know, they belong to Alma. She never mentioned what was in them." He hesitated a moment. "Is it okay if I drop them off with you, and you can give them to her when she returns?"

"I don't know why not," I answered. "After all, I have to return her kid to her also."

"I'll drop them at your hotel," Da Vinci said. "I have to return to Liechtenstein today."

"Okay." I put down the telephone and said to Kim, "Da Vinci has two valises for Alma. I told him he could leave them here."

She picked up the phone, called her sister, and spoke to her for a few minutes. "My sister knows a girl who can take care of Angela. She's sending her right over."

"Thank God," I said.

Angela came into the breakfast room. "Good morning," she said.

"Did you sleep okay?" I asked her.

Angela nodded. "Really well."

Kim said, "What would you like for breakfast?"

"*Petit pain du chocolat* and coffee."

Kim laughed. "Number one, we don't have *petit pain du chocolat;* number two, you're too young to drink coffee."

Angela frowned. "My mother always lets me have coffee."

"Look," Kim said, "this is America. In America kids drink milk, not coffee. I can't get a *petit pain du chocolat,* but I can get chocolate doughnuts. I think you should eat something more substantial, however," Kim said, sounding motherly. "How about ham and eggs, or pancakes and sausage?"

"Pancakes and sausage sound good," Angela said brightly. "But if I don't have a cup of coffee, I won't be able to stay awake for the whole day."

Kim laughed. "Okay, but very weak coffee."

"Okay," Angela said. "I'll have *café au lait.*"

"Okay, that's fine," Kim said, and called room service.

Angela looked at me. "What are we going to do today?" she asked.

"I've got someone coming over here to stay with you. Kim and I have to go to work," I answered.

"You both sound exactly like my mother," she sighed.

JIM HANDLEY WAS waiting for me when I came into my office.

"I've got some word from Aerospatiale," he said.

"What's the word?" I asked. He didn't look happy.

"It doesn't look good. The Dutchmen have offered them more money."

"That's crazy. Aerospatiale offered us the deal," I said.

"What can I say? This is just what they told me."

"I think that the only thing we can do is send them the down payment," I said after pondering the situation for a moment.

Handley looked at me. "You haven't even spoken to the other airlines yet. How do you know how much you can take a shot at? Twenty percent down on that many planes will cost a minimum of a quarter of a billion dollars," he said. "And we haven't got it right now."

"We're fucked," I said. "Someone has gotten a line on our cash. That's why the Dutch company made the offer."

"What are we going to do?" Handley asked.

"We'll fuck the Dutch company," I said. "We'll buy them."

"But they want to buy you," Handley said.

"They want to buy us, we want to buy them," I said. "So they'll give us three billion dollars. I'll offer them five billion for their company."

"Where are you going to get the money?" Handley asked.

I didn't tell him that Uncle Rocco wanted me to head up a tremendous company, probably one of the biggest investment companies in the world. And if I did what Uncle Rocco wanted, I would have the money. Instead, I told him that if it didn't work, we could always merge, or we could get Milken to sell junk bonds for us and get the money.

"And what are you going to do about Millennium

Films?" he asked. "EuroSky has already advanced you five hundred ninety-five million. How do we get any money out of that?" he asked.

I leaned back in my chair. "They advanced me all the money, but the studio still winds up as my company."

"So how are we going to pay back the advance?" Handley asked.

I smiled. "For years I've been watching Kerkorian sell MGM and UA over and over again. And at the end of it he always ends up back in control of the company. What he sells is pieces."

"So?" Handley said.

"It's very simple. I sell them the foreign distribution rights to the film library. That's still fifteen hundred feature films, plus other film inventory," I said.

Handley looked at me. "I thought you didn't want to stay in the film business."

"It doesn't matter," I said. "Didn't we talk about the fact that their real estate and property could sell for as much as four hundred million dollars. That's not bad."

A bemused look of respect crossed Handley's face. "Jed," he said, "you're turning into a real prick."

KIM ENTERED MY office an hour and a half later. "My sister sent the nanny. And I made arrangements for her to take Angela to Disneyland," she said.

"That's nice," I said.

"Also, after they had left for Disneyland and I was getting ready to come to work, Da Vinci came to the apartment and left a couple of large aluminum valises for us to give Alma when she returns."

"Fine," I said. "Did he say anything else?"

"Only that he was catching a flight this afternoon for Europe."

"Well," I said, "I guess that takes care of that."

The phone rang and my secretary spoke into the intercom. "A Mr. Pelleggi is on the phone."

I picked up the telephone. "Yes, sir."

"We didn't really meet last night," Pelleggi said. "But I saw you with Da Vinci, and I was wondering if you had a number for him."

"I'm sorry," I said. "As far as I know he is on his way back to Europe."

"Damn," Pelleggi said. "Do you have any information about Mrs. Jarvis?" he asked.

"No," I said.

He hesitated for a moment. "I'm a friend of your uncle's. We've known each other for many years."

"I'm glad," I said. "I'm very fond of Uncle Rocco."

"I'm also one of the investors in a company with Mr. Di Stefano," he said.

"Yes?" I said.

"It is very important that I get in touch with your uncle," Pelleggi said.

"As far as I know, he's still in Atlantic City," I responded.

"I got no answer at his apartment," he said.

"I'm sure he'll show up in a short time," I said. "If I hear from him, I will ask him to get in touch with you."

"I appreciate that," Mr. Pelleggi said, and hesitated again. "By the way, did you know that Alma's husband, Reed Jarvis, hit on my girlfriend the night of Bradley Shepherd's party?"

"I know nothing about it," I said. Which was the truth.

"The son of a bitch is lucky he got himself killed before I could do him in. I wouldn't have made it that easy for him," he said.

"Well," I said, "all's well that ends well. Now all we have to do is keep our noses clean."

There was silence, then he laughed. "You call me Jimmy Blue Eyes. I like you. You're just like your uncle." Then he hung up.

9

❖

IT WAS LATE by the time I left the office. Kim had left earlier because she wanted to check on Angela and make sure everything was okay. When I got to the downstairs parking lot, it was empty. All the attendants had gone for the day.

I jumped into the Blazer and left the garage. I turned onto Century Boulevard. A voice came from behind me in the back seat.

"Señor Stevens," a man's Spanish-accented voice said. "It's been a long time."

I looked in the rearview mirror. "It has been a long time," I said. The last time I'd seen the man was in Peru. "Captain Gonzales."

The man smiled. "You remember the name correctly, but it is no longer captain. I am now a general."

"Congratulations," I said. "Why didn't you come up to the office?"

"I didn't want anyone to know that I was here with you," he answered.

"What can I do for you?" I asked.

"Señorita Vargas called me yesterday and asked me to get in touch with you because there are some big troubles."

I pulled over to the side of the road and turned to him. "General Gonzales, why don't you get into the front seat? It's easier for us to talk that way."

General Gonzales hadn't changed much. He was still slim and dapper as before. There was a little gray in his hair, but his pencil-line mustache was still black.

I moved back into traffic. "Did Alma say what kind of trouble?"

"She couldn't go into detail. But I know it has something to do with *la cocaina*."

"I thought she was through with that business. After all, she married a very rich man, and she now has a lot of money."

"That's true," Gonzales said. "But she's under a great deal of pressure from the Mafia. They want her to open up her South American contacts for them."

"Christ," I said. "Nothing seems to change."

Gonzales nodded. "She told me that she will be in touch with you, and we'll find out what we need to do."

I looked at him. "Do you know of my uncle, Mr. Di Stefano?" I asked.

"I know of him," Gonzales said. "But we have never met."

"I think that she and my uncle are together in Europe trying to straighten out the problems."

He looked out the window. "Will you let me know the minute she contacts you?"

"Okay," I said. "Where are you staying?"

"I haven't checked into a hotel yet," he answered. "I just arrived here."

"Then come home to dinner with me and we'll find a place for you to stay."

He nodded. "*Gracias,* señor."

I turned north onto the freeway to Sunset Boulevard, and then east to the Bel Air gates.

Gonzales said, "Do you have bodyguards following you?"

"No," I said.

"There are two men in a black Ford who have been behind us since you pulled out of the office garage."

I looked in my rearview mirror. I couldn't see anything.

Gonzales opened his jacket and took out an automatic. "Just in case," he said quietly.

"I wonder what the hell is going on," I said, as I pulled past the hotel entrance to my bungalow.

We got out of the car, but I still didn't see anyone. We went into the apartment. Angela saw me as I came through the door and then she saw Gonzales.

She smiled and spoke in Spanish. *"Buenas noches, Tío!"*

He bent over to kiss her. "Angela," he said in English, "you're becoming a very big girl."

She turned to me. "I would like to get a Big Mac for dinner."

Just then Kim came from the other room. "The nanny says she's been eating hamburgers and French fries all day at Disneyland." she said.

"What the hell do I know?" I said. "If she wants a Big Mac let her have it. Kids are entitled to be kids."

I introduced Kim to the general, but told her that he was visiting from Peru because I had called him.

"I think we should have dinner in," I said. "I think we'll hear from either Alma or my uncle this evening."

"I still want a Big Mac," Angela said.

"Okay. Kim, ask the nanny to take Angela out and get one for her." Then to Gonzales, "You'll join us for dinner and I'll call the desk and get you a room here at the hotel."

We ordered from room service, and while we were sitting at the bar having a drink, Jimmy Blue Eyes called me.

"Have you heard anything from your uncle?" he asked.

"Not yet."

"I put two bodyguards on you," Jimmy said. "I hope you don't mind."

"You worried me a little bit," I said. "I was aware there were two people following me from my office."

"They are my men," he said. "I told them to stay nearby in case you had any problems."

"Why should I have any problems?" I asked.

"Da Vinci is going to screw you," he said.

"How is he going to screw me? He's nothing but a fucking messenger."

"He's more than a messenger," he said. "He's a hit man."

"Who is he after?" I asked. "He didn't bother me."

"He's after your uncle," Jimmy said. "I'm guessing that's why he went back to Europe. I have a feeling that your uncle has gone to Sicily to talk to the commission." Jimmy Blue Eyes was quiet for a moment. Then, "Did Da Vinci leave anything with you?" he asked.

"Yes," I said. "He left two valises that he said belonged to Alma."

"Okay," Jimmy Blue Eyes said. "Sit tight, I'm on my way over."

We were in the middle of dinner when the desk clerk called and told us we had a visitor, a Mr. Pelleggi.

"Send him over," I told her.

When I opened the door, Jimmy Blue Eyes looked at Gonzales. "Who the hell is he?" he asked.

"He's a friend of Alma's from Peru," I answered.

He looked at me. "Is he okay?" he asked.

"He's on our side," I answered.

"Good," he said. Jimmy opened the bungalow door, asked his two bodyguards to come in, and then turned back to me. "Where are the valises that Da Vinci left?"

I looked at Kim. "Where did you put the valises?"

"In the guest closet," Kim answered.

I opened the door and took out two twenty-eight-inch aluminum valises.

Jimmy gestured to one of his men. "Open them."

The man took out a big pocket knife. He pushed the flat side of the blade against a valise lock and hit it. The lock fell open. He lifted the top of the valise.

We looked inside. It was packed with cellophane-wrapped bags of white powder. Jimmy had his man jab one of the packages. Jimmy dipped his finger in the powder and tasted it.

"That's heroin," he said.

Kim turned to me. "What are you doing? You're going to wind up in jail."

"Look, this isn't my business," I said.

"Now what do we do?" I asked Jimmy.

"This was part of the deal. Da Vinci was to bring heroin from Sicily in return for cocaine from Colombia," he answered.

"What has this got to do with Uncle Rocco?" I asked.

"Your uncle has been out of this business for a long time. And there are some people who want him back in it," he replied. He told his men to lock up the valises.

"How much heroin do you think is in there?" I asked.

"I think each valise has about forty kilos," he answered.

"What's that worth?" I asked.

"Wholesale about seven million dollars. On the street, after it's cut, maybe a hundred and fifty million."

"Now what happens to it?" I asked.

Jimmy smiled. "I'll take care of it," he said. "Can I use your phone?"

"Be my guest," I said.

Jimmy punched numbers into the telephone. In a few seconds he was talking to someone in Italian. He spoke so quickly I couldn't follow what he was saying. After he hung up the phone, he turned to me.

"Da Vinci is already in Sicily," he said. "I think it is

important that as soon as we hear from your uncle, we let him know that." He then motioned to his two men to take the valises out.

Jimmy Blue Eyes held out his hand. "Keep in touch, I'll leave my two men here in case you need help," he explained. "You never can tell what those shitheads will do." He shook his head. "Now that the pizza connection trial is over, there is a whole group of new 'zips' moving in, and I think they are after the old men. The only way they can be controlled is by the Sicilian lords."

I watched as they left the bungalow. Then I sat down at the bar and looked at General Gonzales. "What do you think?"

The Peruvian general spoke quietly. "They're all crooks," he said.

10

❖

IT WAS ELEVEN o'clock. We had finished dinner and were having coffee. Angela had returned and gone to bed. The general looked across the table at me. "Do you have a gun?" he asked.

"No," I answered. "I don't need one here."

"I think you need one now," he said. He reached inside his jacket and handed me a small 9mm automatic. "Keep this just in case,"

"Do you think there will be a problem?" I asked.

"I have a feeling that something is not quite right," he answered.

"What do you mean?"

He looked at me. "Jimmy Blue Eyes didn't seem surprised that the heroin was here at your bungalow," he said. "It didn't take him long to take off with the valises.

How much did he say that it would be worth? Seven million dollars?" he said.

"Yes," I said.

The Peruvian nodded. "That is not a bad night's work."

"What are you saying?" I asked.

"He said they were exchanging *cocaina* for heroin. But he didn't tell you where the *cocaina* was coming from. I have a feeling that we will hear more from the Mafioso this evening."

"He said he would leave me two men here as bodyguards," I said.

Gonzales smiled curiously. "I don't know whether they are bodyguards or executioners. Jimmy Blue Eyes is playing with seven million dollars. If I were he I would not leave any witnesses behind."

I thought for a moment. "Maybe you're right."

The telephone began to ring. Kim answered it. "Your Aunt Rosa is on the phone."

"Aunt Rosa?" I asked. "I haven't heard from her in a long time." I reached for the phone. "Aunt Rosa, how are you?"

"I'm fine," she answered.

"You're up very late," I said.

"I just remembered," she said. "Your father used to always send flowers for your grandparents' anniversary mass in Palermo," she said. "I thought it would be nice if you would send flowers this year."

I thought for a moment. This was the first time I had ever heard about this. I knew Aunt Rosa was telling me something.

"I don't mind," I said. "When do I need to send the flowers?"

"The mass will be in Palermo in three days," Aunt Rosa said. "We have a cousin who is a florist in the Villa Igiea Grand Hotel. He'll know where to send the flowers."

"Good. I'll arrange it right away."

Aunt Rosa's voice was serious. "Don't forget. It's really important."

"Don't worry, Aunt Rosa, I'll take care of it," I said.

"You always were a good boy. I know you will. Goodnight."

I turned to Kim and Gonzales. "Now we know where to meet Uncle Rocco."

Gonzales looked at me. "I think it would be a good idea if I stay here with you. After all, I'm a professional and I'll know how to handle any trouble."

"All I can offer you is the sofa, since Angela is in the guest room."

"That's no problem," he answered.

"Where are you going to meet your Uncle Rocco?" Kim asked.

"In Palermo in three days. So we'll arrange our travel plans in the morning. Let's go to bed now."

At three o'clock in the morning the telephone rang again. I picked it up. This time it was Alma.

"Is Angela with you?" she asked.

"Yes," I said.

"Is she all right?" she asked.

"Yes," I answered. "Where are you?"

"I'm in Paris," she said. "Did General Gonzales arrive?"

"He's here now," I said.

"Good, let me talk to him."

I went into the living room. He was sitting on the couch, wide-awake. "Alma's on the phone," I said.

He picked up the phone. I listened for a moment and I realized they were not speaking Spanish. It was probably a Peruvian argot.

Finally he said to her, "Okay, I'll be there too." He put down the telephone.

"What did she say?" I asked.

"She has arranged to rent a yacht in Cap d'Antibes, and she and your uncle will take the yacht to Palermo. Your uncle thinks it is the safest way for them to travel."

"Did she say anything about us meeting there?" I asked.

"Yes," he answered. "She confirmed your Aunt Rosa's message."

"Good enough," I said. "I'll arrange to get the plane tomorrow."

He looked at me. "What do you want to do about the bodyguards outside?"

"Screw them," I said. "If they don't bother us, we don't bother them."

I went back to the bedroom. Kim was sitting up in bed. "What's happening?" she asked.

I smiled at her. "We're going on a honeymoon. To Europe."

WE ARRIVED IN Palermo the day before I was to meet Uncle Rocco. The hotel was comfortable, and Kim and

I had a nice suite. Gonzales had a room across the corridor from us.

At 7 P.M. we went downstairs to the cocktail lounge to have a drink.

"It seems like a quiet town," I said.

The general nodded. "It reminds me of some of the towns in Peru. They always seem to be quiet, but always there are problems below the surface."

The waiter came to the table. Kim wanted Asti Spumante. The general and I ordered scotch.

Earlier in the day we had had lunch at a restaurant not far from the hotel. We had decided to have dinner later this evening at the hotel. The menu was completely Italian. Pasta, pasta, pasta.

We were sitting quietly, not talking, when I heard a voice behind me. "Mr. Stevens."

I turned around. Jimmy Blue Eyes stood there with his two bodyguards.

"Do you mind if I join you for a drink?" he asked.

"Be my guest."

He moved into a chair. "I didn't expect to see you here," he said.

"Neither did I expect to see you here," I said.

"Are you meeting your uncle?"

"I haven't had any messages, I'm just traveling a little. And I've come to attend the anniversary mass for my grandparents," I said. "What brings you here?"

"Business," Jimmy Blue Eyes said.

I didn't ask him what the business was.

Jimmy Blue Eyes smiled. "I know this town very well. Why don't you let me take you to dinner tonight?"

"If it's not an inconvenience to you," I said.

"Not at all," he said. "It would be my pleasure."

I looked at him. "By the way, you mentioned the other day that Da Vinci was in Italy already," I said. "Do you think he might be here?"

Jimmy Blue Eyes shrugged. "I don't know. But anything is possible. I think we should keep our eyes open," he said. "I will pick you up in the lobby at eight-thirty."

"You've got a date," I said.

Jimmy rose from his chair and left the cocktail lounge, his bodyguards following.

I looked at Gonzales and Kim. "What do you think?"

Gonzales didn't look happy. "I think we're in trouble. We don't know who's on our side."

JIMMY BLUE EYES picked us up in a Mercedes 600 limousine. It took us about twenty minutes to reach the restaurant on the outskirts of the city. The restaurant was in what had been a private mansion. We sat on the terrace overlooking the water.

After we had been seated for only a few minutes, the waiters brought a large plate of antipasti to our table. Jimmy Blue Eyes ordered two bottles of red wine. I opened a package of breadsticks and started to laugh.

"What are you laughing at?" Jimmy asked.

I handed him the wrapper from the breadsticks. Printed on the outside was "Made in Brooklyn, New York."

Jimmy smiled. "It's a small world," he said. "Tell me, what do you think your uncle is planning to do now?"

"As far as I know," I said, "Uncle Rocco wants to retire and stay out of things completely."

Jimmy shook his head. "They'll never let him do it totally. He knows too much."

"He's an old man," I said. "I think they could let him have his last few years in peace."

Jimmy didn't reply to that. He said to Kim, "The food is very good here. They have wonderful veal and great fresh fish. Anything you want you will find very good."

"I like fish," Kim said.

I looked around the restaurant. There were about twelve tables on the terrace, but we were the only customers. "They don't seem to be very busy," I said.

"It's Sicily, nobody eats before midnight," Jimmy said. "We're Americans, we came early."

The waiter gave us menus. "I think I would like some veal," I said. "With a side order of fettucini."

"I'll have whitefish," Kim said.

"I'll have fish, too," Gonzales said.

Jimmy looked at the waiter. "I'm going to have mussels."

I hated mussels. To me, just looking at them made me nauseous.

Suddenly the sun was gone and it was dark. The waiters were putting candles on all of the tables.

We were on our main course and Jimmy Blue Eyes seemed in a good mood. "You don't realize how important Sicily is," he said to me. "We're a poor country. And a poor people. But somehow we have managed to work our way to a level of importance. Don't forget, if it wasn't for us, there would not be a Las Vegas. And I've spent my life keeping everything there in order."

"But you don't have the casinos anymore," I said.

He laughed. "We don't need them. There are many other businesses that make a lot more money for us."

I looked at him. "Aren't you worried that someone will take them away from you?"

"People have tried," he said. "But nobody has been able to do it.'"

He looked toward the door. "What the hell is going on?" he said, glancing toward his bodyguards.

Gonzales and I turned to follow his gaze. Two men were coming toward the terrace from inside the restaurant. Jimmy Blue Eyes's bodyguards looked frightened, then quickly disappeared. Jimmy reached into his jacket as I pushed Kim out of her chair and onto the floor. I rolled on top of her to protect her.

I didn't see if Jimmy Blue Eyes had got his gun out of his jacket. But an Uzi seemed to play a tattoo on his body. The two men turned toward us, but this was where Gonzales was really a professional. He held two Colt 45 automatics, one in each hand. He blew off the head of each of the two men.

"Jesus," I said.

Gonzales said, disgusted, "They're assholes. If they were going to hit, they should have hit everybody at the same time."

I got up, and we helped Kim to her feet. She looked pale and nauseous. "Don't look at them," I said.

Gonzales spoke. "Let's get out of here before the police show up."

I looked at Jimmy Blue Eyes. He was lying on his stomach, blood soaking his jacket from the bullets that had gone right through him.

Gonzales and I held Kim by her arms, and we started

to leave. I looked down at the two dead gunmen. One of them was Da Vinci.

Da Vinci is not going to play his computer games anymore, I thought. As a matter of fact, he had a very stupid expression on his face.

The restaurant staff didn't say a word as we went out the front door. I looked for the bodyguards. I didn't see them anywhere. The Mercedes was still there, with the keys in the ignition.

"Let's go," I said. "We'll manage to find our way back to the hotel."

Gonzales looked at me. "I don't know who they were after, Jimmy Blue Eyes or you."

11

❖

UNCLE ROCCO DIDN'T show up at the hotel until seven the following evening. By that time, I was ready to get out of Sicily. Palermo did not appear to be the friendliest city in the world.

He came to our suite. "How was your trip?" he asked us.

"The trip was fine, but I didn't realize that I was going to get in the middle of a war."

"I'm sorry," Uncle Rocco said. "I heard about it."

"How did you hear about it?" I asked.

"The commission," he said. "You know that Da Vinci was after you as well as Jimmy Blue Eyes?"

"Why the hell was he after me?"

Uncle Rocco shook his head. "They thought that was the way they could get to me. But it doesn't matter now. I've got everything resolved. I've had the meeting with the Sicilian commission, the head of the most important families in Sicily. They've sent the okay to the five families in New York."

"What does that mean?" I asked.

He looked at me. "I'm out. Now, all we have to do is to have you take over Inter-World Investments."

"And when do we meet with them to do that?" I asked.

"Back in New York," he said. "Their offices are in the financial district."

"Then what the hell did I come to Sicily for? To get myself shot at?"

"No," Uncle Rocco answered. "We have a dinner to attend tonight in your honor. The commission wants to look you over."

"What happens if they don't like me?" I asked. "Do they kill me?"

"Don't be silly," Uncle Rocco said. "This will be a very pleasant evening."

I met his eyes. "I'll feel better if you can give me a machine gun."

He laughed. "You won't need it. We've got all the protection we need."

Kim said, "I've got to get a dress. I didn't know we were going to have an important dinner to attend." She looked at Uncle Rocco. "Is Alma going to be dressed up?"

"Of course," he said.

"Where can I get a dress?" she asked.

"Don't worry. All the stores are open until ten P.M. And we won't have dinner until midnight."

General Gonzales said, "I'd like to see Señorita Vargas."

Uncle Rocco nodded. "That will be no problem. You can join me when I leave here and return to the boat. She's there."

The general nodded.

Uncle Rocco looked at me. "You better go shopping, too. You'll need a tuxedo. This is really a formal occasion."

"How many people will be there?" I asked.

"Twenty-four, twenty-five. They're really curious to meet you. Most of them knew your father when we were young."

"Where will the dinner be held?" I asked.

"Here at this hotel. I arranged for one of the private party rooms." He looked at me. "You don't look very happy."

"I'm still not sure that I like this whole idea," I said.

"Don't be so nervous," he said. "Just remember, you and I are family."

General Gonzales followed Uncle Rocco as he left the suite.

I looked at Kim. "Call the concierge. He'll probably know the best stores to go to."

KIM AND I started to laugh as we dressed for dinner. We had had to rent our clothes at a wedding boutique. Even though my tuxedo was Giorgio Armani, it was still a three-year-old style. Kim had on a very Sicilian long lace gown.

"I think we can go to the mayor's office and get married in these clothes," she remarked.

"Anything's possible," I said. "I haven't seen a tuxedo like this in a while. What the hell, when in Sicily, do as the Sicilians do."

I looked at my watch. "Christ, we're early. We have another hour to kill before dinner. Let's have a drink."

There was a knock at the door. I opened it. It was Uncle Rocco. He looked fantastic. And why shouldn't he? He, at least, had brought his own tuxedo.

"Where are Alma and Gonzales?" I asked.

"They are not coming to dinner," he said.

"I thought you said Alma was coming," Kim said.

"I changed my mind," Uncle Rocco said. "In Sicily, at business dinners, the women are not invited."

"Then why am I going?" Kim asked.

"First of all, you're American. Second of all, I told them that you were Jed's fiancée and that you also speak Italian, which is helpful to Jed."

"Okay," I said. "Let's have a drink."

"A short one," Uncle Rocco said. "Because we need to be in the dining room before our guests arrive." He turned to Kim. "That's a very pretty dress."

She smiled. "I feel like a Sicilian bridesmaid."

He laughed. "What the hell, nobody will know the difference."

At a quarter of twelve we were in the private dining room. Exactly at midnight the other guests began arriving.

Respectfully, Uncle Rocco introduced me to each man as he arrived. Four of them were older men and in wheelchairs. Each was wheeled into the room by a younger man.

Uncle Rocco sat at the head of the U-shaped table. I

was seated on his left, and Kim was next to me. On Uncle Rocco's right was one of the older men who was seated in his wheelchair.

I had been introduced to each, but there was one problem. When they spoke to me in their Sicilian dialect, I could scarcely understand a word. Rocco tried to translate for me, but this was difficult as he was also busy talking to the other guests. Kim, too, tried to help translate, but her Italian was far better than her Sicilian. When the guests realized our predicament, they politely changed to Italian so that we could communicate.

The older men spoke to me about my father—how much they had respected him because he was one of the few who went his own way. They also said that they were pleased that I had followed in his footsteps.

Kim whispered to me, "What these men said about your father is really very nice."

"Yes," I said. "But don't forget one thing: probably all of them are killers."

By two o'clock in the morning dinner was over, and we were all toasting each other.

Uncle Rocco made a speech. I didn't really catch all of what he said, but the feeling I got was that he was thanking them for allowing him to retire with honor.

The man in the wheelchair on his right said a few words and handed Uncle Rocco a velvet-covered jewelry box.

Uncle Rocco opened the box. He took out a beautiful diamond-studded Patek Philippe watch. He kissed the old man on each cheek and then turned to the other guests. It was hard for me to believe, but I could see tears rolling from his eyes as he thanked them.

Everyone applauded, then began to rise from their seats to depart. A handsome young man came to the table and stopped in front of Uncle Rocco. Uncle Rocco smiled and held out his hand. The man said something in a harsh voice, pulled a gun from his jacket, and shot at Uncle Rocco.

Automatically, without thinking, I jumped over the table and wrestled the young man to the floor. At the same time, two other men appeared right beside me, held him down, and took away his gun.

I got up and moved quickly to Uncle Rocco. He was leaning against Kim. He looked very pale.

"Have somebody get a doctor," I said.

The two men pulled the assailant to his feet. The old man in the wheelchair who had been seated at Uncle Rocco's right was speaking in a rough voice. He then took a gun from his own jacket and shot the assailant in the head.

I pulled open Uncle Rocco's jacket. "I wanted to die peacefully in bed, not by a bullet," he said.

I looked down at him and smiled. "You're not going to die because of this wound. You've just been shot in the shoulder."

The old man in the wheelchair turned to me, and this time, I was surprised to hear, he spoke to me in perfect English.

"I apologize," he said. "It is men like this who bring dishonor to all of us."

WE WERE IN the hotel suite and Uncle Rocco groaned as the doctor picked the bullet from the flesh of his shoulder. Then he quickly swabbed the bullet hole with iodine and dressed the wound, put a sling around Uncle Rocco's neck, and carefully placed his arm inside. He spoke to Uncle Rocco in Italian.

"What did he say?" I asked him. "I didn't quite get it all."

"He told him to keep his arm still—and the bandages needed to be changed every day for the next few days," she said.

"That's not bad."

The doctor took out a hypodermic needle and loaded Uncle Rocco with penicillin. He spoke again to Uncle Rocco in Italian.

Again Kim translated. "He said that's enough for the moment, and that he should take two aspirin every four hours for the pain."

The doctor stood up and put his instruments back into his case. He said something to Kim. She nodded.

"He said that he would come by in the morning to check on him."

"Ask him how much I owe him," I said.

Kim did so. The doctor smiled and answered quietly in English, "One thousand dollars."

I looked at Kim. "This is an expensive doctor," I said.

The doctor turned to me. "I've not reported this to the police, and that alone is worth something."

I opened Uncle Rocco's jacket and took out his wallet. Quickly I counted out ten one-hundred-dollar bills and handed them to the doctor.

"Thank you," I said.

"No problem," the doctor said. "You are welcome." And he left the suite.

Uncle Rocco stared at me. "You didn't have to give him that much money. He would have taken half. In Sicily you always bargain."

"Why should I bargain?" I asked. "It was your money."

"Shit," Uncle Rocco said.

I pulled a chair up to the bed. "Now, why don't you tell me what was going on here tonight? Every time I'm around you, somebody is shooting at you," I said. "The only problem is that they may be shooting at me as well."

"They're assholes," Uncle Rocco said.

"I don't care who or what they are," I said. "I want you to tell me what we're going to do about it."

Uncle Rocco shook his head. "You're not going to do anything about it. The men of honor will take care of them."

"How can you be sure?" I asked. "Maybe they are the ones after you."

"Don't be stupid," Uncle Rocco said. "Now we're all in legitimate business together."

"Do you want to stay here at the hotel tonight?" I asked. "I think you would be more comfortable here than on the boat."

"That's a good idea," he said. "Besides, it's very late, and I think that we all need some sleep. Tomorrow we'll talk to Alma and Gonzales. After the doctor dresses my wound again, we'll start for home." He looked at me again. "You'll have to stop in New York at Inter-World Investments. They have two floors of offices at Eighty Broad. You can start meeting your executives."

12

❖

THE DOCTOR ARRIVED at ten o'clock in the morning to change Uncle Rocco's bandages. He took Uncle Rocco's temperature and seemed satisfied—there was no fever. He quickly gave Uncle Rocco another injection of penicillin and carefully replaced his arm in the sling.

"You're pretty good," he said to Uncle Rocco. "All you have to do is keep changing the bandages daily, give your shoulder a rest for a while, and it will be as good as new."

Uncle Rocco thanked him and walked him to the door. After the doctor had gone, Uncle Rocco came back and sat down at the table where we were having our coffee. "Have you heard anything from Alma yet?" he asked.

"No."

"That's strange. I'm surprised that she hasn't called, or come here looking for me," he said. "I'll call the boat."

"Do you have a number?" I asked him.

Uncle Rocco nodded yes. He took a piece of paper out of his pocket and gave the number to the hotel operator. He waited a few moments as he listened to the phone ringing. He looked at me with a worried expression. "There's no one answering. There should be an answer."

"Maybe she and Gonzales are on their way here," I said.

"I think we should go over to the boat," he said.

"Okay," I said, and called the concierge for a car. Fifteen minutes later we were on the quay in the harbor where the boat had been docked. The *Empress of Beaulieu* was a 120-foot motor yacht built by the Chantier D'Esterel in Cannes.

We got out of the car and looked up at the boat. We saw no one. Uncle Rocco silently took a gun out of his jacket. "Let's go aboard," he said, then to Kim, "You'd better stay in the car."

"Why? Do you think there is a problem?"

"I don't know," he said. "But I don't take any chances." He looked at me. "Do you have a gun?"

I did—the 9mm that Gonzales had given me. I followed Uncle Rocco up the gangplank. We boarded the boat and walked through the salon and then to the bridge.

Uncle Rocco held his hand up in front of me and pointed. A sailor lay crumpled on the floor under the wheel.

Uncle Rocco turned back and led me down a small spiral staircase that led us to the cabins. As we reached the corridor, I looked down. General Gonzales was lying on the floor, two bullet holes in his head. Quickly Uncle Rocco opened the first cabin door. Alma was sprawled across the bed, her throat cut, blood spread all over the sheets. I felt nauseous.

Uncle Rocco pushed me back into the corridor and up the staircase. I looked at him. "Why?"

He shook his head grimly. "It's the drug trade. I told her not to try to play games with it. She wanted out, but she was trying to make a final killing."

I still felt sick. "What do we do now?"

We left the boat and were still silent when we reached the car. I squeezed Kim's hand as we silently pulled away and headed back to the hotel.

Kim looked at me. "What happened?" she asked as we sat in the back seat.

"They're dead," I whispered.

A look of horror crossed her face. She began to cry. "Oh, my God," she said. "What will happen to that sweet child?"

THAT WAS FOUR years ago. We spent several weeks in New York, while I met with Inter-World executives. Then we went back to California.

A month after that, Kim and I were married in Las Vegas. And I lost thirty-two thousand dollars at baccarat.

A month after we were married, we adopted Angela, and two years later we had our own child. A boy. I named him John after my father.

Meanwhile Uncle Rocco left Atlantic City and moved back to New York City. He rented the house he had sold me. He seemed to enjoy his life. But I had a feeling that he missed the action.

I worked all the time, and in a few years Inter-World climbed near the top of the Fortune International 500 and became as well known to the public as IBM.

It was late one evening when Aunt Rosa called me. She was crying.

"Rocco is on his deathbed, and he wanted to see you before he goes."

I was in New York the next morning. Aunt Rosa sat outside the bedroom, crying. Her two daughters were sitting with her. Inside the bedroom, a young priest was praying. He had already given Uncle Rocco his last rites.

My uncle was gasping for breath. A nurse was sitting in a chair next to the bed. She had connected him to a heart monitor. Oxygen was being fed into his body from a portable oxygen tank. His face was pale, and he seemed to be in extreme pain. I touched his hand carefully so that I would not dislodge the IV attached to it.

He turned slowly and looked at me. After a moment he spoke. "I'm really fucked," he said.

I tried to cheer him up. "I've seen people in worse condition."

"I'm sure you have," he said. "But they were dead."

"Uncle Rocco, what are you complaining about? You said you wanted to die in bed. Well, here you are."

"You are really a prick—after everything I have done for you. I've made your life. You're one of the richest men in the world."

"That's not true. I just owe more money than any-body else."

He laughed. "You're really Sicilian. Your blood may be half Jewish, but in your heart you are pure Sicilian," he said quietly. "You are family. You are the son that I lost."

"I could never replace Angelo, but thank you for saying that."

"At one time," he said, "I really hated you."

"Why?"

"I know," he said, "that you shot Angelo."

"I saved him from pain," I said, "because I loved him, and he told me that I should help him because I was family."

Uncle Rocco was silent for a moment. "I know that," he said finally. "Alma told me many years ago. She told me that you tried to save him, but there was no way that you could."

He moved his other hand. "I have a ring on my fin-ger, take it off."

Slowly I removed the ring. It was an old-fashioned heavy gold ring with a large square diamond set in the center.

"Put it on," he said. "I want you to have it. I was go-ing to leave it to Angelo. But you are Angelo to me."

Silently I slipped the ring onto my right hand. It felt very heavy.

"The doctors told me," he said, "that I will not wait too long."

"Doctors do not always know everything," I an-swered.

He smiled at me. "I really don't give a shit," he said.

"I don't want to wait." He squeezed my hand and closed his eyes. Then his eyelids opened again and he was gone.

IT WAS THE day after Uncle Rocco's funeral, and I was sitting at the dining-room table in his apartment with a number of papers spread out before me.

I had the last check from the "Chairman." I was arranging to transfer them to Uncle Rocco's foundation.

The maid came in. "There are some friends of Mr. Di Stefano's to see you," she said.

"Ask them to come in," I answered.

Three old men entered. I remembered I had seen them at the funeral, but I had not spoken to them there.

Now they spoke to me about Uncle Rocco, whom they had known since they were young. They also had known my father. They said they felt sad because there were not many men of honor now.

"But Rocco," one of them said to me, "was an extraordinary man. He never betrayed the trust. He truly was a great man of honor."

I thanked them for coming. They rose to leave, and one of them noticed the ring Uncle Rocco had given me. He reached to hold my hand. "I know that ring," he said. "It was your uncle's ring, and it was his father's ring—your grandfather's. It was a symbol of a true Don."

Before I could move my hand away, he bent down and kissed the ring. A moment later the other two did the same. They looked up at me and there were tears in their eyes.

"May God be with you, Don Jed," they said, and they left.

I sat there for a few moments and looked down at the papers. The tears began falling from my eyes.

I knew that I was a very ordinary man. And I was an American, not a Sicilian.

But to these three old men, I was the Godfather. . . .